WHERE
IS MY
HUSBAND?

WHERE IS MY HUSBAND?

A JAKE AND MALLORY THRILLER

IVANKA FEAR

LeVel
BEST BOOKS

First published by Level Best Books 2023

Author Photo Credit: Amanda Belec, Instagram @thirteen13designsnphotography

First edition

ISBN: 978-1-68512-446-5

Cover art by Level Best Designs

This book was professionally typeset on Reedsy.
Find out more at reedsy.com

For my husband, Brian, the better half of the Brian and Ivanka team
You are the spark that inspires me.
And
To my family, for their support as I write my stories
With all my love. Family is everything.

Praise for Where Is My Husband?

"A twisted story of lies and obsession, this riveting psycho-thriller kept me flipping pages into the night. Be sure to keep the lights on!"—Sue Jaskula, romantic suspense author

"*Where is My Husband?* is a well-crafted thriller that will draw you in on page one and keep you hooked until the very end. If you liked *Gone Girl* and *Girl on the Train*, then you'll absolutely love this book. It's perfect for fans of domestic thrillers who enjoy suspense and tension and stories that aren't what they seem. Since this is the first of three books, I can't wait to see what happens next to the 'happy' couple!"—Gayle Brown, author of *A Deadly Game*

"*Where is my Husband?*, Book One in a new series by Ivanka Fear, author of *The Dead Lie*, follows a young woman struggling to find her missing husband. Part mystery, part psychological thriller, *Where is my Husband?* moves quickly, dragging the reader in a slipstream behind it. Don't get too comfortable. You may think you've solved the mystery, but then the entire plot shifts and you realize that you haven't understood anything at all. A dramatic fast-paced ride, *Where is my Husband?* is a great read for those looking for a book crammed full of twists, turns and unexpected outcomes."—Kim Herdman Shapiro, author of The Wynter Island Mysteries

"A masterful tale of suspense with layers and secrets you won't see coming."—Michelle Godard-Richer, award-winning author of *Fatal Hunt*

"In this piece of domestic suspense, Fear's deliberate unraveling of a

i

seemingly perfect marriage has you wondering, how well do we know the person closest to us?"—Natalie Carter-Giles, author of *Hunting Helena*

"Fans of Mary Kubica and Shari Lapena will enjoy Fear's atmospheric thriller that will have you guessing what and who you believe at every turn."—Brianne Sommerville, author of *If I Lose Her*

Chapter One

I'm early. Or maybe I'm too late.

I've never been good with time. In fact, I almost didn't make it to my own wedding three years ago, too busy looking in the mirror to see whether I was presentable enough. But Jake waited for me, handsome as ever, standing tall with that air of calm self-assuredness he exudes. Smiling as I walked down the aisle on my uncle's arm, blue-green eyes sparkling, he winked to let me know everything was perfect as I stressed about tripping over my own two feet. Jake's patient manner is one of the things that attracted me in the first place. It's a virtue I lack, like so many others. Why I'm thinking about that now is beyond me. Just something to pass the time. I could open the paperback mystery I brought, but he'll be out any moment. Maybe if I count to 100…

And breathe, Mallory, just breathe. Jake's voice whispers in my head.

The space surrounding me is dark, in spite of the few lampposts that stand guard along the grassy boulevard bordering the country road, their light casting shadows of trees and cars on the parking lot where I sit. A few vehicles have their engines running; air conditioners fight the heat of the summer evening as their occupants wait for a family member or friend. We're surrounded on three sides by the gray cement block building that's home to The Auto Supply Warehouse and the 300 or so employees who, as Jake would say, *pretend to work there*. Jake works the 3 to 11 shift. He should be coming out any time. I fix my eyes on the nondescript employee back door. And wait.

My car windows are down, letting in the humidity. Sleeves rolled up, my flowery, chiffon blouse hangs loosely over the elastic waistband of bleached denim capris. Jake picked out this blouse for me. It's one of his favorites, and mine, of course. I don't want to run the air conditioning and waste precious gas, but I've got the blowers on full blast, along with the radio, which is tuned to some song about love gone wrong. But it's all hot air.

I check the display on my dash to ground myself—10:57. Jake will be coming out in a few minutes. I can't wait to see him. Nearly four years of being together, and we still can't bear to be apart, even for work. Since I'm off from my kindergarten job during the summer, I have a lot of time on my hands. Time to fill. Time to miss my husband.

Jake knows how lonely I get without him. He understands I need company. When I dropped him off at work this afternoon, he kissed me goodbye. "Have fun. Enjoy your visit with my mom."

"Thanks, I will. We'll probably binge-watch some more of that medical series she likes."

Since Jake's mom retired from nursing last year, she's been filling her time with hobbies. Living alone and being a homebody at heart, she's glad to see visitors. Even me. And I'm grateful to spend time with her. After leaving Jake in the warehouse parking lot just before three p.m., I drove ten minutes to the city to spend the rest of the afternoon playing cards with Gloria and sipping iced tea on her shaded veranda, overlooking her gardens and flower beds. Following a delicious dinner of barbecued skewered chicken and baked potatoes, we went inside and spent a couple of hours watching television.

It's a routine I follow once a week. Drop off Jake at work, visit his mom, pick up Jake at work, stop at the Frosty Bar for an ice cream treat, drive twenty minutes to our country home where we soak in the hot tub, drink wine coolers, and watch a romantic movie on our outdoor screen before heading to our king size bed. I love summer Fridays.

Right now, though, sitting in the heat of the car and waiting patiently, trying hard not to chew off the tips off my fingernails, watching as the clock clicks over to the 11th hour, I'm more than a little apprehensive.

I've been keeping something from my husband. A secret. Or two. When he finds out, he won't be happy.

Chapter Two

Before the clock clicks to 11:01, the back door swings open, and employees rush out, eager to get away for the weekend. The quiet parking lot suddenly swarms with people, like flies around the lampposts in front of me. It's hard to identify faces from a distance, but I'd know Jake anywhere from his walk. Sometimes, he saunters; other times, he strides at a good pace. What makes him stand out is his confidence, his sense of purpose. So unlike my own walking posture (and standing, for that matter).

My timid little mouse, Jake affectionately calls me.

I open the driver's door of our Honda, and step out, ready to greet him. My eyes concentrate on the door, anticipating the vision of my husband breaking through and heading toward me. He'll plant a quick kiss on my lips, then escort me to the passenger side. Jake likes to drive, and I don't, so it makes sense that he takes over the wheel whenever we're together.

Cars pull out of the lot; yellow headlights and red tail lights brighten up the vast outdoor space. The procession heads out down the country road toward the main highway leading to Brampton Heights. Jake is obviously a bit late tonight. Not unusual, considering he's the evening shift supervisor and takes his job seriously. During the weekdays, the night staff comes in for the 11 to 7 shift. As it's the start of the weekend, the lot empties and no new vehicles enter the area. By 11:06, I'm alone, surrounded by a few stray cars still awaiting their owners.

A shiver creeps up my spine, and goosebumps stand at attention in spite of the warm air. The shadows of trees and shrubs close in, and I imagine someone running out to grab me. My paranoia gets the better of me, and I slide back into the driver's seat, roll up the windows most of the way, and lock the doors.

"Hurry up, Jake! What are you doing in there?"

The employee door opens in response, and I breathe a sigh of relief. Finally. I'm about to open the car door when I realize it's not him. The lone figure walks in the opposite direction, a car roars to life and drives off. Starting up the Honda, I pull up to the back door of the nearly vacant lot. No point in having him walk 30 seconds in the heat. He'll laugh when I tell him that.

It's 11:12, according to the digital display on the dash. I check my phone just to confirm it's the correct time. He's not usually this late. But there have been a couple of occasions I've waited for Jake and wondered what was taking him, times I've panicked thinking something's happened. He hates it when I do that. Just like when he's late driving home from work, and I'm standing at the front window, having bitten my nails down to the quick, convinced he's been in a car accident.

"I was just talking to Craig and lost track of the time," he said the last time he was late coming home. "I'm sorry I worried you. But you need to stop letting your imagination get the best of you. Seriously, you're going to drive yourself around the bend if you think the worst every time I'm a couple of minutes behind schedule. Chill, will you?"

I try to chill. He'll be out any minute. If I stare at the door long enough, he'll burst through. But he doesn't. Nor does anyone else. I send a text.

Hey, what's keeping you?

I add a smile emoji to show I'm not freaking out thinking someone has him tied up in there. With the seat reclined and air conditioner running, I try to calm myself. Sooner or later, he has to come out.

At 11:21, I exit the car and pull the warehouse door. It doesn't budge. My fist pounds on the metal. It's ridiculous, for a couple of reasons. One is that I'm acting irrationally. Jake's just finishing up something. There's no reason to be worried. What could possibly happen to him at work? Then there's the fact no one will hear me unless they're right by the exit. The warehouse is huge. Jake is likely at the other end.

Back inside the car, I check my phone again. He's not answering. There must have been some problem tonight. It's probably not the best time to tell Jake what I've been keeping from him. He'll sense I've been anxious because he didn't let me know he was running late. Even if I don't say anything, he'll notice my agitation, feel my pulse racing, see the sweat glistening on my forehead. There's no point adding to the tension by confessing that I've been lying for the last several weeks. Not really lying, just holding onto a secret. Which amounts to the same thing. He deserves a stress-free night after his long work week.

I can't stand the wait any longer. When I call, his phone goes to voicemail. I get out of the car and bang on the door again, harder this time, shouting his name. I don't care how foolish it makes me look. Not that there's anyone around. No traffic on the road, only a couple of other cars parked in the lot. He's probably chatting with whoever belongs to those vehicles. And here I am, the hysterical wife who can't leave her husband alone for twenty minutes. Twenty-seven now.

The solid door knocks me down as it flings open. A man stands above, swearing, then apologizing. He extends his hand to help me to my feet.

"Are you okay? Did I whack your head? I wasn't expecting anyone to be standing on the other side. You scared the shit out of me." He holds the door open with one foot. "What are you doing here, anyway?" He glances toward the Honda, with its open driver's door.

If I met him in a dark alley, I'd turn and run in the opposite direction. His large frame blocks my access to the building. The long hair and beard cover a good part of his face, but he's probably not much older than me. Maybe thirty-ish? Jake's age. I back away toward the car.

"I'm fine. I'm waiting for Jake."

"Jake? Jake who?"

"Shelton. Jake Shelton, my husband. The evening supervisor."

The man strokes his beard and points inside the warehouse. "You think he's still in there?"

"Yes. I came to pick him up, but he hasn't come out. Have you seen him?"

He shakes his head, then scans me from head to toe. "Just me and Mac.

6

Cleaning up. It's against the rules, but you can come in and look for him, if you want."

"Thank you. He's probably in his office finishing up some paperwork." It's obvious that's what's going on. Jake didn't realize what time it was, that the shift was over, everyone had gone home.

"If you don't mind, could I have a look at your ID first? I don't want to get into trouble for letting someone in after hours."

I grab my purse out of the car, holding it close to my body, and remove my ID to confirm I'm not lying about who I am. The scruffy man motions me in, and leads the way through a set of double doors, exposing the warehouse area. The bright blue industrial shelving goes on forever, boxes stacked ceiling-high with automotive parts, conveyor belts awaiting their packages. LED lights bounce off the concrete, the ice-like surface of the main corridor staring back at me, longer and wider than I remember from the tour Jake gave me weeks after we got married. A couple of forklifts mark the end of that section, and we turn right toward the supervisors' offices located above a flight of stairs. I glance up to the mezzanine, expecting to see Jake locking up his office, but the windows overlooking the warehouse floor are dark. I climb the steps to find the door locked.

"I don't know where he'd be." Once I'm back on solid ground, I turn my head in all directions, as though he might materialize.

The bearded, burly guy reaches behind his back. What if Jake is lying dead somewhere, and I'm about to join him? The man pulls a gun out of his back pocket.

"No!" I strike out, almost knocking it out of his hand.

"What the...? What's your problem, lady?"

Upon closer examination, the gun turns out to be a walkie-talkie. "I'm sorry," I step backward. "It was just a reaction."

"I'm gonna check with Mac, see if he's seen your husband around." He stares at me as though I've lost my mind, but averts his gaze for a moment to make contact with Mac. "What did you say your name was again?"

"Mallory. Mallory Shelton. My husband's Jake. He's the evening supervisor. I'm supposed to pick him up." The words come out of my mouth too quickly, sounding rehearsed, but he seems to accept what I say.

He nods and speaks into the walkie-talkie. "Mac? I've got a woman looking for her husband, Jake Shelton. Have you seen him?"

I draw my eyebrows together and part my lips as Mac responds. "There's nobody left in the building. I just finished doing a walk through and everything's locked up. The last person left about twenty minutes ago. You sure he's not in the parking lot waiting for her?"

"No, he's not in the parking lot. He's still inside," I insist. "Can I have a walk around and see if I can find him?"

It occurs to me that I should know who exactly I'm talking to. What right does this man have to be here, acting like he's in charge? "What's your name? Why are *you* still here? And Mac?"

"I'm Toby. Mac and I are the night cleaning crew." Toby runs a hand through his dirty blond hair. "I *guess* you can have a look around." He seems uncertain, scratching his head. "But I'll come with you."

Toby gets back on the walkie-talkie and tells Mac he's giving me a quick tour of the building, just in case Jake's checking up on something in one of the aisles and Mac missed him.

"There's about 70000 square feet in this place," Toby says as we walk along the back, looking down the long aisles. "But it's well organized. If he's still here, we should come across him."

I call out Jake's name as we walk past row upon row of shelving and end up at the loading dock doors. My echoing voice is hollow, coming back lifeless. Why isn't Jake answering? He has to be here somewhere. Turning left to check out the west wing, we find it empty. On our way back, I stop to peek inside the washroom, checking the women's stalls as well. The break room is pitch black, but I switch on the lights in case he's sitting there in the dark. Rows of folding tables and bright blue plastic chairs sit empty.

"What about the main offices?" I can't imagine why Jake would be in there, but he doesn't seem to be in the warehouse. We continue along to the east wing. I'm about to push through the swinging double doors, although the darkness through the door windows indicates the office staff have gone.

"The office janitor took off a couple of hours ago. Trust me, there's no one in there," Toby says as I push on the locked doors. "Look, I really need to get back to work. I've just wasted a good twenty minutes, and I've still got a lot of shit to do." With that, he turns and heads back toward the center aisle, expecting me to follow.

"Wait! I see someone." It's just a shadow and only a brief flash, but out of the corner of my eye, I could swear someone's on the other side of the shelves. Leaving Toby standing with his mouth open, I run along the corridor separating the offices from the warehouse shelving. He's down one of the aisles, sitting on some sort of vehicle. The engine roars to life just in time to drown me out.

"Jake!" As he drives away, I see the back of his head, wavy dark brown hair curling over the collar of a gray t-shirt.

"It's not Jake!" Toby jogs up from behind, tapping me on the back. "Mac's cleaning the floors." He turns on his walkie-talkie. "Hey, Mac," he shouts. "Can you get off the machine? I'm right behind you."

When Mac dismounts and faces us, my heart stops. It's not him. Of course, I knew all along it wouldn't be Jake.

Why would Jake be riding a floor sweeper after hours? The older man looks me up and down as I return his assessment. Apart from wavy brown hair, he looks nothing like my handsome husband with his chiseled jaw and chin dimple. Mac's closer to fifty than thirty, a few strands of gray hair now visible, with a prominent nose and weather-beaten face.

My distress must show on my face. "Everything okay, Miss?" He walks toward me, his brow furrowed.

I back away, bumping into Toby. With floor-to-ceiling shelving on either side and two strange men closing in, I'm trapped. If I were to scream, no one would hear me. As the reality of my situation sinks in, a familiar wave washes over me from head to toe and back again. Blood pounds in my ears, spots dance in front of my eyes.

Calm down, hold it together. I mentally repeat the words Jake uses when I get like this.

But being alone with two strange men in a huge warehouse out in the country, with midnight approaching and my husband nowhere to be found, is just too much for me to deal with. Although it's futile, I scream as loud as I can. "Help! Jake! Jake! Where are you?"

The screaming accomplishes *something*, at least. Both men back away, Toby with his hands in the air. "Hey, calm down, will you? Jake's not here. You must have missed him on his way out. He's probably looking for you out in the parking lot."

"Is there someone we can call for you? A family member or a friend?" There's fatherly concern in Mac's face, but it could all be a show.

"I'm going to call the police." It's meant to be a threat, and it works. They back off a little more.

"I don't think that's necessary," Toby says evenly, his hands still in the air. "I'm sure there's just been a misunderstanding."

"Misunderstanding?" I fumble around in my pockets and purse, trying to fish out my phone, but it's not there. "What kind of misunderstanding?"

"Maybe your husband got a ride with someone else."

I hadn't thought of that. He does catch a ride home with Craig sometimes. When Jake's car is being serviced in town, he goes to work with Craig. It's a bit out of his way, but Craig's his best friend, and Jake's returned the favor on numerous occasions. Sometimes, they drive into the city for a drink after work and take one car, leaving the other behind in the warehouse lot to pick up on their way home. Or, they just drive in to work together. The problem is *I* have Jake's car. It's not at the garage being serviced. He didn't drive himself to work. Craig didn't pick him up today. I took Jake's car to get an oil change in the city after dropping Jake off, then visited Gloria. Maybe Jake forgot I was picking him up and got a ride. Maybe I'm not the one who's mixed up.

"Yeah, maybe. Maybe he did." I need to get out of here. I don't know what these two are capable of doing. No one will be around the warehouse till late Sunday evening to start off the new work week. That's two whole days. "I'm just going to take another look out in the parking lot, then head home."

Mac doesn't look like he's ready to let me go. "Are you sure you don't want us to call someone for you?" He advances again. "I don't like the idea of you heading out to the parking lot by yourself in the condition you're in."

"I'll take her out." Toby's hands sit loosely by his side. "Make sure she gets to her car safely."

"Um, yes. Okay." Better Toby than Mac. He's closer to my age and pretty laid back. "Thank you."

"Hold on a second," Mac says, and I'm ready to make a run for it if he comes near me again. "I've got an idea. Let me try the intercom."

Intercom? Mac hops on the floor sweeper and takes off down the aisle. A few minutes later, his voice reverberates through the loudspeakers. "Jake, Jake Shelton? Are you still in the building?"

Toby and I wait, but silence overtakes an underlying hum. When Mac returns, he shakes his head. "He'd have answered if he was here."

Shrugging his shoulders, Toby indicates it's time for me to leave. My eyes scan the warehouse aisles at each intersection on our way to the exit. The double warehouse doors open to the main lobby at the employee entrance, and it occurs to me I haven't looked in the most obvious spot. To the left is the locker room, where the warehouse staff keep their personal belongings. Not waiting to get permission, I barge through the door into a room filled with medium-sized gray metal lockers. Number 78 is Jake's. I know his combination, though Jake's not aware of it—they're the same numbers he uses for everything—our wedding date. He might as well use 1,2,3,4,5,6.

Toby seems to have no objection to my going through Jake's stuff, as I have the combination. "I'm guessing you and Jake don't keep anything from each other," he comments as I check out the contents of my husband's locker.

"No, never. Are you married?" Since he's indulging me, I might as well engage in some polite conversation. Jake would want me to be friendly to the staff.

"I am. Got a kid on the way, too." He smiles, putting me at ease. Toby's not a serial killer, after all. But something weird is going on. "I guess my wife would be upset if I wasn't where I was supposed to be. You guys have a fight or something? Jen takes off for a couple of hours to cool down when I piss her off. Sometimes spends the night at her mother's."

"No. No fight." Jake and I don't fight. Staring at his locker full of safety equipment, I do wonder, though, if Jake took off on me. His hard hat, safety goggles, work gloves, steel-toe shoes, and ID badge are in his locker. He's obviously left the warehouse.

Yes, there's definitely something not right.

Chapter Three

My first thought when I'm back outside is that Jake must have panicked when he came out and saw the Honda, driver's door wide open, keys in the ignition, my phone sitting on the passenger seat.

"Oh, my God! He's probably going crazy wondering what happened to me." I spin around, looking in all directions. "Jake! I'm right here!"

"Hand over your phone," Toby demands, his hand extended. Is he going to steal my car and make sure I can't call for help?

"What?"

"Your phone. I'm going to put in my number so you can call if you need help. But I really need to get back to work."

Keeping my eyes on him, I walk around to the passenger side and reach in for my phone, bringing it to the driver's side. I'm not about to lean through the driver's door and risk him attacking me from behind. How do I know he's telling the truth? He may not even have a wife. He could be lying.

Toby's last words make me wonder what he sees when he looks at me. "Look, I don't know what's going on here. I don't know if you're high or something or if you're just confused, and it's none of my business… but I think Mac's right. You *should* call somebody. Get a ride home. Jake's probably at home wondering where the hell you are." He hesitates, then adds, "But if you can't get hold of anybody, give me a call. I'll make sure you get home safe."

I know I'm an attractive twenty-eight-year-old, blue-eyed, long-haired blonde woman with curves in the right places. Even though I doubt my own attractiveness much of the time, I know this because of the looks I get from men—the ones I know and the ones I don't. Jake says I'm a man magnet.

Yet the look Toby gives me as his face disappears isn't like that at all. It's a look of genuine concern. While he took me around the warehouse, I was worried about my safety, being alone with a man I didn't know. It turns out he was worried about my safety, too.

He tilts his head and asks, "Are you sure you're okay?" I nod. He closes the warehouse door.

I'm alone again in an empty parking lot. Somehow, I've managed to miss Jake. He obviously left work, didn't see me parked here, and now we're looking for each other. We'll have a good laugh about this tomorrow. We're like the Three Stooges, only there's just two of us. Me and Jake.

With the darkness and humidity closing in, I grab my keys, slam shut the car door before the battery dies, leaving me stuck here with no one to call, lock up, and head around the side of the building where the offices are located. Fortunately for me, there are lights on that section of the building, illuminating the warehouse signage. I check my phone for messages, but finding none, call him again. No answer. Using the flashlight app on my phone for extra guidance, I navigate my way along the perimeter of the huge facility. It's surprisingly quiet. Only the sound of my own voice, calling for him.

Maybe I *am* crazy to think that Jake's wandering around the building looking for me. Toby indicated as much when I called out for Jake when we got outside. He clearly doesn't think Jake is anywhere near the warehouse. But I'd never forgive myself if I left him out here in the dark.

When I get to the back of the building, it's downright spooky. No parking lot lampposts. No lit up sign. No outdoor lighting. By the light of the moon and the stars, along with my phone, I inch my way across the grass, sticking close to the building. Every once in a while, I call out, but the sound of my voice scares me. It's as though hearing myself makes the fact I'm alone all the more evident, and a shiver runs through me, precipitating me into a jog around the trucks at the loading doors.

By the time I reach the end of the building and work my way back toward the lit parking lot out front, I'm convinced this is all a dream. It's so impossibly surreal. I left Jake off at the start of his shift. I came to pick him up at the end of it. His stuff is in his locker. He left the building. I was waiting for him in the parking lot. How did I not see him? How did he not see me? Why isn't he answering his phone?

As I approach the Honda, I think I have my answers. Toby is right. Someone else has given him a ride. That someone has to be Craig. Who else could it be? We've gotten our signals crossed. He probably told me he was going out for drinks after work with Craig, and I just wasn't listening. It wouldn't be the first time.

If they're at the bar, he wouldn't hear the phone above the music. I won't let on that I've been worrying. If I do, he's going to be concerned. My memory *does* sometimes play tricks on me. I forget things.

Kind of like an absent-minded professor, Jake jokes.

Craig and Jake have been best buddies since Jake started working at the warehouse, ten years ago. That's six more years than I've known my husband. Craig is still single.

"I can't let him down," Jake says whenever the two of them go out. "Just because I'm happily married, I can't not go out with my best friend anymore."

I'm completely understanding, of course. I would never expect Jake to give up his best friend. Besides, Craig's a great guy. Some girl is going to be very lucky one day. I'm not jealous of the time they spend together without me. You can hardly have a guy's night out with a wife tagging along.

I drive the car to the parking lot exit, stop, and let it idle for a while, just in case Jake is still out here somewhere wondering what on earth happened to me. It wouldn't be the first time. He lost me once before. He couldn't bear it if he thought he'd lost me again.

"I can't live without you," he tells me every day. I feel the same way. It's like we're not two separate people. From the moment we met, we became one—Jake and Mallory. There was no more just Mallory.

It's time to go home. Forget about this little mix-up. He'll be home before I know it, back in my arms, holding me tight, telling me he's sorry. Telling me it's his fault I got mixed up. Telling me I'm not crazy, just a little confused.

Telling me how much he loves me.

Twenty minutes go by in agony as I drive to the home I share with my husband, hoping to find him there waiting for me. Trees and bushes pass by on my left when I turn down our road. Jake and I love our little piece of heaven in the country. We're just on the edge of town, within a reasonable walking distance of the small town's business area, but blessed with the quiet and beauty of nature. I pass our only close neighbor, on the same side of the road as our home, but far enough away that we have our privacy. The Winstons, Linda and Paul, are an older couple in their fifties, so we don't have much in common. Still, we'd be more than happy to socialize with them. They've just never invited us over. I suppose we could have made the first move.

There are a couple of lampposts on the other side of the street, but as usual, the one in front of our house is out of commission. Only the headlights tell me when I reach our driveway. No lights are on inside or outside of the house. Turning right, the gravel crunches under the tires as I ease down the long lane toward the beautiful old red brick building set on several acres of grass, flower beds, and trees. Home.

Except, it's not home if Jake's not here. And I know for a fact he's not home. The security light comes on in front of the garage as I kill the headlights. Jake installed the three motion-activated lights along the front of the house for my peace of mind. When we first moved here three years ago, it terrified me to be home alone at night while Jake was at work. I called him at the warehouse every time I heard a noise outside.

It's just some stray cat, he'd say. *Chill, Mal.*

He said the lights were a small price to pay for my peace of mind. Not only do they warn me when someone's coming, they also light my way as I run to the front door and struggle with my key in the lock on the few occasions I'm out on my own. Tonight is one of those nights. Only I'm not coming home from the grocery store in town. Tonight, I'm coming home alone because I've stupidly managed to misplace my husband.

As I stumble into the house, I flip on the light switch and lock the door behind me. Our black and white long-haired cat, Nellie, runs up to greet me and rubs against my legs, purring for attention and food.

"Hey, girl. Did you miss Mommy?"

Once she is fed, I settle myself on the couch in my PJs with Nellie and a calming cup of chamomile tea. The air is on, the T.V. is on, and my nerves are on edge. This was supposed to be our night. It's nearly one in the morning. I call Jake one more time. He doesn't pick up. I try another number. He picks up on the second ring.

"Hi, sorry to bother you guys. I just wanted to check that everything's okay. I think we got our signals mixed up. I thought I was supposed to pick up Jake tonight. My mistake. Anyway, can I talk to him for a minute?" I need to hear his voice. I never thought I'd be one of those needy wives, but I just love my husband so much.

"Mallory?"

"Yes?"

"What are you doing? Are you okay?"

"I'm fine. I'm sorry to interrupt your guy's night out."

"What are you talking about?"

"You and Jake. What do you mean, 'what am I talking about'? I guess I forgot the two of you had plans tonight." Has Craig had too many drinks? He sounds groggy, a bit out of it. I don't want him driving Jake home if that's the case.

"Should I pick you guys up? Sounds like you've had a little too much."

"Mallory."

Something in his tone frightens me. Hearing him say my name that way makes me think something has happened to Jake. Is he hurt? Is he ill? Was there an accident?

"Craig? Put Jake on now." If he's drunk, too, I don't want to take any chances. I'm going to go pick him up.

"Mallory. I'm home in bed. I went straight home after work. Alone. What's going on?"

Chapter Four

Craig insists on coming over to check on me and breaks the connection. I hold the phone in my hand, not understanding. I pinch myself to make sure I'm awake. This can't be happening. If Jake's not with Craig, then who *is* he with?

For a moment, an absurd thought goes through my head. Maybe Jake isn't real. Maybe I'm not married. Maybe I've created some fantasy based on my desire for a perfect life. Jake says I have an overactive imagination. I prefer to consider it a sign of creativity.

The wedding photo on the bookcase confirms Jake is very real. He's everything I've ever wanted in a man. The image of the two of us stares back, so perfectly happy on that June day three years ago. I'm wearing my mother's organza wedding gown with its long beaded lace train and lace and pearls on the sleeves and bodice. It had been stored in a metal trunk in the basement closet for so long, awaiting my big day. My blond waves are loose (the way Jake likes them), with a long lace veil topping them off, the diamond and pearl earrings and necklace Jake gifted me adding a final touch. I look like a princess. Beside me, Jake is my Prince Charming, handsome in his black tux. We had a small, intimate ceremony and reception, but it was a traditional wedding, just like Jake wanted. It was perfect.

Setting down the framed photo, I climb the stairs to our bedroom and step into the walk-in closet. Jake's clothes are hanging there, neatly organized, pants on the bottom, shirts on top, casual clothing on one side, the few dressy items he owns on the other. His sweaters lie folded on the shelves, his pajama bottoms and t-shirts, socks and underwear in the drawers, shoes arranged on a wire rack, belts and ties hanging in their spot. Nothing seems to be missing. Why would it be? Jake would never leave. How that thought could have entered my mind for even a fraction of a second is unfathomable. He loves me. He would rather die than lose me.

Gazing at our antique cherry four-poster bed, sheets flawlessly tucked in, with the elegant gold and dusty pink floral and plaid duvet turned down, and tons of pillows artistically displayed, I wonder how I could possibly go to sleep with Jake missing. I'll wait for him to come home. Rest won't come till he's back in my arms.

We've never spent a night without each other since we got married. Except for that one time. He thought he'd lost me. It was during our first year of marriage, and it was, of course, *my* fault.

* * *

Two and a half years ago

"Jake just called. He's on his way here," my friend Heather had warned.

"What are you doing here? I texted you, saying I was staying over," I explained when he banged at Heather's apartment door.

"I didn't get any text from you." Jake's tight face held back his emotions. He looked like he was about to cry, but he wouldn't embarrass himself in front of Heather. "I was worried that something bad happened. I was ready to call the police."

It was understandable he would feel that way. I had gone to visit my old roommate from university. It was a wintry weekend, and I shouldn't have set out on the three-hour drive that Saturday morning, especially without saying goodbye. Jake had been out picking up some supplies at the hardware store. The bathroom faucet was leaking, the toilet wouldn't stop running, and there were no light bulbs left to replace the one burned out in the kitchen. Saturdays we usually clean the house and do any repairs or maintenance. However, I made other plans for that weekend—plans that didn't include

Jake.

I hadn't seen Heather for a couple of years. When I called her that morning, she invited me to visit. I didn't bother to pack anything. We'd have lunch, chat for a bit, reminisce about the good old days.

But things didn't go quite as planned. By the time we exited the restaurant, snow poured from the sky, blanketing the roads, the wind whipping our faces. I wouldn't be driving home till the storm abated.

"I'm sorry I worried you," I said to Jake as he stood in Heather's doorway the next day, waiting for an explanation. "It won't happen again." Seeing him so distraught, I realized I could never leave him again.

Heather suggested I skip school and stay another night, but Jake wouldn't hear of it.

"I've just driven all this way to get my wife back. I'm not leaving without her." His arm protectively around me, he kissed my forehead. "Sweetheart, I know how forgetful you can be, but the next time you go away for the weekend, you really need to let me know."

"I… I… yes, I'm sorry."

Heather's eyes flitted between me and Jake, and she touched my arm. Her brow furrowed, she opened her mouth, then closed it as though she wanted to say something but thought better of it. I was sure she wondered what Jake was doing with a wife who could be so inconsiderate.

We drove home Sunday afternoon, me following Jake in his Honda to make sure I got home safely in the snow. We didn't speak to each other on our phones during the drive. We didn't talk until we were alone inside our home.

"Do not ever—I mean it, Mal—ever do that to me again."

He was shaking, his bottom lip quivering. "I thought—I know it sounds crazy—but I thought you'd left me. At first, I thought maybe you'd stepped out to get something at the store. But when you didn't come back, I started to go nuts. I called everyone to find you. It's a good thing I remembered your friend, Heather. It was the last place I thought of looking before calling the police. You can't just walk out on me, Mal. We're married."

"I… I know… I'm sorry. I thought I texted you. I thought you knew where

I was last night. I wouldn't leave you. You must know that. I'm so sorry I worried you."

"I do. Worry about you, Mal. Sometimes, you get so caught up in your own little world and lose touch with reality. I couldn't bear it if something happened and I lost you. We're meant to be together, you and I. Till death do us part. I meant those words we said on our wedding day."

"Me too." I tried to reassure him that I loved him, that I would never leave him. One thing was clear right then and there—I never wanted to see that expression on his face again. I'd give anything to make up for the stupid mistake I made that weekend.

* * *

Now the tables are turned. Jake didn't come home tonight, and I'm the one going nuts. Did I not get a message he sent? Has he left me? He wouldn't, though.

So where, oh where, is my husband?

I'm sitting on the bed trying to understand when one of the security lights comes on, sending a sliver of light through the curtains.

He's home. Jake must have gone out with some of his other work buddies. I'm so relieved I won't say a word, even if he is drunk. Even if he did spoil our Friday night.

Chapter Five

The doorbell rings before I reach the bottom of the stairs. He must be too drunk to get his key in the door. That's okay. He deserves to let off some steam now and then. Especially being married to me. How he puts up with my anxiety and fantasies, I don't know. Love really does conquer all, I suppose.

I swing the door open, ready to put my arms around him. If he's not too drunk, we'll head straight for bed and make love. I'll tell him it's my fault—I made a mistake. I need to show him how much he means to me. The thought of losing him, even though he's only been gone for a couple of hours, kills me. I can't imagine living without Jake.

When the door opens, I'm shocked to see Craig standing there, his eyebrows drawn together. He steps inside and closes the door. "Mallory? Is everything okay?" He pulls me into his arms.

"I thought you were Jake." I step away from him.

"You sounded confused on the phone. I told you I was coming over to check on you."

Craig's expression tells me he's as worried as I am. His brown eyes are warm and sympathetic, brown hair curls down over his crinkled forehead as he looks to me for a response. At 32, he's fit and nice to look at, but not as good-looking as my husband. Not that I should be noticing how attractive another man is, especially Jake's best friend. I lower my eyes.

"It's Jake. He's not home."

"I know." Craig takes my hand and speaks gently. "But his car's in the driveway. So is yours. He must have left work with someone else."

"But why didn't he text me? Why didn't he answer when I called? Why isn't he home yet?" The growing hysteria in my voice fills the entryway. "What if something's happened to him?"

"Mallory." He says my name and stares at me, trying to make eye contact. But I can't. I just can't. "Think. About the last time you saw him."

I don't want to think about the last time I saw him because I'm afraid it may very well be the last time I ever see him.

"He kissed me and told me to have a good time at his Mom's. Nothing else." I'm hyperventilating, and I know how hysterical I must seem, considering Jake's probably going to stumble through the door after a night out at some bar. He's done that before. I should be used to it by now.

Craig responds calmly. "I've got an idea."

"What?"

"Did you try tracking his phone?"

How stupid can you be?

Why hasn't that occurred to me? "No... I guess I didn't think of that."

When I sign into our account, it shows our house as his last location. "He's here?" My head spins around the room, and I almost expect him to jump out and have a good laugh at my expense.

Craig takes the phone from my hand. "He must have turned it off. That's not like him, but maybe after last night, he needed to take a break."

Last night? Craig's thumb wipes away the tears rolling down my cheeks. "Hey, it's going to be okay. Why don't you and I check out a couple of his usual drinking holes? If he shut his phone off in the bar and he's had too much to drink, he probably doesn't realize how late it is."

That sounds logical. "But why aren't you with him?"

"I had a headache all night. The last thing I needed was to get plastered, so I went straight home and popped a couple of pills. Besides, I'm not Jake's favorite person right now. I thought he'd be with you tonight anyway. It's Friday. So what happened, Mallory? You need to clear your head so we can figure this out."

"Let's go find him." I'm out the door first. Despite being upset, I remember to lock up. If Jake beats me home, I'm sure he can figure out the key into the keyhole thing sooner or later.

Craig's Jeep sits behind my Toyota. As soon as I get into the passenger seat, I turn around and check the back.

"He's not there," Craig says, following my gaze, "if that's what you're thinking."

"I know." Of course, he's not there. If he was, Craig would have said so. My husband is not passed out in the back of his best friend's vehicle.

I can hear Jake's reaction. *Where do you get these crazy ideas, Mal?*

"It'll be okay." He's trying to keep me calm and focused on what we need to do, but I know it's not okay.

Half an hour later, we're in the city, parked outside one of Jake's usual haunts. The neon sign flashes, open at 1:34 a.m. As we pass through the door, sound and lights assail my senses. It's not something I'm used to, being in a bar. When I attended university, I went out with friends, but that seems like a lifetime ago. Craig seems to know his way around, though.

"Hey, Matt," he greets the young bartender, taking a seat on a stool, indicating I should sit next to him. "Just a couple of orange juices, when you get a chance."

Matt nods and pours our drinks. As he sets them on the counter, Craig asks if he's seen Jake tonight.

"Last time I saw Jake was with you last night, at closing."

"Any of our usual crowd around?"

"Yeah." Matt points to one of the booths where three guys are conversing and laughing.

"Wait here," Craig says. I'm about to protest when he adds, "I'll just be a minute. Matt, keep an eye on my friend. Make sure no one hits on her." He winks.

I sip my orange juice, waiting patiently while Craig talks to his work buddies. They shake their heads in response to Craig's questions. When Craig returns, I say, "He hasn't been here, has he?"

It's a rhetorical question. I know he hasn't been here tonight.

"No. They haven't seen him all day."

As the words come out of his mouth, a jolt courses through my body and my eyelids flutter. Who was the last person to see Jake alive? Was it me?

Have you lost your f...ing mind?

Of course, he's alive. Why would I think such a stupid thought?

"Let's head out. Maybe we can check another spot before closing time." Craig escorts me to the door.

A couple of blocks away, we pull into a similar-looking establishment. The lot is almost empty. "Sometimes, we come here. It won't hurt to check it out."

It doesn't take long to confirm what I know. Jake's not here. Neither is anyone who might know him. "Now what?" I ask as we pull out of the lot.

"Call him. Maybe he's home by now. Use my phone."

I know it's futile, but I do exactly as I'm told. Craig knows Jake well. Maybe he thinks Jake won't pick up for me because he's afraid I'm going to lecture him about going out drinking instead of taking me to the Frosty Bar and the hot tub. Jake probably decided I didn't need an ice cream treat this week.

Have you put on a few pounds lately? His concern for my health is endearing, and he's right, of course. I do need to watch my weight.

"No answer. Now what?"

"We go back home and call people. He has to be somewhere."

Yes, he does. Unless he's dead.

We drive in silence, turning into our driveway at 2:28 a.m. The house is dark. If Jake were home, he wouldn't go to sleep with me missing. "He's not here," I state the obvious.

"No."

Once we're inside, I collapse into Craig's arms. "Where is he? Where is my husband?"

"Oh, Mallory." Craig rubs my back. "I think it's time for you to face some hard truths."

Chapter Six

"Truth?" What is the truth?

"You and Jake have been having some problems lately. Maybe Jake's with another woman." Craig holds my hands in his as we stand facing each other in the entranceway. "Especially after what happened last…"

"An affair? No, no, he wouldn't do that. Did he tell you he was seeing someone?"

Craig shakes his head. "He didn't say anything to me, but he wouldn't, would he? He'd know I wouldn't want him breaking your heart. Do you have any idea where else he might be?"

I don't know. Someone ran him over and left him on the road? Or he's in a hospital and has amnesia? Maybe someone kidnapped him? I'll get a ransom note soon. Maybe someone mugged him? He's lying unconscious somewhere. Maybe someone killed him? His body's in a dumpster or some other godforsaken place. Maybe he got drunk and wandered off? He's going to wake up in an alley with a big hangover.

"Mallory?" Craig leads me to the brown leather sofa and snaps me out of my crazy thoughts with his firm voice. "Could this have anything to do with Jake's… problems? Has someone been threatening him?"

"No, I don't think so. But maybe…"

"We need to call people, see if anyone knows where he might be. Who do you want to start with?"

I have no idea. Jake and I have few friends. We like to spend time alone. Mostly, it's just the two of us. There's Craig, of course. He's become as much a friend to me as he is to Jake. Craig spends more time here than anyone, including Jake's mom. Then there's Vicky. I met Jake through her. When I reconnected with her.

"What about Vicky?"

Craig hesitates. "He wouldn't be with her." But I hear doubt creep into his voice.

I nibble the skin around my long, pink nails. "No."

But, of course, I know it's a very real possibility he's with her right now.

Although she *was* my best friend, we lost touch. Vicky and I attended the same high school and hung around with the same crowd. But like most high school friends, we went our separate ways after graduation. On to different universities in different cities, with Vicky building a whole new social network, while I concentrated on my studies, venturing out to local bars and restaurants with schoolmates now and then.

* * *

Nearly four years ago

I ran into her at an upscale restaurant nearly a year after I returned home to settle my parents' estate following the house fire. As my date, Brad, and I ate our starter salads, Vicky tapped me on the shoulder.

"Mallory, hi." We hadn't seen each other for a few years, although we still commented on each other's posts on social media now and then. She had changed her looks since high school, unlike me. Her long auburn hair was styled straight, and she wore a form-fitting black dress that showed off her figure and stilettos. Kohl lined her brown eyes, which were offset with a soft purple shadow and long, thick lashes. She pulled off sexy, but elegant.

"Vicky. I didn't know you were in town."

"I actually moved back home. A couple of months now. An articling opportunity with a prestigious law firm presented itself, and I missed my family, so it worked out perfectly."

The smile left her lips as she remembered I no longer had a family. "How about you? How are you doing?" She placed a hand on my shoulder.

I told her I was fine, though it was far from the truth.

When she suggested we get together for lunch on the weekend to catch up, I wanted to decline the invitation. I had nothing noteworthy to catch up on. My parents were dead, my home was gone, I had no boyfriend, no siblings, no friends. What I had was a class of kindergarten kids by day and a lonely apartment by night. This date was my first in a long time. Brad teaches Grade 6 in the school where I work as an early childhood educator. I doubted Vicky and I had anything in common anymore.

Just as Vicky was about to leave us to eat our meal, she was joined by a tall, nicely built guy with wavy brown hair, a handsome, unshaven face, and the most dazzling blue-green eyes I've ever seen. A girl could never forget those. He put his arm around Vicky and smiled at Brad and me. "Do you want to introduce me to your friends, honey?"

He had me from that very first smile and the spark in those eyes.

Vicky called the next day and said she'd made reservations at Chez Juliette for Saturday at 1 p.m. I accepted, not wanting to be rude. But as it turned out, I enjoyed Vicky's company, and she seemed to tolerate mine.

When Vicky broke up with Jake a couple of months later, I just happened to be at her place when he came around to talk her into getting back together.

"It's over, Jake," Vicky said when she opened the door. "I told you I don't want to see you again."

"You can't break up with me without an explanation. You owe me that much."

From my spot on the living room sofa, I observed him push open the door and pull Vicky toward him. When he noticed me, he released her. "Oh, you have company."

"Yes, you remember Mallory." Vicky backed away from Jake and turned to me. "Mallory and I were just about to head out to the mall, weren't we?"

I didn't recall any plans to go to the mall that afternoon, but I nodded. "Yes, we were."

"I came here to talk to you," Jake reminded Vicky, stepping farther into the apartment. "The least you can do is give me a few minutes of your time."

"Five minutes." Vicky headed to the kitchen, Jake following. I was embarrassed when I heard their conversation through the closed door.

"We have a good thing going," Jake said. "I don't want it to end."

"We had a few months of fun. It ended when you..." I didn't catch the next part.

"I told you I was sorry. Every couple has their ups and downs, their disagreements. Just because we had a little fight..."

"A little fight?"

"Yes. It doesn't mean it's over. It's not over for me."

"Well, it is for me. Look, we had some good times. The sex was great. But let's just call it quits before things get ugly."

"Vick, please."

The kitchen door opened, and I grabbed a magazine off the coffee table, pretending to be engrossed in reading. Jake left with a final plea. "Can we at least be friends, Vick? I'll call you in a few days."

Vicky didn't respond. She slammed the door behind him. She turned to me. "Some guys get too attached and don't know when it's over. You know what I mean?"

I didn't know at all. I'd never had a serious relationship. No one had ever been too attached to me. I remember thinking I would have loved to be in Vicky's shoes, having a gorgeous hunk of a guy begging me to stay with him.

A few weeks later, Jake and I bumped into each other getting our morning latte at the Cafe Mozart. "Hey, it's Mallory, isn't it?" Jake approached me in line.

I gazed into the deep sea of his eyes and was lost in a turquoise paradise.

* * *

I'm still lost to him, arms flailing in deep waters now that he's gone. How could anyone ever break away from those eyes and that smile?

"No," I answer Craig now, trying to convince myself as much as him. "I don't think Vicky would know where he is. But I can't think of any other friends we have in common."

"Okay, give her a call, then." Craig knows Vicky from when she and Jake were together. They also hooked up at our wedding, then dated for a few months. The break-up was tough on Craig, according to Jake. But Vicky told me they didn't want the same things in life. She wanted to settle down, and he wanted to play the field a little longer. Oddly enough, the four of us have managed to remain friends.

The phone rings several times before Vicky answers. "Hello? Do you know what time it is?" There's some rustling, and it sounds like she's about to hang up.

"Vicky? Are you there?"

No answer.

"Vicky? It's Mallory. Can you hear me?"

"Mallory? Just a minute." A few seconds later, she continues. "Why are you calling at this time of night? Is everything okay?"

"No, it's not. Jake's not home. I don't know where he is. You wouldn't have any idea, would you?" I'm grasping at straws. Or, I hope I am.

"Jake? Why would I know where he is? I haven't seen him since the four of us went out for dinner last month."

She's talking about my birthday dinner six weeks ago—me, Jake, Vicky, and Craig. We had a good meal, followed by an evening of bar hopping. I woke up with a whopper of a headache and gaps in my memory. "You know Jake. He's probably out getting shit-faced with Craig and his work buddies."

"No, Craig's with me now. We checked out the bars together. No one saw Jake tonight."

Silence on the other end. Then Vicky voices the same conclusion Craig came to. "I'm sorry, Mallory. But do you think it's possible he's with another woman?"

"Jake would never do that to me." The stoniness in my voice is something I can't control and hope she doesn't pick up on. He may have cheated on her, I don't know, but he told me when he asked me to marry him that he was a one-woman kind of guy.

"No, I know," Vicky tries to placate me. "But he's a man, Mallory. They're all the same." A huge sigh comes through my phone.

"So you haven't seen him? And you have no idea where he might be?" I want to end the call, but not before I'm convinced she can't help me find Jake.

"Sorry, but I'm sure he'll be home soon. Try not to worry. He'll likely have some explanation. Car trouble, maybe?"

I don't bother to tell her both our cars are in the driveway. "Okay, thanks anyway."

"Send me a text tomorrow. Let me know how it goes. And if you need a good divorce lawyer, give me a call at the office."

She laughs, but I don't join her. I know my husband better than she does. He hasn't had car trouble; he's not having an affair. And divorce is out of the question.

Craig sits, elbows on his knees, on the chair across from me, watching my every move. He raises his eyebrows. "Well?"

I shake my head. It's barely perceptible, but I swear he looks relieved. Did he actually think…? "She hasn't seen him since my birthday."

"Oh." A brief flash of something crosses Craig's face, as though that brought a memory forward. "The birthday."

I change the subject abruptly. "So, who do we call next?"

"What about Terry?" The night of my birthday celebration, we ran into Terry, Jake's best friend from high school, at one of the bars. "Have you got his number?"

Although it's unlikely Jake wandered five hours away from home, I pull out our Christmas card address book from the antique desk in the den and read out Terry's number as Craig enters it into his phone. Maybe Terry is in the area, visiting his parents in Brampton Heights.

But, of course, Terry hasn't heard from Jake in the last six weeks.

Craig and I stare at each other for a long time, trying to think of who else Jake could possibly be with. "His brother?" Craig suggests.

Contacting his family sounds like the next logical step, but I hate the thought of worrying them. Jake's older brother, John, is married with two boys. We visit them every couple of months.

"He didn't have a car. How would he get there?" I remind Craig that Jake's car isn't missing, only Jake. "It's an hour and a half away."

Craig shrugs. We've exhausted the list of friends. Family is next.

"I'm going to wait till morning to call John. Same with Jake's mom." I'd just left Gloria a few hours ago. As far as she knows, he's home in bed with me right now.

"I don't want to leave you alone, Mallory. But it's not going to look good if I stay all night." Craig bends down to plant a kiss on the top of my head. "When Jake comes home...or if someone sees my car parked here..."

He opens the door, and we stand on the porch, looking toward the road. "You need to be strong. Let's wait till morning, and we'll go from there."

I know he's right. There's nothing else to do at this point. As Craig's car heads down the dark country road, I lock the front door, wondering how it ever came to this. One minute, I was a happily married woman; the next I'm a woman whose husband has left her without an explanation.

Since Jake's not here to do the nightly rounds, I double check the back door and the patio door to make sure they're locked up tight, Nellie trailing me. Pouring hot water over my teabag, I gaze out the kitchen window to our huge back yard. Although it's too dark to see much of anything, the solar lights provide some illumination along the flower beds. The shovel still sits where I left it the last time I used it. At the very end of the lawn, in the right corner, is the garden shed, broken bits of ceramic pots, gardening tools, along with a mixture of dirt, fertilizer, and bird seed covering the wooden floor. I can't see it from here, but I know what's in there. Just like I know what's next to it—beautiful rose bushes to the left, every one filled with thorns ready to draw blood. The ground's nicely mounded, nothing to mark what lies buried beneath. Sipping calming chamomile, my thoughts wander to the last time I saw Jake, and I wonder what he's doing, what he's thinking.

Chapter Seven

Dark. Damp. Dank. I thought hell was supposed to be hot. If this is heaven, it's been overrated. Maybe it's purgatory, but I've gotta feeling there's no one praying for me. Where the hell am I? Why the hell does my head hurt like a son of a bitch? Why the hell can't I move? Just dreaming. A nightmare. Wake up.

My eyes won't open. Too heavy. Need to get some rest. Need to sleep... just drift off.

Light coming through my eyelids. I'm in the hospital. Maybe in a coma. Car accident? Yeah, that's why everything hurts. Need to call a nurse. Water, pain meds. Need... Mallory. Mallory will be here, by my side, like she always is. Need to open my eyes, see Mallory.

Slowly, just a little slit, open. Look for the light. I'm so damned confused. So alone. Where is she? Why don't I sense her presence? What is that chirping? Birds? Outside my window? Forcing my eyes to open, I look up. A halo of light at the end of the tunnel. So this is it. This is how it all ends. I need to go to the light. Close my eyes and float to the light. My head. Why is it hurting if I'm dead? My body aches. Why can I feel pain if I've left my body?

NO! My eyes fly open. I won't. I won't go to the light. I won't leave Mallory. She needs me. Jake and Mallory—we're a team, till death do us part. I won't leave her. I look around the dark space, moving my head with great effort; my eyes scan the shadows. Whatever this place is, it's no hospital. No beeping, no buzzers, no alarms, no intercom, no moaning. And the smell is wrong. Rot, wet, mold. Not antiseptic, not sterile. More earthy.

My fingers creep over the bed I'm lying on. Something wet, slimy, squishy. Cold. Where is the warm blanket?

Why am I alone? How long have I been here? As my eyes adjust to the near darkness and the fingers on my other hand grope the bed under me, I come to a realization.

I'm underground. In the cold, wet ground. But not dead. No, not dead. Yet.

Chapter Eight

J ake planted those rose bushes for me. Just before we got married, we spent one morning at the nursery and loaded up several garden carts with perennials and annuals. I felt like a real wife, my husband-to-be pulling the carts after me as I planned which plants would go in which flower bed. "Whatever you want, honey. I'll love it. Just like I love you," he'd said.

He had already dug up and manured the flower bed, prepared the hole for me to place the first rose bush into the ground. "Ouch! Oww…!"

Jake took my finger into his mouth and sucked the blood, his hand stroking the length of my arm, his kiss caressing my cheek. "Let me take care of that." He led me to the shed and removed antibiotic cream and a bandage from the first aid kit.

As I stand in the kitchen staring at the dark, I imagine him with me now, comforting me, taking care of me. His lips on my cheek, his hand on my hand, his body next to mine. Just like he always has, right from our first real date, he reassures me, makes me feel safe.

* * *

Three and a half years ago

We went to a movie that night, one I chose. During our conversation the day we met at the coffee shop, he'd asked me out.

"I'm not sure it's a good idea. You've just broken up with Vicky, and she's my friend. I don't know how she'll feel about the two of us going on a date." I didn't mention that I broke up with Brad the previous week because he wanted our relationship to move faster than I did.

"I really don't think Vicky would care," Jake had said, setting down his latte. "It's over between us. She's moved on. I'm ready to do the same."

He took my hand, and his eyes locked on mine. "How about dinner tonight? You've got to eat. I've got to eat. We could eat together."

He wasn't going to take no for an answer, and besides, I couldn't possibly turn him down when he looked at me with those eyes. "What about a movie instead? There's one playing that I kind of wanted to see, if you're up for it. It's one of those sappy ones, though, so I'll understand if you're not interested."

My hope was to let him down gently. As attracted as I was to Jake right from the first moment I saw him, my hand pulled away from his. Once he learned about my baggage (and he would, sooner or later), he'd run for the hills, and I'd be left heartbroken.

He smiled and said, "Oh, I think I'll be quite interested, if it means I get to spend time with you." How could I refuse?

Although the movie had been billed as a romantic comedy, it ended on a sad note. As much as I tried to hide my tears, Jake was attuned to my emotions. His left hand moved up and down my arm, and he reached over with his other hand to place it on mine. It was so sweet, I didn't feel the need to pull away.

"They'll always have their memories," he whispered in my ear. "No one can take that away from them."

When Jake dropped me off at my door after the movie, he gave me a chaste kiss on the cheek, as though he knew it was all I could handle.

"What do you want to do on our second date? How about something that doesn't involve crying?" He laughed and put me at ease. I decided if he could put up with a chick flick and a crying jag, the least I could do was have dinner with him.

* * *

Looking back on that first date now, and how I fell in love with Jake, I remember thinking that I couldn't for the life of me understand why Vicky would let him go. Her loss, my gain. Except now, it's my loss, too.

Chapter Nine

The grounds of our estate are beautiful, as is the old farmhouse itself. Jake and I moved in right after we got married. The house had belonged to his grandparents on his mother's side. After they retired from farming, they didn't want to sell the family farm, so they rented out the land, but kept a three-acre parcel with the house for their own use and lived there until his grandpa passed away. When his grandma followed, the year after, the house sat empty. Jake's mom graciously offered to sell the property to us at a fair price, including all the furnishings, before putting it on the market. She even held the mortgage for us at a really low rate so we'd have enough funds to decorate and make it our own. The large farmhouse did need some renovations, but I could imagine the two of us building a life there together. It was perfect. Three good-sized bedrooms, one for each of the kids, I'd said at the time, plus the main bedroom for us. Jake convinced me to turn one of the bedrooms into a walk-in closet and ensuite for ourselves.

"The kids can have bunk beds. We'll have a boy's room and a girl's room," he'd said with a wide grin. "We're going to need our own space once the house is overrun with three or four rugrats. Besides, we can always build on later if we need to."

I thought we had the perfect life, Jake and I. But maybe I missed the signs of trouble in our marriage. Maybe I ignored them. I should have known it was all *too* perfect. I wanted the perfect husband, the perfect home, the perfect family. And I was willing to do whatever it took to get it. Because the perfect family I used to have went up in smoke.

From the moment I fell so deeply in love with Jake, I knew he was the answer to my dreams. He was the fresh start I desperately needed.

You never know how traumatic events in your life will affect you. When I lost my parents, I lost myself. I was living up north, having just finished my university degree. When a job came up there at a local school, I didn't hesitate to take it. Like so many other young people, I had moved out of my parents' house and was making my own life. After the fire, I kept wondering if things might have turned out differently if I had made alternate choices. What if I had moved back in with my parents? What if I got a job and a place close to them? What if I checked on them more often? Would they still be alive? Or, would I have died in the fire with them? Would I have survived and blamed myself for not checking the smoke detectors? Would I have lived and wondered why I wasn't there for them at the exact moment when they needed me?

What could I have done differently? I'm well aware there are things that are simply out of our control. I'm also a firm believer that the choices we make have consequences. The consequence for me was that I found myself so utterly alone and guilt-ridden after their deaths that I couldn't function. I was in that state from the moment I learned my parents were gone until the moment I met Jake. He saved me and brought me back to life.

* * *

Four and a half years ago

The memory of the police at my apartment door that day is one I will never forget. It was early morning on a frosty December day, just weeks before Christmas. I knew they were dead before the two officers had the opportunity to say anything.

"Miss Mallory MacIntosh?" They looked so somber, there was no doubt they weren't there to ask for a donation to the toy drive.

When they asked to come in and had me sit down on my living room couch, I rocked back and forth, hands over my ears and my eyes closed. I didn't want to hear it. If I didn't hear it, if they couldn't make me listen, then it wouldn't be true. But I heard them.

"We're so sorry, but we have bad news." I didn't envy them their job. They were kind enough. The empathy showed on their faces, in their voices, in their words. But since then, every time I see a police officer, I feel the beginnings of a panic attack.

Mom and Dad had left the fire in the wood-burning fireplace in the living room and gone to bed. They had done that many times, and it was a constant source of anxiety for me as a child growing up in a house with flames. I worried about other things, too; this was just one more thing to add to my list of scary things in life.

"It's almost out," Dad used to say when there were still embers burning, and it was time for bed. "It's fine."

He never seemed to worry. Mom, on the other hand... I guess that's where I inherited my anxiety disorder. But Mom trusted Dad, and Dad was as much an authority on mental health as anyone, being a psychiatrist. He did everything he could to help the two of us live a normal life. Mom was vehemently against taking medication; our anxiety was kept at a manageable level with alternate therapies.

Every night the fire was left burning, I'd get out of bed to check it. The red embers glowed in the dark, warmth emanating from the hearth. Sitting in front of it, staring past the iron screen, I imagined that was what hell looked like. When I was a young teen, I loved watching horror movies. I still do, but I never watch alone. Only with Jake, who protects me and keeps me safe. Only with Jake, who jokes about the absurdity of them. The premise of one of the movies I had seen was that evil creatures lived inside the fireplace chimney. Once you've got an image of that stuck in your head, it's hard to get out.

As much as I worried, I felt safe because Dad was there. When the police came to my door to tell me my safety net was gone, that Mom, who had been my best friend, was gone with him, I lost it completely. The officers looked on as I wailed and rocked my body, trying to convince myself this was simply one of my nightmares.

If I could pinpoint one moment in my life that destroyed me, that was it. Coming home to a burned-out house where most of our belongings were gone or damaged, dealing with funeral arrangements, the lawyer and the insurance company, the relatives who were supportive for the first few months, that was the aftermath of the trauma. I moved in with my mom's brother and his family. In the spring, I found a job in a new school, then an apartment of my own. I went through the motions of living without actually *living*.

When I met Brad at work, he went out of his way to make me laugh. After we had gone on a couple of dates, he confided he saw a sadness in me.

"I've been going through a tough time. My parents died this past Christmas." I found it hard to talk about, even though Brad was a good listener.

"That's terrible, Mallory. But you need to go on. You're still among the living."

I knew he was right, but it was easier said than done. About a month following my parents' deaths, my aunt took me to see Dr. Falcon. She prescribed medication for my depression and something to help me sleep. I didn't put up a fuss. If pills were going to help me deal with my loss, then bring them on.

"We'll put you on a benzodiazepine for a while, Mallory, to treat your anxiety and help you relax, but I'll want to see you regularly to monitor your condition." Dr. Falcon warned me to use the pills as prescribed as they could become addictive, and there might be side effects. "And the best thing for you, really, is therapy."

Dr. Falcon and Brad had something in common. They thought they could cure me if I just talked about my problems. But talking doesn't change anything. I could talk till I was blue in the face, and my parents would still be dead.

I enjoyed Brad's company. We'd go out for lunch and dinner, to the movies, to the park, the lake, or just for a walk or a drive. He was a nice distraction from work and a lonely apartment. The night he brought over pizza and suggested we stay in to watch television, I knew I had to break it off.

He came over with thoughts of spending the night for the first time, and I had no intention of allowing that. I enjoyed the pizza and the movie. I really liked the snuggling and kissing, but that was where I drew the line. Because I was afraid.

"I appreciate that you want to be with me," I explained when he suggested we go to bed. "But I can't get involved with anyone right now. I'm just not in the right place."

I confided that I was still grieving and not sleeping well, that I suffered from anxiety disorder and depression. "I need to deal with my issues first. I can't cope with any complications in my life. And this—it's definitely a complication for me."

When I broke up with Brad, I used the cliche 'It's not you, it's me.' Because it really was me, not him. "You're a good friend, Brad. But I'm just not ready for anything more than that."

He looked disappointed at the time. "I understand. I'll give you a bit of space, if that's what you need. Give you time to grieve. Maybe you'll feel differently in time."

I was relieved he took the breakup as well as he did. The truth was that as much as I longed to have someone love me, I wasn't prepared to reciprocate that love. If I loved someone, there was a good chance I would lose them, just like I lost Mom and Dad.

But when Jake entered my life, he put the fire back into it, in a good way. He ignited a spark I didn't know was there. For the first time since I'd lost my parents, I actually wanted to live. I was ready to see the world without looking through a lens of drug-induced calm, and hazy memories.

On our third date, Jake said the words I longed to hear, but feared. "I think I'm falling in love with you." He held my hand, gazed into my eyes with his crystal blue-green irises, and swept the hair off my forehead.

"I love you, too." The words slipped out before I could think about the implications of what I had said. When he kissed me, I didn't want him to stop. He was the first man I loved, and I loved him in every way.

Dr. Falcon noticed the change in me. "I think we can cut down your meds,

Mallory. You seem to be doing well. I've never seen you so happy." When I told her the reason for my euphoria, she was pleased to see me eager to move on with my life. Before long, I decided I didn't need the meds at all.

Yes, Jake saved me and brought me back to life. If I had the chance to do the same for him, would I?

Chapter Ten

I 've known Jake isn't perfect for a long time. Even before we married, I saw the signs of imperfection in him. But I wasn't about to back out of the wedding because of lurking doubts. I told myself it was normal to panic about whether I was marrying the right person, that it was simply wedding jitters. Everyone gets them. Jake would have had doubts, too, if he knew who he was marrying…

* * *

Three and a half years ago

"Let's just keep it simple, honey," he said once we began the wedding planning. "Just family and a few close friends."

I didn't have a problem with that. I had few family members and only a handful of people I could even consider friends of any sort.

"There's no point in going overboard and spending a ton of money," Jake said, and I agreed, of course.

All we really needed was each other. Together, we selected the venue. Jake suggested the farm property. "There's lots of room to set up a tent in the back yard, kitchen, and bathroom facilities, and my mom will make sure the gardens are perfect for photos. And one of the guys from work does photography as a hobby. I'm sure he'll give us a great deal."

The menu, the wine list, the wedding cake, flowers, the decor, music—Jake and I made our selections together, holding hands and smiling at each other. No disagreements, no second guessing. We wanted the same things. Jake even went to the dress fittings when I had Mom's gown altered, so grateful it had been saved from fire, yet devastated my parents wouldn't see me wear it. Jake didn't complain once about having to wait around, or having to put up with my tears.

Jake surprised me with tickets for our honeymoon. "A week in Jamaica. I know how much you love the beach." He anticipated my every need.

Jake knew my deepest desires. It was like he read my mind. I seemed to want exactly what Jake wanted.

"You know me so well," I said at the time. But I already knew both of us were keeping secrets from each other.

A week after our engagement, I bumped into one of Jake's friends on one of the rare occasions I was out on my own. "I'm glad to see he's found his perfect woman. I guess the third time's the charm."

When I asked what he was talking about, he told me Jake had been engaged twice before. I acted as though I knew, but didn't think it was important.

"I didn't tell you because it wasn't serious. We broke it off when we realized we weren't right for each other," Jake said when I asked why he hadn't told me about his previous engagements.

"I don't want any secrets between us," I insisted. "No secrets, no lies. Ever."

It made me wonder what else he wasn't telling me. He had a past I knew little about. "Maybe we should hold off on the wedding for a while. We've barely known each other for a couple of months."

"No, I don't want to wait any longer. I don't need to know you for two years or three or more to know you're the one for me." Jake wouldn't hear of postponing the wedding.

Until that time I'd managed to keep the severity of my anxiety disorder from him, telling myself that no man wants a wife who's mentally unstable. Besides, I had it under control. But once I began to worry that Jake wasn't telling me everything about himself, I began to lose that control.

"What are these?" he asked when he found the pills in my purse, a month before the wedding.

"Sometimes I get a little anxious," I confessed. "They're prescribed by my doctor for panic attacks. Don't worry. Lots of people take them. And it's not like I need them very often. I had a hard time after my parents died, but I'm better now. Because of you."

"You didn't tell me you were on drugs. That might have been good to know."

"You didn't tell me you were engaged before. Twice."

"Don't ever lie to me again, Mal. And don't pry into my past. If you want to know something about me, then just ask. No secrets, right?" There was something almost menacing in his eyes at that moment.

We had a bit of a face-off, staring at each other, and I thought he was going to get angry, but then Jake smiled. "Right. So we're even." He kissed me. It was our first fight. Our only fight till after the wedding.

* * *

Couples fight all the time. But Jake and I, we're so finely attuned to each other, disagreements are rare. Which is a good thing, given his family history. As I look around the homey kitchen in which his grandparents and their children once lived and loved, I wonder if this has always been a place of refuge.

When Jake first brought me here, I doubted I could live in the countryside. The openness of the fields juxtaposed with the constricting nature of the woodland was disconcerting. I didn't voice my opinion to Jake, not wanting to offend him. He was so excited at the prospect of owning our own property, especially such a sizable chunk of real estate, and his mom was thrilled it would stay in the family.

This time of year—with the tall stalks in the cornfield to my left and out back, the copse of evergreens to my right, woods out front—the house is trapped in the middle. Being raised as a city girl, I never envisioned myself living so alone. But I've grown to love it. The solitude is peaceful. And, besides, the two of us need only each other. Jake allowed me free rein to decorate inside and out (within our budget, of course), and we made it our own. Jake and Mallory's place.

As I climb the stairs, my feet heavy and my heart gripped with fear, I think about where Jake is right now. At the doorway to our bedroom, I stop and place my hands protectively on my stomach and look at the empty bed in the middle of the room I decorated to my tastes. I've made this place my own, and now I need to lie in my bed. Alone.

Chapter Eleven

T*hump!*

I wake and reach over for Jake, but he's not there. Something slides from my chest onto the space where my husband should be. By the light of my iPad, the source of the sound is visible. Nellie, who has jumped onto the bed, walks up to my chin, rubbing her face into mine. "Hey, sweetie," I coo as she purrs into my ear.

Jake saved Nellie two years ago and brought her into our lives. She was just a wee kitten, too young to be taken from her mother, when he found her under our wooden front veranda, behind the lattice. She'd been separated from her family, left behind, the runt of the litter.

* * *

Two years ago

"Come out here, hon," he'd called to me as he came home from work one summer night.

He stood in the doorway, holding the door open, and waited for me to join him on the porch. I thought maybe he wanted a romantic night under the stars, like we used to do the first few months after we got married. We'd sit on the porch swing and gaze at the sky, talking about our future.

But when I tore myself away from the Rom-Com I was watching and stepped outside, he put his finger to his lips to indicate I should be quiet.

"Shh... there's something out here," he whispered. "I think it's a ghost. Listen. It's coming from under the porch."

Still upset from our conversation about having a baby that morning, the fact that he was putting it off, I was in no mood for one of his jokes. Sometimes, he just liked to scare the bejesus out of me for fun, so I'd run into his arms and cling to him. Assuming this was probably one of those times, I turned around to go back inside.

Then I heard her. I jumped at first, understandably, given that Jake had put the notion of ghosts in my head. But he told me to turn on the porch lights and get a flashlight. "I think there's an animal down there. Sounds like a cat."

From the front hall closet, I grabbed a flashlight from the shelf and handed it over, then stood on the front lawn as he shone it through the lattice. The mewling continued, with Jake crouched down, staring through the diagonal slats.

"I'm going to need a screwdriver," he said. "Do you want to go fetch it? Or do you want to wait here?"

He already knew my answer. There was no way I was going to the basement. I'd only been there twice. Once, when he gave me the grand tour of the property before we bought it, and then again when we moved in and stored stuff down there. It's an older house, with an unfinished basement. The stone walls, the old wooden beams, pipes in the ceiling, the monster of a furnace, are reason enough for me to stay away from the basement. The bricked-in windows and partially dirt floor with a pile of rubble are guaranteed to keep me out. I'm convinced someone buried bodies down there. Rows of shelving along the walls hold plastic tubs full of stuff we don't need but don't want to throw out. Jake also keeps his tools on a workbench and on the pegboard.

Fortunately, I have no reason to go down there. Before we got married, Jake had a main floor laundry room, mudroom, and bathroom built onto the back of the house, adjoining the kitchen. When a fuse goes out, Jake goes downstairs to take care of it. When the furnace or hot water heater quits running, Jake gets it going. The basement is his domain.

I waited on the porch while he fetched his set of screwdrivers. I could hear the poor thing crying underneath me. I just hoped it was a kitten and not some wild animal. As I watched, Jake unscrewed the lattice, donned a pair of work gloves, and crawled under the porch, sweeping the flashlight from side to side.

"There you are." He spoke gently, coaxing it to him.

I crouched down, looking in. Bright eyes glowed in the back corner.

"Bring a bowl of milk, Mal. I'll bet he's hungry."

Jake was so sweet with the little kitten, so loving.

When he finally brought out the tiny ball of fur, he asked, in a silly baby voice, "Can we keep it, Mal? Please can we? Huh, huh, can we? I always wanted a little kitten of my own."

I couldn't help but laugh. I knew he was kidding around, and he knew I would insist on keeping it no matter what he said.

"We'll call her Nellie," I said, once she was safely inside, given some milk, and tucked into a little box by our bed for the night.

"How do you know it's a girl?"

"I just know. But if it's a boy, we'll call him Jakey."

That was how Nellie joined our family. And how I got over the depression I'd been sinking into the last many months. Once again, I was temporarily off the meds.

"I know how much you want a baby, Mal," Jake said as I held little Nellie for the first time. "And it'll happen someday. In the meantime, let's just be happy with what we have. The two of us, that's all we've ever really needed. And now we have Nellie. The rest will come. You just have to be patient."

Jake went out early the next morning to buy cat supplies. He came home with everything we needed and stuff we didn't need. The rest of the morning, he set up the litter box in the mudroom, the cat dishes on the kitchen floor, the cat bed with a blanket and stuffed mousie in the living room, along with the scratching post tower and a ton of cat toys. He showed Nellie everything he'd bought, and played with her until she was worn out, setting her in his lap to curl up and sleep until it was time for him to go to work.

"Your turn to babysit," he'd said with a smile as he kissed me goodbye.

* * *

For a while, I stopped grieving the fact that I wasn't pregnant and became a Mom to Nellie. As much as I've always loved Nellie, every month I missed out on getting pregnant, I felt myself slide back into a deeper depression. Jake understands my need to have a baby, but I need to be patient, he keeps saying. It will happen when it's the perfect time.

With Nellie clutched to my chest, I close my eyes and pray. **Now I lay me down to sleep. I pray the Lord my Soul to keep.**

And I float off into my dream world, where Jake somehow finds his way back home to me.

Chapter Twelve

Something wakes me. I can't get back to sleep without Jake by my side. All I can do is think back to when our troubles began. Our first fight as a married couple.

* * *

Three years ago

The first week after our honeymoon, he headed to the convenience store one night, saying we needed milk. I told him it was okay, there was enough for our morning coffee and cereal. "I'll get some tomorrow. We're in need of other groceries, anyway."

"I've got a craving for hot chocolate, hon. The Bailey's Irish Cream flavor. I'll pick up some whipped cream while I'm at the store. And some microwave popcorn. We can sit by the fire pit and have a movie night outside."

He wrapped me in his arms and whispered in my ear, "Then we'll get in the hot tub, naked."

I could hardly argue with that.

We had a romantic evening, one of many to come. But, the next morning, cleaning out the pockets of his jeans before stuffing them into the wash machine, I found a debit receipt dated yesterday. Last night's milk? Upon seeing the total, I dropped the jeans and ran into the living room, where Jake sat flipping through channels.

"What is this?" I demanded. "$114.94? What kind of milk and whipped cream was that? Was it gourmet popcorn?"

"I picked up a few other things while I was there."

"I told you I was going to the grocery store today. You know we can't afford convenience store prices. What did you buy?"

He studied me, then shut off the television. "Okay. I didn't buy groceries," he confessed. "I picked up a couple of lottery tickets."

"A couple of tickets? At $50 a piece?" I screeched. "Were they made of gold? You just blew our grocery budget for the week."

"Relax, Mal. It's not that big a deal."

"Relax? You just threw a hundred bucks into the garbage. What were you thinking?"

"I was thinking we'd be able to take a lot more trips and do more renos on the house when we win, for starters." He said it so seriously I convulsed with laughter.

"When we win? Are you *kidding* me?"

"I used different combinations of our birthdays and the day we met and our wedding date for my numbers. There's bound to be a winning ticket in there somewhere." He was so flippant about it, I seethed, my eyes ready to bulge out of my head.

"Are you crazy? We're supposed to be saving for fixing up the house, especially the nursery. Don't you ever waste money like that again!"

He remained calm while I lost my cool. That made me angrier.

"I'm sorry, honey, I didn't realize a few tickets would upset you so much. I won't do it again." His eyes pleaded with me to forgive him. How could I be angry with those turquoise irises?

"It's okay." I cooled down after breathing through my nose and counting as far as 27. "This time. But don't do it again. I thought you said we were going to be open with each other and make decisions together. I don't think spending money on tickets is wise, especially since we don't have extra cash to go around, with the mortgage and car payments, the wedding and honeymoon expenses, plus the money we already owe on the renovations. You know things are tight."

Just before we got married, Jake had insisted we keep all our money in joint accounts. He said he'd take care of the bills, which was fine by me. But his irresponsible behavior with the lottery tickets gave me second thoughts.

"You got it, sweetie, no more lottery tickets. I'll run everything past you from now on. I guess I've just been used to being single for too long." He kissed my forehead, telling me not to worry. He'd keep a tighter rein on his spending.

And he kept his promise, which must have been hard for him, since he came to me three days after our fight and showed me the $200 he won. It turned out our wedding date was lucky, in more ways than one. But there were no more suspicious purchases or withdrawals from our accounts. Only the regular payments for the house, cars, insurance, taxes, and other bills necessary for the running of the house. Jake even provided me with receipts for his gas and grocery purchases, takeout food and bar bills, and for household items and repairs. We went to the mall together to shop for clothing, books, and games. All major expenses had to be approved by both of us. That's what married couples do. They work together. Or so I thought.

The first time I found his hidden stash of tickets, about a week later, I didn't say anything. I waited for him to confess that he'd had a moment of insanity and beg for my forgiveness. He never mentioned them. I left them where I'd found them, stuffed between the mattress and the box spring in the guest bedroom. He would be forced to tell me when I asked why there was an unaccounted expenditure in our bank account.

The second and third time I found tickets hidden in the house, I wanted to see how long he would go on lying to me. I did wonder, though, how he was paying for them. There was no record of money missing from any of our accounts. All the receipts he gave me, all the household expenses, the bills—everything added up. Where was he getting the extra money?

Keeping secrets tends to erode a marriage. I wasn't about to let that happen. One day it all came to a head.

"I know about the tickets," I confronted him a few weeks into our marriage. "I know you're hiding them from me. What I don't know is where you're getting the money."

Jake apologized profusely for lying, promising he would never keep anything from me again. "I borrowed it from Mom. When I won the two hundred bucks the night we had our first fight, I figured if I could win once, it was only a matter of time till I won again, so I spent my winnings on more tickets. But I lost, and I knew the only way to get the money back was to keep buying tickets. So I went to Mom."

I suspected then that Jake had a bit of a problem. Since I'd had some problems of my own in the past, I knew he needed help, not another argument, so I let it go.

Gloria was the one who introduced me to a side of Jake I didn't know existed. When I visited her the next time, I asked about the loan.

"Oh, I see you're wearing it," she said, pointing to the bracelet on my wrist. "Yes, Jake borrowed a couple of thousand from me to buy your birthday present. It's lovely. Diamonds are a girl's best friend, they say."

Except, I knew Jake spent under a hundred dollars for the zirconia bracelet and gardening gloves he gave me for my birthday. The money came out of our account. Did that mean Jake spent two thousand dollars on lottery tickets?

"There's something you should know," I told Gloria. She *is* his mother, after all. If he was spending money foolishly, especially if he was borrowing it from her, she had the right to that knowledge. "Jake's been spending a lot of money on lottery tickets. I confronted him about it when I found out, and he promised he would stop, but he's still doing it and keeping it from me."

Gloria's mouth hung open, her eyes fell to the floor, and she walked to the window, her back to me. "I didn't know about the lottery tickets."

Turning to face me, she added, "And I don't want to interfere in your marriage, but there's something you should know about Jake. He's my son, and I love him more than I can express, but... he's not without his issues."

I stared at my mother-in-law, trying to anticipate what she was about to say. "What sort of issues?"

"You're his wife. You should know." Gloria took me by the hand as she sat beside me on her couch. "Jake's an addict."

"It's just a few lottery tickets," I sputtered, wild thoughts running through my mind. *Is he on drugs? Coke? Meth? Why haven't I noticed the signs?*

"He gambles. It started several years ago. Jake had a big win at the casino. His friend, Terry, was the one who got him started. He and some of their school friends took Jake out for his 21st birthday."

Gloria explained how Jake won a small amount that night, how he kept going back every weekend and eventually won tens of thousands of dollars. "I told him he should invest it for his future. Jake said there was a lot more to be won."

Gloria heaved a pensive sigh. "He lost it all. I thought he'd quit at that point. Then, one day, he told me he'd hit it big again."

"What did he do with the money?" I knew our bank account didn't reflect my husband's good luck.

Gloria shook her head. "Oh, Mallory. He just spent it on drinking and more gambling. It was a vicious circle for him—he'd win, he'd lose, he'd win again. I was so happy when I heard the two of you were getting married. I thought maybe he'd settle down and save up for the family I know you want so badly."

Gloria's eyes glistened as she held mine. "Please don't tell him that I told you. I don't want to lose my son's confidence. But I really think you need to know the truth."

Once I understood Jake had a serious problem, I kept a closer eye on him and hoped to wean him from his addiction. "I think maybe I've been too harsh about the lottery tickets," I compromised. "You can buy seven tickets a week. One for each day. Everyone's entitled to a little fun."

Since I knew he wasn't going to the casino anymore, I decided to let him indulge a little. That and one or two nights a week out drinking with his work buddies was something I allowed him to have for himself. In exchange, he allowed me to go solo for a big grocery trip once a week, and to visit his mom. The rest of the time, we spent together, the way it should be. Husband and wife joined at the hip. Jake and Mallory.

Chapter Thirteen

I wake in our bed, curled up, the duvet pulled to my chin, memories of last night's nightmare still fresh in my mind, but with it a sense of relief. Because Jake's back. The earthiness of his scent surrounds me—the freshly dug dirt, wet leaves, pools of stagnant water. I'm about to suggest we shower, but wet fabric scratches my cheek, and my eyes sting. Something's off. My eyes open in alarm to find Jake's t-shirt scrunched in my hands on top of the pillow. I reach over to him, but I'm met with empty air. Jake's side of the bed is where I fell asleep, facing the edge. I remember now. I'd taken a t-shirt out of the hamper and wiped my tears with it until I fell asleep.

The digital display on the nightstand tells me it's 6:06 a.m. Jake's been gone for seven hours. He's never stayed out all night before. I know what I need to do, but the prospect of doing so weighs me down, and I can't force myself out of bed. Holding onto his scent for a while longer, I close my eyes again and pretend he's with me.

His strong arms hold me, hands caressing my back, voice whispering in my ear, telling me everything is going to be okay. Like always, Jake gives me a sense of security, makes me feel like I belong. I belong to him. As I hold his sweaty t-shirt next to me, I consider how I can possibly go on if he isn't coming back. My phone sits on the nightstand, next to the clock radio. Even before checking, I know there are no messages from Jake. The volume is turned to max, so I would have heard if he tried to contact me. As the clock clicks over to 6:30, I pick up the phone and call Jake's brother, John. I hate to disturb him so early on a Saturday morning, but it's necessary. I need to know when John last heard from Jake.

When he answers, I quickly apologize, then tell him Jake didn't come home from work last night. "I was wondering if he said anything to you, if you might have any idea where he might be."

"Are you saying he's missing?" If he was asleep when I called, he's wide awake now. "You don't know where he is?"

"When I went to pick him up from work, I didn't see him come out. I thought maybe he got a ride with someone, or went out with his buddies for a drink, but he's still not home."

John is silent for a while, and I imagine him trying to process what I've said. When he finally speaks, he says he spoke to him last week on the phone. "It was our usual conversation. He asked about Deb and the boys. Said everything was great with the two of you. We talked a bit about work. That's it."

"So he didn't give you any indication he was thinking of leaving me?" When I hear myself ask the question, I lose control. My throat chokes up, the tears flow, and my body heaves and shakes.

"What? Mallory, no. No way. He'd never leave you. Were the two of you having some trouble lately? Every married couple has problems. But I can't believe he would just take off and not let you know where he is."

"I... I... know."

"Have you checked the hospital? Maybe something happened at work and..."

"They would have called me if he was injured at work. There's no message on my phone. Even if I missed a call, which I didn't..."

"Have you checked with his friends? His co-workers?"

"Yes...I did..."

"Someone must have seen him leave work."

His words stop my tears in their tracks. Of course. Someone must have seen him *at* work. Someone had to have seen him *leave* work. I need to find out who, and what they know. The problem is, it's Saturday. No one's at the warehouse.

"You're right. I'll keep calling people." I hang up after John assures me Jake is bound to turn up sooner or later, and I promise to let him know as soon as he does. Then I steel myself to make the most difficult call of my married life.

"Mallory? What's wrong?" Gloria knows I wouldn't call this early without a good reason. There's no easy way to tell Gloria her son is missing, so I just blurt it out.

"It's Jake. He didn't come home last night." I give her the details, asking, just in case, "He didn't happen to call you, did he?"

Gloria's hysteria comes through the phone immediately. I recognize the feeling, know it intimately. "Where could he possibly be? What's happened to him? Have you called the police?"

"I haven't. I was hoping he'd be home by now. But he's never stayed out all night before." By this time, the two of us are crying. Gloria is sick with worry about her youngest boy, and I'm a basket case, having lost my husband.

"Hang up and call the police now," Gloria instructs, taking charge. "The sooner they start to look for him, the sooner he'll be back. There must be some reason why he didn't come home, though. Did the two of you have a fight? You didn't mention you were having problems."

"No, we weren't. We aren't having problems." I wouldn't tell my mother-in-law if we were. What goes on between Jake and me is our business, nobody else's.

The ringing of the doorbell prompts me to tell Gloria I'll call her back as soon as I hear anything. In my haste to answer the door, I trip over the pile of clothes I tossed out of the hamper last night, lose my balance, and crash headfirst into the sharp corner of the armoire. A jolt of pain pierces through my brain. Instinctively, my hand goes to my forehead and the wet stickiness of my own blood. The sight of red on my hands makes me woozy. I need to get to the front door. Maybe Jake's forgotten his key.

I head toward the ringing, holding the railing. Step by step, I descend until I'm in the hall entrance. My hand unlocks the bolt, grabs hold of the door handle, and I find myself face to face with Vicky.

"Oh my God, Mallory!" Vicky pulls her phone from her pocket. "I'm calling 911."

"No!" I stop her just in time. "There's no need for that. I'm okay."

She gives me a good, hard look, eyes narrowed, and walks past me. "Where's Jake? Jake! Jake! Where the hell are you? Get out here now!"

"He's not here. He still hasn't come home."

Vicky looks up the staircase. My eyes follow hers along the banister, streaked with blood. "Mallory. What's going on here?"

"I bumped my head on the armoire. I'm okay."

"Mallory." Vicky climbs the stairs, and I follow. "There's a lot of blood."

Standing in the doorway of our bedroom, I see what she's talking about. It looks like a murder scene. "Oh…" The sight of blood makes me woozy again, and I need to sit. Vicky helps me to the bed. The cool, wet towel she places on my head feels good.

"I'm taking you to the hospital," Vicky states. "Do you think you can make it down the stairs?"

"No. No hospital."

Vicky takes out her phone again. "Then I'm calling an ambulance."

When I protest, Vicky explains there are two options—she can drive me to the hospital or I can go in an ambulance. I graciously accept her offer of a ride.

"Please… don't say anything about Jake." The last thing I need is for the world to know.

"What exactly is going on with you and Jake?" Vicky helps me down the stairs. "Are the two of you having problems?"

"No, no problems. Everything's fine." The only problem is my husband is missing and I have no idea where he is. "I thought you were him. I thought he was finally home."

"Let's get this head injury dealt with first, then we'll figure out where he's gone."

"My purse. My phone." I point upstairs. Leaving me on the couch, Vicky retrieves my stuff. It only takes her a minute, but in that moment, Jake's voice reaches out to me from a corner of my mind. As she comes down, darkness surrounds me, and the walls close in. A wetness pulls me under. I'm drowning or being buried alive. Jake calls out for me, asking where I am. And there's an overwhelming sense of guilt because I can't help him. He's lost to me. I wish I could go back a week to last Friday, when Jake and I were in the hot tub, warm and relaxed. My last thought is how cold I am. Then everything goes black.

Chapter Fourteen

T he voices are far off, and I know I'm dreaming. No, not a dream. A nightmare. My eyelids are too heavy to open, as though they're glued shut. My subconscious wants to keep floating away in the shadows, aware that my waking world is even more terrifying. But I need to wake up sooner or later and face reality. What that reality is, I don't know. I'm light as a feather, but my heart hammers in my chest. I'm about to drop onto concrete. No! I have too much to live for.

"Mallory, wake up." It's a voice I know.

Through the ringing in my ears, the voice calls me. If I could just force my eyes open, I might stop myself from free-falling. My fingers grip a cold hard surface and hold on for dear life.

"That's good. I know you can hear me. Now open your eyes, Mallory."

Through the slit, light filters. A hand touches mine and squeezes, causing me to unclench my fingers slightly. A bit of assurance that someone's there prompts me to open my eyes further, but it's too much of an effort. The hand slips away, and I slip away with it. "It's okay, Mallory. Just relax. You're in the ambulance. You hit your head and passed out. I'll meet you at the hospital."

The doors close, and Vicky's gone. A steady hum purrs underneath, almost lulling me back to sleep, but a piercing sound jolts me to action. An alarm? Is there a fire?

I struggle to get up, but something presses me down. In my mind, Mom and Dad sleep in their beds as smoke fills their room. There's nothing I can do to stop the flames from engulfing the house because I'm not home. I'm three hours away, living my life without them. And it suddenly dawns on me that I'm going to have to live without Jake. My eyes fly open, and I try to sit up, without success. Coldness assaults my veins. As I pull away, someone holds me in place.

A strange voice says, "It's just the IV. You're okay. I'm going to check your blood pressure so you'll feel some tightness on your arm."

The interior of the ambulance is foreign to me. I've never seen the inside of one firsthand, and it's frightening being fastened down and closed up in the white and gray box with its medical equipment and supplies. The only thing that keeps me from panicking is the uniformed female paramedic who asks questions, not just about my symptoms, but any medical conditions I have, medications I take, and whether I remember how I got the bump on my head. Instinctively, my hand goes up. I want to go back to sleep, but she keeps talking, expecting me to respond.

One of the questions she asks about my medical condition forces me to fully wake. "Yes, I am. A couple of months." She records my responses while trying to calm me.

By the time we arrive at the hospital, I'm alert enough to observe my surroundings. The glass doors slide open, and they roll the gurney to the emergency area. The antiseptic smell and sterile white walls greet me, and I'm deposited into a small curtained area where they transfer me to a bed. A nurse takes over the interrogation and checks my blood pressure, heart rate, temperature, and oxygen levels.

"Everything's looking good," she assures me. "Head wounds tend to bleed a lot. But the doctor will be with you shortly to give you a complete examination."

"Will I have to stay in the hospital?" With Jake missing, I need to be home waiting for him when he comes back.

"We'll have to wait and see what the doctor says." As she leaves to tend to other patients, Vicky appears.

"Thank God you're awake. You were in and out of it for about ten, maybe fifteen minutes." She takes a seat, and we wait for the doctor to arrive.

Because it's a small-town hospital, there usually aren't long wait times. I know that from my previous visits to the hospital, the other couple of times I've fallen or bumped into something. My clumsiness is a direct result of my daydreaming. The number of times I've clunked my head on a cupboard or bumped into a doorway, both at home and at school, is too many to count. Walking down the hall at school, I often stop midway, trying to remember where I'm going. Leaving my car in a parking lot is a traumatic experience. It takes a lot of mental effort for me to remember where I've parked. And it's a wonder I haven't been struck by a vehicle during my walking excursions, as I think about anything but the traffic.

While we're waiting, Vicky asks if I feel up to talking. "Do you want to tell me exactly what's going on with you and Jake? I know he didn't come home last night. How have things been between the two of you the last few days?"

"Fine. Everything's…." What can I say to Vicky? She knows Jake. "It's been good. I can't believe he would leave like this without a word."

"No, it's not like him. Not to come home all night."

The doctor interrupts our conversation, and Vicky leaves. The young male doctor smiles and cheerily checks me over, asking more questions. I ask a few of my own. By the time he's done, I've been poked and prodded, both physically and mentally.

"Can I go home?"

"I don't see why not. You should have someone stay with you for at least the next 24 hours." He rhymes off a list of symptoms to watch for and gives instructions about what to do in case I experience any of them.

When the nurse escorts me to the waiting area, Vicky rises, linking her arm in mine. "I'll take it from here."

I shake my head in an effort to clear the ringing in my head, but it won't stop. "Is that my phone?"

"Oh, yes, sorry. You've had some texts and calls come through in the last hour or so." Vicky hands me my purse, and I rummage through it to locate my phone. It has to be Jake, wondering why I'm not at home.

"Hello?"

"Mallory? Thank God! Are you okay? Where are you?"

Disappointment sets in. "Yes, I'm okay. I'm at the hospital. Vicky's with me. We're just about to head home."

"The hospital? What happened? Has Jake been found? What did he say about where he's been?" The voice on the other end is frantic.

"No, no, it's not Jake. I had a fall, that's all. It was stupid. I wasn't watching where I was going, but I'm fine. I need to get home and see if Jake's there."

"A fall? Are you sure you're okay?"

"Yes, a mild concussion. I'm supposed to rest for a couple of days. I just want to get home."

"I'm there right now, Mallory. I've been ringing the doorbell and walking around the house, but I don't think Jake's here." Craig sounds a bit calmer now that he knows I'm okay. "I'll wait for you."

"Who were you talking to?" Vicky asks when I finish the call.

"Craig. He's at our house right now. He was worried about me."

"What did Craig say? Has he heard anything?"

"No." It's barely a whisper.

Vicky's eyes light up. "You don't think...? If Jake got hurt last night or had an accident, he might be in the hospital. Maybe he's right here."

John had already suggested Jake could be in the hospital, but why didn't someone contact me? Vicky steers me toward the reception desk. I feel like we're checking out of a hotel, waiting in line with other guests. Jake and I were planning a vacation out east next month. That's not going to happen now. Not unless Jake miraculously shows up and says he wants me back. I'd take him back in a heartbeat, even if he did leave me for another woman.

Once we're at the front of the line, Vicky explains that we're looking for my husband, who didn't make it home from work last night. "We wondered if maybe he'd been injured and couldn't call home. Would it be possible to check if he's here?"

The middle-aged woman behind the counter checks her records, makes a phone call, and shakes her head. "Sorry, he's not here. There's no record that he's been here."

"Has anyone with amnesia been admitted?" I ask, just in case.

The woman confirms there have been no John Does in the hospital the last few days.

65

As we head for the exit, Vicky has another idea. "If he'd been injured at work or at one of the bars or en route, they'd take him to the city hospital. I'm sure he's fine, but it wouldn't hurt to check."

"Could you call Grandview for me?" I sit back down on a black leather chair in Emergency while Vicky makes the call. I'm on the edge of my seat as she inquires whether Jake Shelton was admitted late last night or early this morning. She provides his description as well as his name, in case he forgot it, and asks whether he visited the emergency department.

Vicky shakes her head after ending the call. "No, he hasn't been there either. Sorry, it was just a thought."

Vicky leaves me inside the glass doors and pulls her car up to the emergency exit. As she gets out to help me, I wave her away, indicating I can manage.

Vicky doesn't say anything more about Jake on the drive home. We both know it's out of character for him to just take off like this. Whatever thoughts we have about where Jake is and who he's with, we keep them to ourselves.

At 10:36, we pull in next to Craig's Jeep. Craig jumps up from the front porch swing and jogs to the passenger side, opening the door to help me out.

"I was going out of my mind for the last hour, wondering what happened to you," he says as he guides me to the house, Vicky following. "I thought maybe Jake…" He stops, takes the key from me, and opens the door to the house where Jake and I thought we would spend the rest of our lives raising a family.

As we enter the main level, Craig leads me to the spacious living room on the left. To the right is the formal dining room, the large eat-in kitchen straight ahead at the back of the house, with an adjoining den that will become the kids' playroom.

"Let's get you settled on the couch," Craig says, plumping up the pillows for me.

"What happened to *you*?" Vicky stares at Craig's face, but he waves his hand in the air and says he bumped into something, and it's no big deal.

"There's a lot of that going on, apparently." Vicky sets my purse on the floor by the bookcase and sits next to me. She explains to Craig how I ended up in the hospital and says she plans on staying overnight to keep an eye on me. "I just need to drop by my place to get a few things first, if you don't mind waiting till I get back."

"That's not necessary," Craig says. "You're farther away. And besides, I don't need to go back home for anything. I can stay and take care of Mallory. Jake would want me to keep an eye on her, with that head injury. It's the least I can do for my best friend."

Vicky asks if I want her to stay as well. "I'm not sure how Jake will feel about…"

"It's fine," I say. "Go home. You've done enough. Thank you for being here for me. If you hadn't come along when you did, I don't know what I would have done."

Vicky and Craig exchange a look that makes me wonder. Are they seriously going to fight over who gets to take care of me? "I'll call you if I need anything," I tell Vicky, who seems unsure she should leave me alone with Craig.

"I don't mind staying," she insists.

"Well then, I guess we're all having a sleepover," Craig says. "If Mallory loses consciousness again, you're going to need help carrying her to the car. I doubt she wants another ride in an ambulance any time soon."

"There's only one guest room," I point out. The other bedroom is Jake's office for now.

Craig catches Vicky's eye. "No problem. You take the bedroom. I'll stay on the couch in the den."

Once the sleeping arrangements are ironed out, I remind them my top priority is finding Jake and ask what they think we should do. Vicky checks her social media to see if Jake has posted since last night. Craig decides it's time to call his boss and have him talk to some of the other employees.

"You need to get some rest." Vicky reads over the generic head injury instruction sheet we were handed upon leaving the hospital. "It says you can sleep, but I'll be right here keeping an eye on you. Don't be upset if I wake you now and then."

As an afterthought, Vicky adds, "What about Gloria? Do you want me to call her and explain what happened to you?"

"No. There's no need to worry her any more than she already is. Besides, if you call, she might think you have some news about Jake." I'm sure Gloria would think the news was bad if I needed someone else to make the call for me. "I'll talk to her myself later today."

Craig brings me a cold glass of water and a couple of pain pills. "Here you go. Get some rest. Vicky and I will see if we can track down any leads on Jake. We'll wake you for lunch."

Knowing I'm in good hands with our two best friends taking charge, I allow myself the luxury of sinking back into the pillows. Vicky covers me with the light throw, and I realize I'm still in my PJs. As far as I'm concerned, it's still the night before. I close my eyes and slip back into dreamland, where Jake waits for me.

Chapter Fifteen

Crystal eyes, a mix of blue and green, bore into mine as I float off to sea. He's with me on a raft he built, and I hold a baby wrapped in yellow. As I gaze adoringly into the blue-green eyes of our child, then back at Jake, he disappears. I search the water, which moments ago was calm and has now turned choppy, wondering where he is. Did he go for a swim? Did he jump overboard? Will he climb back any minute, laughing, telling me the water's great? I scream his name, holding tightly onto our child.

"Mallory, it's okay. Wake up. You must be having a nightmare."

I open my eyes, grateful to be out of the dream world. Vicky rubs my arm, and I loosen my grip on the throw I've scrunched into a bundle. Nellie lies on my chest, purring.

"What time is it?" I ask.

"After one."

"Did you find out anything?"

"No. I went to your neighbors, just in case they saw him. I know it was a long shot, since he went missing from work, but still—"

"And?"

"And nothing. Linda says the last she saw Jake was yesterday afternoon as he drove past their place on his way to work."

"The two of us were in the car. Jake was driving."

"She did say the two of you go together on Fridays. Nothing seemed out of the ordinary, according to her."

Vicky heads to the dining room table where a vase sits, filled with lilies and phlox from my gardens. She retrieves my laptop from the table. "Why don't you check Jake's accounts and see if he's been active on messenger or email in the last day? Maybe there's a clue there. I'm going to fix lunch."

Taking Vicky's advice, I log in. The usual junk mail pops up. He subscribes to every newsletter that's offered. I flip through them. One looks different, more personal. Although I don't recognize the name, I have a bad feeling about it. Glancing up to make sure Craig and Vicky aren't in the room, I click on it.

Two words taunt me: **Tick Tock.**

Chapter Sixteen

"Time for lunch." Vicky sweeps into the room with a tray of sandwiches and cookies. Craig follows, carrying a pitcher of lemonade in one hand and three plastic glasses in the other. I realize I'm actually hungry, in spite of everything.

"Did you find anything?" Vicky sets the tray on the table and motions to the laptop.

"No, nothing."

Craig pours a glass of lemonade and hands me a napkin with half an egg salad sandwich on it. "Eat. You'll feel better with something in your stomach."

Vicky sits next to me, with Craig across from us on one of the club chairs. He takes a bite of his sandwich and watches while I do the same. Swallowing, he says, "I called Bob." Bob Townsend is the warehouse manager. "He's been on the phone the last couple of hours, talking to people from the evening shift. No one saw Jake at work yesterday, Mallory."

Craig waits for me to meet his eyes, and I dread what he's going to say next. "It occurred to me that maybe he'd gotten himself into some sort of trouble, so I called the city jail, but he's not there. I think it's time for us to contact the police."

My mouth flies open; some of the egg salad I was slowly chewing spills out. Bringing my napkin to my lips, I swallow. The food sticks in my throat. "The police?"

I turn to Vicky to see her reaction. The dark circles under her eyes tell me she's stressed. The whole morning has been about me, and I haven't given any thought to how this is affecting my friends. I'm sure Vicky has other things to do with her weekend besides babysitting me and worrying about her ex-boyfriend cheating on me. And poor Craig. I dragged him into this whole mess. I should never have called him. If Jake has left me, it's my own fault.

"I think Craig's right," Vicky agrees. "Since Jake hasn't contacted you by now, maybe it's time to let the police know he's missing."

"No, no police." The last thing I need is for the police to ask questions.

Vicky raises her eyebrows. "Is there something you're not telling us?"

"I'd rather not have everyone know our private business. If he did leave me…." Tears flow down my cheeks.

Craig takes my hands in his. "It's okay, Mallory. We just need to file a report, that's all. He'll be back before you know it. But it will look strange if he stays away much longer and you don't take action."

I nod. Yes, it will look suspicious if I do nothing. But calling the police makes it all too real.

Craig phones the station, his tone somber. "I'd like to speak to someone about a missing person."

The sight of the police cruiser in my driveway an hour later, with two uniformed officers exiting the vehicle, brings a tightness to my chest, and my throat constricts. This is really happening. The police are here because Jake isn't.

Craig invites the officers inside, explaining who he is and pointing to Vicky and me. "This is Jake's wife, Mallory, and her friend, Vicky. Mallory hasn't seen Jake since yesterday afternoon when she dropped him off at work."

One of the officers is about our age, tall, clean-shaven, with short blond hair; the other is closer to middle age, with a bit of a paunch around the middle, lines around his blue eyes, and streaks of gray through brown hair. Neither looks intimidating. In fact, it's only the uniforms that make me uneasy. After introducing themselves, they each take a seat on one of the club chairs while Craig joins us on the couch.

"Tell us about the last time you saw your husband." Officer Heinz, the older man, takes a small notebook out of his pocket. "And what happened to your head?"

My right hand moves to the gauze as though I'm not sure what he's talking about. Vicky sets her hand on my left knee to encourage me. I repeat my story, trying not to leave out important details. When I get to the part about bumping into the armoire, Officer Heinz turns to his colleague, Officer Rombough, and nods toward the staircase.

"Do you mind if we have a look around the place?" Officer Rombough rises.

Knowing it will look odd if I say no, I give him permission. I don't know what they could possibly find that would tell them where Jake is. They won't find Jake's blood on the banister; it's obviously mine. If they check it out, they'll find my fingerprints mixed with the blood.

Officer Heinz asks who Jake might possibly be with. I give him the short list. Then he adds, "Did the two of you have a fight before he went missing?"

"No, not at all. We rarely disagree about anything."

"Do you have children?"

"No, not yet."

"Has anything out of the ordinary happened lately? Was Jake upset about something?"

This is where I'm not sure how much to tell him. The secret I've been keeping from my husband—could it possibly have anything to do with his disappearance? "Well, there is one thing."

Officer Heinz gives me a quizzical look, while Craig tenses up, applying pressure to my right hand. Vicky's eyes are on me, and I know she's wondering how much I'm going to tell the police. With the support of my two best friends, one on either side of me, I expose some truth. "It's his father."

"Something happened to his father?"

"No, not his father. His mother."

Officer Heinz tilts his head. "What happened to his mother?

It's a difficult story to tell.

I recall when Jake told me why his father wasn't part of his life anymore.

A few days after he proposed, he confided in me.

* * *

Three and a half years ago

"There's something I think you should know about my past," Jake began. "It's not pretty, but it's bound to come out sooner or later, so I want you to know before we get married."

At the time, wild thoughts went through my head. Had Jake been in prison? Had he done something illegal? Was it about his sex life? Had he done something he was ashamed of? Did he have an addiction of some sort?

"Your past doesn't matter. I love you. Whatever you did before, it's not who you are now," I said, thinking I knew Jake well.

"When I was eighteen, something happened."

Eight years ago, I remember thinking. He was just a kid.

"My dad didn't treat my mom well. Me and John, either." He stopped for a moment as though searching for words. "That's not entirely true. He treated us very well when he was himself. When he wasn't, he beat the crap out of us. When we were kids, I thought the way he acted was normal. I thought all dads were like that, that he was just a good disciplinarian and that we deserved it."

My heart had gone out to him, and I hugged him, saying no one deserves to be beaten. I also confided that I'd had an occasional spanking myself. "I think we grew up in a generation where that was acceptable."

"I'm not talking about a bit of a spanking," he said grimly. "My dad literally beat us. All three of us were in the emergency room more than once. Until the day I stopped him."

The shock must have shown on my face.

"It's not what you're thinking. I didn't lay a hand on him. But I did make a serious threat. I told him to get the hell out, or I'd kill him."

"What happened?"

"He was dead sober when I confronted him with the ultimatum. There was no talking to that man when he was drunk out of his mind. I said I never wanted to see him again, and if I did, he'd wind up dead, and I'd go to juvie hall, maybe prison, for a few years. Dad broke down crying and promised he'd never hurt us again. When I picked up the phone to call the police, he packed his bags and left."

"Oh, Jake." I held him close. "I'm so sorry that happened to you. It sounds like it was for the best that he left."

"It was. He sent Mom money for John and me for several years, longer than he needed to, till we turned 25. But he never came back. Mom never divorced him. She said he was the only man she could ever love." Tears flowed freely down Jake's cheeks.

"You did the right thing. It sounds like he was poison for your Mom. She couldn't face the truth about who he really was. You took charge. Someone had to."

"John sided with me. Mom did, too, but she was sad after he left. Depressed. She tried to…." Jake choked up. "She took too many pills about a month after he left. I found her in bed. I thought she was dead."

"Oh, no, Jake." I couldn't imagine what he'd gone through as a child. My own life was tragic enough, losing my parents to the fire when I was 23, just out of university, with no siblings to help me through my grief. But until then, I'd been raised by two people who loved me and wanted the best for me. Like every teenager, I'd caused a bit of trouble, but we were a solid family unit. Until the house fire shattered my world and left me alone.

"She pulled herself together after getting counseling," Jake continued. "It was hard for her to ask for help, especially since she was a nurse—she felt she shouldn't be having these kinds of problems, I guess, being a professional herself. Things got better after she faced the fact her husband was abusive and she was clinically depressed. Her doctor prescribed meds, and things got better."

There wasn't much else for me to say, or if there was, I couldn't find the words.

"I've always worried… that I'd be like him. That I'd lose control and hurt someone," he confessed. "Especially when I have too much to drink. I get so angry sometimes."

At that point, I hadn't seen any signs to indicate Jake could be violent. On the couple of occasions when I'd seen him drink a few too many, he was still the same old Jake—loving and with a good sense of humor. Perhaps a bit louder and more boisterous.

"You're nothing like him, Jake."

* * *

Officer Heinz waits for an explanation, his sharp eyes watching me.

"It's his father *and* his mother." I give him the condensed story. Jake's father walked out on his family years ago, and now he's back. Jake is going to be furious when he finds out his mother is giving him another chance.

Officer Heinz nods and writes in his notebook. "How long has he been back?"

"A few weeks. His mother has been seeing him without Jake's knowledge. She told me in confidence, and I suggested she let me break the news to him."

"I take it you haven't done so. Is it possible Jake found out for himself?"

Is Officer Heinz suggesting Jake's disappearance has something to do with his father's reappearance in his mother's life?

* * *

When Gloria first told me Steve wanted another chance, I couldn't believe she would even consider it. What kind of woman forgives a man who has abused her, a man who abused his own children?

"He says he's a changed man," Gloria justified her decision. "He wants to make things right, bring our family together. Says he's given up drinking completely, and he's going to AA regularly."

"Have you forgotten how he treated you? And Jake and John?" I knew Jake would hit the roof when he heard he'd returned. He wouldn't tolerate his dad worming his way back into his mom's life, AA or not.

"He's so sorry. Steve says he's ashamed of himself and what he did all those years ago. He wants to make amends. Everyone deserves a second chance," Gloria said. "And I still love him. Always have."

My mouth hung open at her words. "How could you love a man who would hurt you?"

"It wasn't him. It was the drink. He's a good man, Mallory."

When Gloria insisted I meet him and judge for myself, I refused to have any part of it. If Jake wanted him out of their lives, that's where he needed to stay. But Gloria broke down sobbing, begging me to intervene between Steve and Jake, asking me to convince Jake to let his father apologize to him. I finally agreed to one meeting.

"On one condition," I said that Friday night three weeks ago. "After I meet him, if I decide I don't want him back in Jake's life, you promise not to see him again." I was positive there would be no possible way I could be convinced Steve deserved a second of Jake's time.

But the man I met two weeks ago was nothing like I expected. He looked a lot like Jake, which was disconcerting, but what really threw me for a loop was his personality. Like Jake, he was charming and easygoing. There was nothing about him that shouted 'abusive father.'

"So you're the young lady who's stolen Jake's heart," he said with a smile as he took my hand and leaned in for a kiss on the cheek. "It's so nice to finally meet you."

I'm not sure what I had expected. Someone who had a permanent scowl on his face, someone filled with anger? Maybe I would see murderous intent in his eyes, some sign he was a psychopath. But Steve's blue-green eyes gave off only warmth, just like his son's. His smile put me at ease instantly, and his demeanor was gentle.

We went out for dinner that Friday night, the three of us. Steve wanted to know all about Jake and me. "I'm so glad he found you. He deserves the best. I visited John and his lovely family a few days ago. My boys have done well." Tears welled in his eyes as he added, "It was for the best that I left when I did, that I didn't come back. Even though I missed them so much."

He put down his fork, bottom lip quivering, and cried shamelessly, blowing his nose into a napkin.

I almost felt sorry for the man. Almost.

It was Gloria who convinced me to keep an open mind. "Steve's had a rough time, being away from us for the past twelve years," she said, placing a hand on his. "But he pulled himself together, and he wants to reconnect with his boys before it's too late. He spent the last few years looking after his sick father, who passed away a few months ago."

"Your father was sick?" I turned to Steve for further details. "What was wrong with him?"

"Nothing in particular. He drank and smoked himself to death. Didn't eat properly or exercise. Apart from going to work, he spent most of his time passed out in front of the T.V. When he retired, he hardly left the house anymore. Just before he died, he said he didn't understand why he was still alive at eighty-four, when the wonderful woman he loved was dead at forty-two. He was a miserable old coot. Hell, he was a miserable human being, always was. But he was my dad."

"So you looked after him in his final years?"

Steve explained he returned to his childhood home after being kicked out of his own house. "When I asked Dad if I could stay with him for a few weeks till things settled down at home, he just grunted, opened the door wide, and pointed to the stairs. I lugged my stuff up to my old room, grateful to have somewhere to crash till I got myself straightened out. I think he was grateful, too, just to have someone around. Mom passed away when I was a teenager. Cancer. Then, I moved out a couple of years later for university, leaving him alone. I should have tried harder to make more time for him, but I got caught up in my own life."

As much as I tried to harden my heart against Steve, the more he talked, the more I felt sad for him. He'd had some bad breaks in his life. Not that it was any excuse for his behavior.

"Anyway, I ended up staying more than a few weeks. He needed me, even if he wouldn't admit it. And as much as I wanted to go home to my family, I knew it was best if I stayed away."

I had to ask. "Did you ever hit your father?"

Steve's hands covered his face. "Once. A few months after I left my family."

"What happened?" I wasn't surprised he had hit his own father. If he was capable of hurting his wife and sons, it only stood to reason he would do the same to his old man.

"I'd been drinking. He told me I was a miserable chip off the old block, and I needed to get my act together, or I'd end up like him. I was furious. I was nothing like my old man, I said. And I shoved him. Sent him flying against the stone fireplace, where he hit his head. Put him into an induced coma for about a week."

"Oh my God," I said, "You could have killed him."

Steve looked directly into my eyes. "I almost did. That's when I knew I could never go home to my family."

At that point, Gloria put her arms around him and told him she loved him. "So you see," she said to me, "Steve chose to stay away to protect us."

"It was the hardest thing I've ever had to do in my life."

"But you're back now," I pointed out.

"Yes. After Dad's accident, I turned myself in to the authorities. I knew it wasn't safe for me to be around anyone. I spent a couple of years in prison for aggravated assault, got out for good behavior. That's when I started to attend AA meetings and get counseling. Dad forgave me and visited me at the prison. He told me he was proud of me for finally getting the help I needed, especially since he had never been able to do so himself."

"And when you got out?"

"I moved back in with Dad and took care of him. His general health was deteriorating as he got older; his lungs and liver weren't in the best shape after all the years of abusing his own body."

"And why now? Why have you come back?" He'd better have a good reason, I'd thought. No way was Jake going to welcome him back with open arms. Even if he happened to be on his deathbed.

"Seeing Dad so lonely for the last forty years, I didn't want to be him. With Mom gone, he retreated into himself and never learned to live again. He tried to drink himself into the grave to be with her. When Dad died, I realized I *would* end up like him. I'd die alone with no one to mourn me if I didn't reach out to the people I love. I've only got a few years to go till I'm sixty. I don't want to waste any more time."

When Steve was done telling his story, I considered that Jake might be willing to forgive and forget. I just needed to find the right time to talk to him about letting his Dad back into his life.

Chapter Seventeen

"I don't think Jake knew. That his dad was back." Without getting into the whole issue of abuse, especially since I don't know how much Jake told Vicky and Craig, I give Officer Heinz some insight into Jake's family discord.

Officer Rombough asks to speak to his colleague privately. When they return to the living room, Officer Heinz states, "There's a lot of blood. Quite the head injury. What exactly happened here?"

After questioning me about my run-in with the armoire, the officers turn their attention to Vicky and Craig. "They're our best friends," I explain. "When I told them Jake didn't come home, they came to check on me this morning."

Officer Heinz catches me off guard. Instead of questioning them about where Jake might be, he asks, "Is your friend, Mallory, prone to accidents?"

Craig and Vicky turn to me and then steal a look at each other. If they're put in the position of choosing sides, will they support me or Jake? Vicky speaks first. "Mallory is a bit clumsy. But this is the first time she's hurt herself this badly."

"It's probably the stress she's dealing with," Craig adds. "With Jake missing."

"Yes, that's right. She told me she was kind of out of it from lack of sleep and tripped into the armoire," Vicky agrees. "But she's fine. At the hospital, they said head wounds can bleed a lot."

Once they've confirmed with Craig and Vicky that my head wound occurred this morning, the officers concentrate on when Jake was last seen. I repeat that I dropped him off for work yesterday afternoon at 2:40. "I had an appointment to have the oil changed in Jake's car at 3. He said he'd go in early and have a coffee before his shift started. Otherwise, it was our regular routine for a Friday. I drop off Jake at work; I visit his Mom; I pick him up after work. Except he wasn't there after work."

Officer Heinz nods and turns to Vicky and Craig. "And when did the two of you last see Jake?"

"I haven't seen him for six weeks," Vicky answers. "Mallory's birthday party. The four of us went out to celebrate."

"I saw him Thursday. Jake and I work the same shift at the warehouse. We drove in to work together, like we do sometimes. Went out for a drink afterwards. Then I dropped him off at home," Craig says.

"What about yesterday? Didn't you see him at work?" Officer Heinz stops recording in his notebook to observe Craig's response.

"No. And I just checked with my boss. Apparently, no one saw him at work yesterday. It's as though he never showed up."

Officer Rombough raises his eyebrows. "Didn't you wonder why he wasn't at work yesterday? Had he called in sick?" His eyes go from Craig to me, and I focus on Craig's answer.

"I didn't really think about it, to be honest. I don't run across him every day. We often work in different areas. Sometimes, he doesn't even show up in the break room. If he's busy with paperwork, he'll eat supper alone in his office."

Officer Heinz asks a question that brings deep furrows to Craig's normally smooth brow. "That's quite the shiner. How'd you get that?" He's referring to the bluish tinge around his right eye.

Craig brings his hand to his eye as if he's forgotten about the incident that caused it. "Oh, that. Got into a bit of a fight in the parking lot Thursday night after we closed down the bar."

"With Jake?"

"Jake and I closed down the bar, yes. The fight was me and some other guy who thought I was trying to pick up his girl. It happens. It all got straightened out. He kept the girl, I got the shiner." Vicky flinches beside me, and Craig shakes his head, adding, "It was just a misunderstanding."

82

Officer Rombough nods as though he's been there himself, and Officer Heinz records the fact in his notebook, as if it might be relevant to Jake's disappearance. "Are you interested in pressing assault charges?"

"Charges? For what? It was no big deal. He took a drunken swing at me, that's all. It looks worse than it is. Besides, I don't know him from Adam."

The police leave my house, saying they'll file a missing persons report and let me know when they have any information about Jake. "If you hear anything in the meantime, call the station," says Officer Rombough. "In most cases, missing spouses turn up within a couple of days. Usually, it's just a fight or misunderstanding."

"What do I do if he doesn't come back?" As much as I don't want to face this particular scenario, I can't sit here and do nothing.

"Keep calling him. Keep contacting family and friends, yours and his. Even if they don't know where Jake is, they might say something that gives us a clue where to find him, and it's also good for you to have some support." Officer Heinz motions toward Vicky and Craig, the emotional support team on either side of me. "You can also check online, see if he's been in contact with anyone. If you have access to his finances, check out his bank accounts, see if there have been any withdrawals. Maybe call his credit card companies."

The rest of the afternoon is spent on the phone. Craig contacts his boss again, calls their drinking buddies personally, once again checks in with the bars they frequent, and talks to Jake's brother, John, to fill him in about the police report. Vicky hauls out the phone book to call Jake's old high school buddies, some of whom still live at home, and to get contact info from the parents of the ones who have moved away. "You never know," she explains. "Maybe he met up with one of them. He used to talk about his high school friends when the two of us were dating. Have they stayed in touch?"

His best friend from school, Terry, sends an email once in a while, along with photos of his family. They get together and have lunch once or twice a year. "Just Terry, but Craig's already called him. And he hasn't heard from him since my birthday party."

Vicky raises her eyebrows at the mention of the party.

Terry lives in Kingston. If Jake went to visit him, it would be a five-hour drive. I think back to the time I visited my friend, Heather. Jake was out of his mind with worry. It's possible this is payback for what I did, putting me in his position.

After checking Jake's social media sites again and finding nothing, I send a plea to our online friends to let me know if they have any idea where my missing husband might be. Then I take a look at our bank account. Nothing there. Just a few hundred dollars. We have a couple of joint credit cards. When I call to check the balance, I know Jake hasn't used them since he's been gone. Jake and I don't keep separate accounts or cards. Our finances are jointly held. For the most part, anyway. The mortgage, cars, credit lines, everything belongs to the two of us. We're one entity. Jake and Mallory.

I wrack my brain, trying to think of who else to call. Heather comes to mind again. When she picks up the phone, I explain what's happened. She doesn't seem surprised. "He'll be back. Guys sometimes need a breather after a fight."

"We didn't fight," I insist.

There's silence on the other end for a few seconds, then Heather reminds me how upset Jake was when I left him. "You walked out on him, remember? But you went back."

"That was different."

"I don't know. Was it? You got upset and took off for a while. That's probably what's going on now. Let me know when you hear from him."

After speaking with Heather, I call my work friends, for support, like Officer Heinz suggested. "Sue, something's happened." Sue is the kindergarten teacher I've worked with for the past four years. She's the closest I have to a friend, other than Vicky and Heather. When I explain what's happened, Sue offers to come over.

"Thanks, but I have a couple of friends here already. I just wanted to let you know."

"What about Brad? Does he know? Do you want me to call him? Is there anyone else you want me to contact?"

"Thanks, I'll call him myself. But I don't want everyone at work to know.

Not just yet. I'm sure he'll be back."

"Okay, but let me know if there's anything I can do."

I debate whether to call Brad or not. We've remained friends since our breakup, when Jake and I started seeing each other. Brad and I work closely together. His Grade 6 students are 'reading buddies' to our kindergarten kids. They spend twenty minutes with us every day. While the kids interact, the three of us observe and chat. During school social events, Sue, Brad, and I stick together. When we go to a workshop or conference, it's the three of us at a table, the three of us having lunch. Jake gets a bit jealous of my 'work husband,' given the fact that Brad and I dated briefly. It's kind of cute how he always wants to know when I see Brad and what we talk about.

"Oh, Mallory." Brad sighs when I tell him Jake's missing. "Do you want me to come over? What can I do—"

"No, no. Don't be silly," I cut him off. "You don't need to come. I've got a couple of friends here already. There's nothing else you can do."

"Don't worry. He'll come home when he's ready. Just give it some time."

My last call is the hardest. "Hi, Gloria. No, he's not back. I haven't heard anything. Listen, I don't want you to panic, but I think you should know. I called the police."

Gloria's gasp is audible. "You did it? You contacted the police?"

I know exactly how she feels. "I think we need to consider that maybe Jake has run off." That's as far as I get before I start to blubber. Gloria joins me. In between sobs, I manage to tell her about my head injury and my trip to the hospital.

She stops crying abruptly. "Mallory? When did this happen? Are you okay?"

"I'm fine, just a little concussion. Just me being clumsy, that's all."

"Do you want to come stay with me? I'll pick you up. You should have someone looking after you." Gloria takes on the role of the mother I lost years ago. "You have to be careful with a concussion. When did it happen? Before or after Jake went missing?"

"Be… after." I was fine when she saw me yesterday; she knows that. "After I came home last night, I finally fell asleep, then woke up groggy in the morning and bashed my head on the edge of the armoire on my way out of the bedroom." My brain's still fuzzy. The last 18 hours have been a nightmare. "I have Vicky and Craig here with me. I want to stay home, so I'm here when Jake comes back or tries to contact me."

There's a sigh of relief on the other end of the line. "Well, I'm glad to hear you're okay."

"I did want to ask you something, though. Did you tell Jake his dad was back? Does he know?"

Chapter Eighteen

The conversation with Gloria is a wake-up call for both of us. Two men with a tendency to violence possibly meeting up?

"No, I don't see how he could know. He didn't hear it from me or from John," she answers, then there's a moment of silence on her end. "Steve claims he hasn't tried to approach him. You don't think he'd hurt him, do you?"

I'm a bit confused by what she's asking. Who would hurt whom? I know we're both thinking it's tough to break the cycle of domestic violence.

"Maybe you should warn Steve to keep a low profile for now, till we find out where Jake is," I suggest. Neither of us wants to consider the possibility of what might happen if Steve and Jake come face to face.

We end the conversation, promising to call the minute we hear anything. I wonder why she married a man like Steve. Why did she stay with him? Why does she still love him? Which leads me to wonder what people think of *my* marriage.

Maybe it's time for me to come clean. Stop deluding myself and face what everyone knows to be the truth. My marriage isn't the perfect fairy tale I've wanted it to be. Jake and I are a normal married couple, like any other, with the same types of problems everyone else has. There's some consolation in my admission. It means people might be right. He could have taken some time away because he was angry with me. It's possible he spent the night in a hotel just to give us a break from each other. Even so, there must be some logical explanation why he hasn't contacted me. Maybe he lost his phone.

Or maybe he *has* contacted me. I open my laptop and check his email messages again. There's the one I saw earlier, indicating that time was running out. **Tick Tock**. Did Jake send that? I don't have my own email or social media accounts anymore. We share everything. If he did write that message, what is he trying to tell me?

As I begin to doze off, the pain pills dragging me under, my mind considering what the message means, a loud banging on the door startles me. Jake! Vicky heads for the door before I can get up.

"No, I'm just a friend," she says, her voice shaking, when the visitors ask if she's Jake's wife. I struggle toward the door. "This is Jake's wife, Mallory. What's this about? Is it Jake?"

The mid-afternoon sun shines on their backs. They're dressed in black pants and black t-shirts, in spite of the heat. The taller, black-haired one says, "Would Jake happen to be home?"

"No, he's not here." I examine their faces. "How do you know Jake?"

"We're old friends from way back, went to school together. I'm Nick, and this is Adam," he says, pointing to the stockier man next to him.

My body relaxes. For a moment, I thought…

"Do you know when he'll be back? We could wait for him," suggests his friend, stepping closer to the door.

"No, sorry. Maybe another time. I'll tell him you stopped by." I close the door, but Adam puts his foot out to stop me. We make eye contact, and it's clear he's not taking no for an answer.

Turning around, I holler with enough volume to raise the dead. "Craig! Can you come out here?"

A chair scrapes across the floorboards, and Craig races to the entrance. Smiling, Adam explains they're old friends of Jake's. "We were just in the neighborhood, down by Heart Lake, doing some fishing. Then we thought of our old buddy, Jake. His grandparents had a farm here, from what we remembered. So we looked him up."

Jake has never mentioned a Nick or an Adam. But then, I don't have the best memory. And I'm sure I've never told him the names of everyone I knew during my school days. But maybe Craig knows who they are.

"Sorry, who did you say you are?" Craig asks.

"I'm Adam, and this is Nick."

"Last names?" When they tell him, Craig shakes his head. "Jake's never mentioned you."

"It was a long time ago," Nick explains, his hand moving to his back pocket. Thinking he has a gun, I scream. I've been reading too many paperback thrillers lately. Added to the fact that my husband is missing, I have every right to overreact. He pulls out a wallet, and I feel foolish, everyone looking at me like I'm nuts.

"I'll just leave a number where he can reach us," Nick says, "if you have a pen." Vicky grabs one out of her purse, and Nick writes a number on the back of a restaurant business card.

"Let Jake know Nick and Adam were here to see him. We'll be back next time we're in the area. We expect to be back again real soon. The fishing here is great," Adam says, taking another step forward. "And Jake owes us a visit. It's long overdue. It's been nice to meet you, Mallory."

They drive off in their black sedan, leaving us wondering if they had anything to do with Jake's disappearance.

"Have you seen these guys before, Mallory? Did Jake ever mention them?" Craig locks the door and helps me back to the sofa. His face registers nothing, though I sense his fear.

"No, never. But I don't know all Jake's school friends."

Two strange men have come to my door asking for Jake the very time he's missing. Is that a coincidence?

Vicky exhales a deep breath. "I thought...when I first answered the door, maybe they were detectives. And that they'd...oh, Mallory." Her eyes glisten. "I thought maybe they'd found his body."

I gasp, then shut my mouth. We had the same thought. And I know that's exactly what went through Craig's mind.

There's nothing more to be said. It was a morbid thought, but given the circumstances, there's a real possibility that something terrible has happened to Jake. My mind is going in so many directions right now, it all blurs together. It's hard to sort out what's real and what's not.

I need to get some sleep. I can't cope with this. Jake's gone, I'm stressed out and exhausted, and my head hurts.

Craig and Vicky must read my mind. "Close your eyes and get some rest. We'll be right here till Jake comes home," Craig assures me.

"I'll make soup and grilled cheese for a late supper. Everything will be okay." Vicky pulls the throw over me.

But it's not okay. It's never going to be okay again. Not unless Jake somehow finds his way back to me. And at this point, I'm beginning to accept the fact that isn't going to happen.

Chapter Nineteen

My mind drifts, but sleep won't come. Voices intrude upon my semi-conscious state, voices that mirror my own thoughts.

"Those guys aren't up to any good." Craig is trying to keep his voice down, but it travels from the kitchen through the hall into the living room. "Gambling buddies, more likely than old school chums."

"You don't think they have anything to do with his being missing, do you?" Vicky's voice is high-pitched. "Why would they come looking for him if they're responsible? That doesn't make sense."

"Unless he owes them money. Maybe Jake took off to avoid these guys. Knew they were coming to look for their cash back—cash he probably doesn't have."

"It's more likely he got totally plastered and woke up in some bimbo's bed, and he's too scared to face Mallory."

"I don't know. I thought that at first, because I know they've been having problems. But he wouldn't risk his marriage. He's too afraid of losing Mallory. I've given it some thought, and I don't really believe he'd cheat on her."

"I guess you'd be an expert on the topic of cheating."

"Vicky…." Craig's tone is pleading. "That's in the past."

"Is it?"

"Can't we put it behind us? Besides, this isn't about us."

In the ensuing silence, I cock my ear to the hallway, straining to hear what that's about.

"You're right, it's not. Just the same, he could be screwing around, especially if what you said is true—that they're having problems."

"If those guys come around again, we're calling the police." Craig's voice is the last I hear before I drift off again.

* * *

"It's been a long, stressful day," Craig says after dinner, his face drawn. "I'm going to hit the sack. Try to get some rest, Mallory. Good night, Vicky." He heads to the den off the kitchen.

Vicky helps me up the stairs, saying she'll leave the guest room door partly open so she can hear if I need help during the night.

"I'll be fine. But thanks." All I want is to get through this. It's like when I lost my parents. If Jake's left me too, I will survive. Somehow.

Thinking I'll feel better after a shower and a change of clothing, I enter the ensuite and peel off the pajamas I've been wearing since last night. I wrap a towel over my head, covering the gauze and the gash underneath. The warm spray feels good on my face, and my tears mix with the soothing water, thinking of where Jake is and whether he's feeling comfort or pain. I don't wish the latter on him, but I know it's a definite possibility. He could be lying battered and beaten, waiting for someone to find him. Vicky thinks he could be finding comfort in another woman's arms, but I know he's not.

After brushing my teeth, I slip into the short-sleeved white linen night-gown Jake bought. "When I saw it in the store window, I thought of you, my angel," he said on Valentine's Day. It's beautiful, even if it is a bit Victorian, and I put it on in hopes that Jake will show up to see me in it tonight. He'll slowly undo the tiny buttons on the lace yoke, slip it over my head....

Someone's in the hall. I hear footsteps, then see the shadow outside my door.

"Just checking on you." Vicky peeks through my open bedroom door. "Oh, that's lovely."

"Jake bought it for me."

Vicky nods in understanding, saying she can't imagine what I'm going through. As she stands in the doorway, it seems she wants to say more, but she wishes me a good night and heads back to the guest room.

Vicky thinks he's not coming back. It's been too long. No matter how much he'd had to drink, he would have come home or called by now. How am I supposed to get through another night without him? The answer lies in the medicine cupboard above the toilet. For the last couple of years, I've had to resort to the meds again, but I only take them when I really need them—and this qualifies as one of those times. The vial of benzos sits on the shelf, half empty, where it's been for more than two months, nearly untouched. I haven't needed them. Everything's been perfect. No anxiety, no depression, no sleepless nights. Until now.

One little pill, that's all I need. I'm about to pop it into my mouth, when I remember. I can't. I shouldn't. Except for a double, maybe triple dose a couple days ago, I've been pill-free for too long to go back. Especially now. I wasn't even sure about the over-the-counter pain pills Craig gave me, but I didn't want to cause a fuss, so I took them. Besides, my head really does hurt. When I think about the side effects I've suffered in the past—loss of balance, loss of memory—I can't help but be wary. Back on the shelf, they go. I need to calm myself in a more natural way.

The blood on the armoire and on the wall has vanished since morning. My hand touches the gauze, a physical confirmation that I haven't imagined the head blow. I remember Vicky's reaction to the blood and the way the officers looked at the banister. Yes, it was real. I didn't imagine it. But, when did I clean it up?

The house is quiet now except for the hum of the air conditioning. I flip the stairwell light switch. The handrail feels cool on my way to the main level entry. No sign of blood on the banister. I check the front door to find it locked. Turning around, I set one foot in front of the other, feeling my way in the near darkness toward the kitchen. This house—its creaks, its moans, its squeaks, its hums—it's part of me. It doesn't scare me. Through the kitchen window, the sliver of a moon glows in a starry sky. When the kettle boils, I unplug it before it whistles, pouring hot water over the Sleepy Time tea bag. Placing a couple of Social Tea biscuits on the saucer next to the cup, I step, stop, step, back to the stairs. Fearful of falling, I hold the handrail with one hand, the cup and saucer in the other, and climb, placing one foot on a step, then the other next to it. Slow and steady.

My door is wide open. Did I leave it that way? I set the tea on the nightstand, fluff my pillows against the headboard, and ease myself into bed. Switching my bedroom lamp to night light mode, I spy my iPad on the night table. One sure way to get myself to sleep is to listen to my audio book. I choose the least frightening of the suspense novels I have downloaded, anything to drown out the quiet. And listen.

My eyelids grow heavy as I sip tea and let my mind drift into an imaginary world where the protagonist deals with a husband who's trying to drive her insane. At least, that's my guess. You never know till you get to the end. Sometimes, it can surprise you.

It doesn't make me forget about Jake, but it does make me sleepy. He'll be back tomorrow. And if he isn't, I'll keep looking for him. I'll never stop. Not till I find him. Dead or alive.

Chapter Twenty

Nellie snuggles with me as I sink into the land of my nightmares, where my parents are burning. A strange buzzing wakes me. Did I get a new phone? I grab my cell off the night table, but there's no incoming call, no voicemail, no record of a text. My cell on the pillow, I close my eyes. I don't want to miss Jake if he tries to contact me.

Before I doze off again, brightness filters through the slit in my curtains. Someone has set off the security light. If Jake were here, he'd tell me it's probably one of the strays that come around, maybe Nellie's mom still looking for her two years later, or maybe a raccoon or skunk. But Jake's not here, and someone's out there. Gently moving Nellie aside, I glance out the window, which faces the front of the property. A movement catches my eye. I don't see it directly, but I sense it's there, just out of my line of vision. And I'm sure it's no cat.

The security light turns off as the curtains fall closed, and I reassure myself there's no reason for alarm. Vicky is across the hall. Craig is in the den, at the back of the house. Nellie is with me. Four cars sit in the driveway. Surely no one would think of breaking in knowing people are in the house. Yet, as always, my mind goes to the most horrifying possibility. You read about it in the news all the time—home invasions. Criminals are getting bolder all the time. If Jake were here, he'd make me feel safe, telling me we're locked up tight, help is just a 911 call away. Joking that his old baseball bat is in the bedroom closet.

But Jake's not here. That fact hits me with a fresh shock every time I allow it past the defensive wall I've erected in my brain. And if something has happened to Jake, then maybe I'm in danger, too. If I were capable of logical thinking in my current state, I would wake Vicky or Craig. They'd look out the windows, open the doors, and take a quick tour outside, set my mind at ease by concluding some animal set off the security light, and we'd all go back to bed.

Since logical thinking isn't my strong suit, and I'm further impaired by a head injury and the stress of a missing husband, I grab Jake's bat and creep down the stairs toward the front entry. Slipping into my sandals, I unlock the door, turn the knob, and ease it fully open. The warm air hits me when I step onto the porch. As I take a few steps forward, the movement triggers the security light. If anyone is out here, they have a good view of me now, bathed in the spotlight. I swing the bat a few times to give the impression that I'm armed and ferocious, just in case I *am* being watched.

Two maple trees loom directly ahead on the edge of the lawn next to the road, their branches casting ominous shadows in the moonlight. No traffic travels down the road this time of night. What lies in the bushes and trees on the other side of the road, I don't even want to think about. There's a darkness in the heart of the woods; it's muted during the day, but at night, it takes a tenacious hold on the natural environment. To my left, the cars sit in the driveway, in front of the two-car garage bordered by rows of evergreen trees. Someone could be hiding amongst the vehicles or trees. The vast space on my right is occupied by farmland, the corn about my height, obstructing my view. If someone is out here, the chance of me seeing them is slim.

Standing on my steps looking out at the darkness, I think of the number of times I sat on the porch swing, reading a book, waiting for Jake to come home from his shift. With all the outdoor lights on and the front door partially open, phone by my side, I'd sit there in my PJs. Alone. Not that I wasn't somewhat afraid, but Jake insisted it was perfectly safe. Living in the country, on the outskirts of a small town, you don't expect robbers or murderers to pop up on your front lawn. Still, I've always been scared a rabid skunk, raccoon, or possum might wander up to me in the dark. Now that Jake is gone, I'm afraid there might be someone or something more sinister wandering around my home.

* * *

Three years ago

I recall one time I had a particularly big scare on the porch. A shadow streaked across the lawn, followed by someone shouting. That sort of thing late at night raises the hairs on your neck, especially when you're home alone. My gut reaction told me to head to the door, get inside and lock it. What I did was remain frozen in my spot, panic coursing from my head down to my feet.

"What the hell, Russ! Get back here!" A voice blasted across the lawn.

My heart pounded in my chest, sweat formed on my brow. But, the sound of heavy breathing as someone hurtled toward me jolted my body into action. I sprang from the swing, yanking open the screen door. The intruder jumped up behind me, nearly knocking me down.

"Russ! Come back here! Now!"

"Arf! Arf! Arf!" Russ barked. As relieved as I was to know Russ wasn't the threat I had envisioned, he nearly gave me a heart attack. When he bounded up the steps, I was sure he planned on taking a bite out of me.

But, the sight of the tiny pup rolling over at my feet, belly up, brought out my motherly instinct. "Hey, there. Where did you come from? You scared me silly." My high-pitched voice pierced the night air.

"Sorry, Mallory." My neighbor, Paul, approached the porch. "We just got him. I took the little guy out for a walk, and he got away from me."

Still puffing, he attached the leash back onto his Russell Terrier pup and gave him a belly rub. "Good boy, Russ. But you can't run away from Daddy like that. It's a good thing there's not much traffic on this road."

Paul wore his pajamas and slip-on sandals. It dawned on me that I was dressed in the same manner. Putting my arms across my chest, I said, "He's so cute."

"Needs to learn the rules, though. Too many places to lose yourself out here with the woods and the cornfield."

Uncomfortable having him gawk at me in my PJs, I didn't know what else to say, but he didn't appear ready to leave.

"Waiting for Jake to come home?" he asked, and I nodded, saying Jake should be home any time. "It's a nice night to be out. Sorry if Russ scared you."

"It's okay," I said, patting Russ on the head. "He just startled me. I'm going to head inside now. Have a good night."

I locked the door as Paul pulled Russ toward the road. My heart rate settled down, but my palms were sweaty. When Jake came home half an hour later, I recounted how our middle-aged neighbor in his pajamas and his new puppy nearly scared me to death. Jake had a good chuckle about it.

* * *

Maybe it was Russ who set off the security light tonight, out for a late-night run. Or a cat. We'll have a laugh tomorrow when I tell Jake I chased a stray cat around the house in my nightgown in the middle of the night. Unless it's not a stray cat and someone's about to drag me off into the cornfield. Staying close to the side of the house as I work my way to the back yard, part of me considers how dangerous this could be, but the other part needs to know if it has something to do with Jake.

The solar garden lights illuminate the yard somewhat, but the effect is less than reassuring. Shadows send a chill down my spine as I creep along the flower beds, listening and searching for whatever set off the security light. There's nothing out here, other than mosquitoes, attacking every inch of my delicate skin. The large yard with recently cut grass, trees, and my flower beds, stretches ahead, the cornfield beyond and to the left, rows of evergreen trees on the garage side. The garden shed sits in front of the cornfield, next to the trees. I don't need to walk all the way back to be reminded of what lies there. Retracing my steps to the front door, a shadow catches my eye.

"Hey! Who's there?" the approaching figure demands.

I run, but not fast enough. An arm grabs me around the waist, and I'm forced to face my assailant, who wrestles the baseball bat out of my hand.

"Mallory? What are you doing out here?" He's so close I could kiss him.

I recognize the voice, look into the face I know well, my panic subsiding.

"You nearly scared the life out of me! For a moment, I thought you were a ghost." Craig's face in the moonlight is as white as my nightgown billowing in the breeze.

"The security light came on out front. I wanted to see what set it off. I was hoping it might be Jake."

Craig wraps me in his arms. "Why didn't you come and get me? You shouldn't be out here on your own. What were you thinking?"

"What are *you* doing out here?" I pull away.

"I was in the kitchen getting a drink of water when I saw movement in the yard. I'm worried those guys might come back. Nick and Adam. I've been thinking about them all night, wondering why they showed up on your doorstep now, of all times."

What if they were out here waiting for me? What if Craig hadn't come along when he did? "Let's get back inside," I whisper, shivering, arms crossed in front of my chest.

Craig leads me in through the back door, turning on the outdoor lights.

"Let's leave these on for the rest of the night. If there's anyone out there, we'll see them coming."

As we walk toward the front entrance, we're greeted by the wide open door. In my haste to get outside, I neglected to pull it closed behind me. While I've been wandering around the back yard, the house has been unsecured.

My eyes move to the staircase. "Vicky!"

The stairs creak as we climb, our eyes fixed on the landing. Craig and I peer into the guest room. The covers on the bed are shoved aside. No Vicky.

Chapter Twenty-One

"Shh…" Craig whispers, easing open the bathroom door to find it vacant as well. He checks Jake's office. No one there.

My door is halfway ajar. Craig swings it open, flicking the switch. The bed is exactly the way I left it, with Nellie still curled up on it and the ensuite door open.

"Where is she?" I ask in a hushed tone.

Craig indicates we should head back downstairs. Gripping the baseball bat, he leads the way through the house. We head into the kitchen, to the mudroom at the back door, checking the other rooms along the way. Vicky isn't in the house, nor is anyone else.

"First Jake, now Vicky? What's going on, Craig?"

"I'm going to take a look out front." Craig strides toward the front door. "Stay here."

"No, I'm coming with you."

It's irrational, but I'm overwhelmed with the fear that everyone I know is being abducted. If I lose Craig, too, I'll lose my mind.

The exterior lights illuminate part of the lawn, but beyond that, shadows of the trees threaten to swallow us. Through the silence of the night, the sound of panting and pounding ripples across the lawn toward us. As a silhouette nears, Craig raises the baseball bat, instructing me to get inside. Before I reach the bottom porch step, a voice slices through the muggy air.

"Where the hell have you two been?"

Craig lowers the bat and breathes a sigh of relief as Vicky enters the lit area of the lawn, bending over, hands on knees, catching her breath.

"What happened to you? Are you okay?" Craig leaps forward and embraces Vicky, kissing her on the mouth. "I was going out of my mind."

"Me? I'm fine. You had me worried sick, Mallory." Her tone implies it's my fault she's running along a dark road bordered by forest. "I can take care of myself," she says to Craig, pulling away.

As though I can't. *Poor meek little Mallory.* That's what she's thinking. She has no idea what I'm capable of, no idea what I can withstand.

Craig tells us to get inside. After checking all the doors are secured, we sit at the kitchen table. "I think we're all overreacting," he concludes, clasping his hands together under his chin. "Lack of sleep, worry, stress—it's getting to us. What were you doing out there, Vicky?" His tone is berating, with an undercurrent of worry. "Did you not stop to think Nick and Adam could be out there?"

"I went to check on Mallory, and she wasn't in her room, so I came downstairs looking for her. When I couldn't find her, I went to tell you, but you were gone, too. I ran around the house looking for you. The cars are still in the driveway, so I thought maybe someone came along and picked you up, or maybe...I don't know, Craig, with Jake gone and those guys coming around, maybe someone drove up and took you against your will. I ran over to the neighbors, but the house was dark."

It's all clear now. The situation is the same as when I sat in the parking lot waiting for Jake, and he wasn't there. I had considered maybe we missed each other, or someone had picked him up, similar to what Vicky thought now.

"The security light came on out front, so I went to check it out," I explain. "Craig saw someone in the back yard and came out to see what was going on, but it was just me. When we went back in, we noticed I'd left the front door open, and we thought someone might be inside. Then, when we couldn't find you, we thought someone might have taken you."

It sounds like a comedy of errors, but not one of us is laughing. If Jake were here, he'd find it hilarious.

"What we need is to get some rest," Craig states. "Everything's locked up. If Jake comes home, he'll ring the bell if he's lost his key. I don't want either of you going back outside. If you think you see or hear something strange, wake me up."

Back in my room, I have a hard time falling asleep after our excursion into the night, but I don't want to disturb Vicky and Craig any more than I already have, so I turn off the lights and lie quietly, waiting for morning.

Left with nothing but my own thoughts, I picture Jake's face and wonder, not for the first time, whether I ever knew my husband at all. Have I been blinded by love? Does the Jake I love really exist?

Chapter Twenty-Two

I can't expect them to stay with me forever. "You've got your own lives. I appreciate you being here for me, but there's really nothing else you can do."

Vicky accepts that and tells me to call her anytime. "I'm so sorry he's gone. You'll hear from him soon, I'm sure." With a sigh, she adds, "If he *is* with another woman…"

"No, he wouldn't do that to me," I say to the woman who slept with my husband.

Vicky nods, but her face shows what she's thinking. If he could cheat on her, he can just as easily cheat on me. I don't know why she broke up with Jake, but I've always assumed it was because he slept with someone else. Although she never confirmed that, she didn't deny it either. Jake told me Vicky wasn't ready for a committed relationship. I think they just weren't right for each other. When you find your perfect person, you're ready to give yourself completely, and you don't need anyone else. That's what happened with Jake and me. No need to fear commitment. No need for anyone else in our lives.

Craig insists on staying a while longer. "Let me talk to the police again, see if they have any leads. But I agree with Vicky. You'll hear from him soon." He shakes his head. "I'm sorry for what he's putting you through. He'll come back begging for your forgiveness."

I don't need their pity. Jake hasn't left me for another woman. It's not a matter of me forgiving *him*. If I'd been a better wife in the first place, he'd still be here with me. "You don't need to stay. To tell the truth, I'd rather just have some time on my own. I'm tired."

After Vicky leaves, Craig calls the police station. He records something on the notepad during the conversation.

"Nothing new. They've given us a number to contact the detective in charge directly if you have further questions or think of something that might help them find Jake. You're to contact them immediately when he comes home. In the meantime, they've put him in their database of missing persons, and they're putting out bulletins in an attempt to locate him."

Craig says he thinks the police probably suspect it's a typical case of a husband intentionally taking off for a while. "That doesn't necessarily mean he's cheating on you, Mallory, in spite of what happened between us, and it doesn't mean he's leaving you. If you ask me, I think it's more likely he took off because of his gambling. He probably teed off someone and went into hiding for a few days. It's no coincidence those guys showed up at your door now. You and I both know Jake's issues. I think you need to face the fact that the two of you have been having some problems lately."

"Everything's fine," I insist. "We love each other. We don't have problems."

Craig lets out a deep sigh and runs his hands over his face. "Okay. Whatever you say, Mallory." Catching my eye, he adds, "But you and I both know why he might have taken off."

I don't want to hear it.

"Goodbye, Craig. Thanks for your help. I'll call when I hear something." I don't need him reminding me my marriage isn't perfect. I show him to the door. It's 9 a.m., nearly 36 hours since I sat and waited for Jake in the Auto Supply parking lot.

Left on my own, I decide it's time to come up with a logical explanation for Jake's disappearance. One that everyone will believe, including me.

Chapter Twenty-Three

Wondering whether Jake's decided to hook up with one of his ex-fiancées, I open my laptop and check his social media sites again.

No new posts. Well, there wouldn't be, would there? If he's been taken against his will, he won't be able to post GIFs of kittens. And if he's hiding out, he won't want to leave clues. If he's left me, he won't be online taunting me. I send out another plea on all our social media accounts, asking for anyone who's heard from Jake in the last two days to let me know ASAP. It's a long shot. For the most part, our online friends are people we've never met. We're not much for socializing in real life.

When I check our email, another message pops up from the same sender as the 'Tick Tock' message yesterday. **Hickory Dickory Dock. The mouse ran up the clock.** Who would send this to us? A children's nursery rhyme?

I click reply. **Who is this? What do you want?**

My head aches. Setting aside my laptop, I climb the stairs, my hand on the banister, and head for the ensuite. Wrapping a towel over my bandaged head, I step inside the glass enclosure, and warm water comforts me. When it runs cool, I shut it off and select a pair of comfortable shorts and a sleeveless button-down white shirt from our walk-in closet. As I don't expect to go anywhere today, it doesn't matter if the marks and bruises on my legs and arms are visible. I give myself a good pinch to make sure I'm awake and conscious, adding another small bruise to my left arm.

Nellie follows me into the den. An idea came to me while I was in the shower. If I want to find out what happened to Jake, I need to contact everyone who knows him. The antique desk in the den holds a list that might help. At Christmas, Jake and I send cards to extended family members, to friends from the past as well as the few friends we're still in contact with, to neighbors in our small town, to co-workers, to people who work in stores and restaurants we frequent together. Jake insists on keeping up with people, saying he wants everyone to know how happy we are. So every year, I spend a couple of weeks and a few hundred dollars worth of postage and photographs of the two of us to send out Christmas cheer and a photocopied note telling everyone how great we're doing.

It's going to take the better part of the day, but I organize myself at the dining room table. Ready to prepare a phone call tree, I start calling people we sort of know.

"Hi, Laura? It's Mallory Shelton. Yes, it's been a while. The reason I'm calling is Jake seems to have gone missing." After explaining what happened, I ask Laura if she could call a few people for me and provide her with a list of five names.

"Oh, Mallory. You must be going out of your mind. Yes, of course, I'll call around and see if anyone has any idea where he might be. You take care of yourself."

Once I've called 20 people, I stand up to stretch. It's exhausting being the wife of a man who's gone missing. Everyone is more than willing to help me, the poor wife who's been left behind. I don't mind their pity and concern for our marriage. Someone's going to be able to help me. Someone's going to come up with a plausible reason why Jake left and where he might be. Someone's going to give me information I can feed to the detective in charge of finding Jake. Then, one of two things will happen. Sooner or later, Jake's either going to be found, and I'm going to have to face the truth and live with it, or Jake will be gone for good, and I'm going to have to live without him. Either way, I need to know. And I want to do everything I can to show what a good wife I am. Jake wouldn't expect any less of me.

Chapter Twenty-Four

I begin to tidy up the mess I've made—the address book, my phone, the pen and notepad, the sheets spread out on the table, my empty teacup and saucer, the cookie crumbs—when it's apparent something's off. One of the drawers in the china buffet is partially opened. I try to think of the last time I searched for something in there. Place mats, napkins, tablecloth? When was the last time we had a dinner party?

Upon closer inspection, some of the cups and saucers in the china cabinet appear out of place. Ordinarily, they're arranged by color and pattern, stacked two high to accommodate them all. Now, there's a yellow-flowered one on top of a blue one and a pink one on top of a green one... and it's just not right. I wouldn't stack them that way. And Jake most certainly would point it out if I did.

Someone's been in here. Someone slipped into the house when the door was open last night. The dining room is just to the right of the entry hall. It would take only minutes to steal something. What could they possibly want? Most of the things in this room were wedding gifts or passed down from Jake's grandma. None of the teacups seem to be missing, just rearranged. I take a good look at the rest of my fine china. There's a set of eight good dinner plates, bowls, dessert plates, two serving plates, and two serving bowls. I can't tell whether they've been touched, but everything seems to be here, including the crystal wine glasses. When I open the drawer, I count the silverware and find a complete set of eight. The partially open drawer contains my linens. It's obvious someone's been rooting through them. Still, nothing appears to be missing.

Although I'm relieved to find no one has robbed us of our fine dining wares, it makes me wonder if they've taken something from one of the other rooms. A quick walk through the rest of the main level uncovers a few things askew here and there. Not really messy, just not quite the way they usually are.

I keep a perfectly clean and tidy house. Jake and I like it that way. Of course, we sometimes make a *bit* of a mess.

Like Jake always says, *A house is meant to be lived in.*

But we both agree it's not very comfortable living in a house that's not in order. Since Jake's been gone, I've let things go. The towel hangs crooked in the downstairs powder room, and there's water splatter on the mirror. Cups sit in the sink from our morning coffee because the dishwasher hasn't been emptied. In the living room, pillows and throws are tossed about. The remote isn't in its usual spot. Magazines lie strewn haphazardly on the coffee table. Quickly, it becomes clear that we haven't been robbed. The house is just a bit more untidy than usual because I've had guests. Vicky probably moved the cups and saucers when she was making tea.

There's nothing to worry about. As I tidy the house, I'm hoping to hear back soon from some of the Christmas list people I've contacted. The rumbling in my stomach reminds me to eat. I need to keep up my strength for the baby growing inside me—the baby whose father is gone.

Chapter Twenty-Five

The stacks of lottery tickets from last night's draw grab my attention as I replace the address book in the antique secretary desk. At some point, I should check to see if there's a winner, but now's not the time. It's not like there's any chance Jake has gotten lucky. In all the years he's been buying tickets, he's never gotten ahead.

I stare at the lottery tickets inside the desk, wondering how he managed to buy all those without me knowing. My stomach reminds me again it's almost supper time, and I haven't had anything all day other than a cup of coffee, a cup of tea, and some biscuits. Once I've tidied the main level of the house, satisfied everything is back in its place and nothing is missing, I open a can of chicken noodle soup for supper, slather butter on a bagel, and grab some crackers and a yogurt. Nellie meanders in and out between my legs, reminding me to feed her, too. "It's okay, sweetie. Mommy will take care of you." The realization that Daddy may never come home hits me anew. How am I going to take care of a baby on my own?

The phone's ringing causes me to jump as I ladle soup into a bowl. Hopefully, the calls to our Christmas card recipients have paid off. Someone has seen Jake or thought of where he might be. "Hello?" I pick up, not bothering to look at the display.

"Mallory, I'm just checking everything's okay." Considering it's been less than eight hours since Craig last saw me, I'm not sure what he expected to be different.

"Yes, nothing new. I'm just having some soup. I need to eat for two now."

The silence on the other end frightens me. What's going through Craig's mind? What am I thinking, bringing that up, especially now, when my top priority should be my missing husband?

"Yes, of course. You need to think about the baby, Mallory."

It's the first time we've talked about the baby. Under normal circumstances, I should be ecstatic to talk about the fact that Jake and I are finally expecting. But these aren't normal circumstances.

"This is really hard for me," I say, trying to swallow the lump in my throat.

"I know."

There's more silence on the other end, and I'm not sure how to fill it. What should I say? "Well, I guess I'll get back to my soup. Thanks for calling."

"Mallory?"

"Yes?"

"Do you want me to come stay with you? Jake would understand. I've been thinking how weird it is that those two strange men showed up on your doorstep right after Jake's disappearance. I'm worried they'll come back when you're alone. There was something about that whole situation that doesn't seem right."

"I'll be okay," I say, even though I have good reason to suspect Nick and Adam aren't who they claim to be. "The doors are locked. I'm not planning on opening them for anyone I don't know."

"What about your head? How are you feeling?" Even through the phone line, his concern is genuine.

"I'll be fine, really."

"Keep your phone with you. I'm going to call and check on you throughout the night."

"Don't worry. I'll call 911 if I need help." I say this to assure myself more than him. "And Paul and Linda are just down the road. I'm sure they'll come if I call."

"I'm here for you. For anything. You know that, right? Call me. Promise."

I don't know how to respond. When I finally speak, I choose my words carefully. "Yes, of course, I'll call you. You're a good friend. To Jake, and me. I don't know what we'd do without you."

After supper, I double-check all the doors, and settle myself in front of the television. The phone rings again.

"I'm sorry to bother you, but I can't just sit and wait," Gloria says. "Has there been any news? Anything at all?"

"Nothing, no. I'll call you right away if I hear anything. I'm just going to lie down on the couch and rest my head."

"Oh, your head. Are you sure you're okay? I can come over." I can almost hear the lump in her throat trying to ease itself down. "Till Jake comes back."

Just as I assured Craig I would be fine, I do the same with Gloria. Except I don't mention the baby. Because she doesn't know.

Nellie and I curl up on the couch to watch the news. Exhaustion settles in, and drowsiness overwhelms me. I drift off to dreamland as the meteorologist reports a storm is expected tonight. Wherever Jake is, I hope he finds shelter.

When I dream, Jake's next to me, the two of us in front of a cozy fire, watching the flames flicker, listening to the crackling and popping of the wood. We sip Baileys and hot chocolate, snuggling into each other. The baby sleeps in the cradle to our right. To our left is a stack of lottery tickets and casino chips. A mobile plays music. A melodic tinkling, a soothing lullaby.

"How much do you think we can get for the baby?" Jake asks, his teeth flashing as he grins and rubs his hands together.

My eyes fly open and scan the room; Nellie jumps off me as I pull myself to a sitting position. At first, I think I'm still asleep because I can hear the tinkling from my dream, then I realize I'm alone in my own living room. A sitcom plays on the television, and through the window the sun sets.

Ping, ping. Tin,tin, tin tin ping. Ping, ping. Tin, tin, tinkle, ping.

It's the wind chimes Jake put on the deck off the kitchen eating area. He bought them for me as a present for our new home. As he hung them, he sang a song about giving me the sun, the moon, and the stars. I rise, walk to the sliding glass doors separating the kitchen and the deck, and peek outside. Flipping on the outdoor lights, I step onto the wooden boards. The tinkling has quieted down as the movement of sun, moon, and stars on the wind chime slows down. Standing just outside the doors, I stare, mesmerized.

What set that off?

There's hardly any breeze. It's a calm, humid evening. Still. Quiet. Like the calm before the storm. A shiver runs through my body, and in my rush to get back inside, I stub my toe into a huge sliver on the wood.

"Ouch!" It bleeds as I hobble back inside. In the bathroom off the mudroom, I disinfect my wound, take a bandage out of the drawer, stick it over the cut. The sight of the toilet triggers my bladder muscles, and I relieve myself. As I dry my hands on the towel, the sight in the mirror shocks me. The bags under my eyes have deepened over the last couple of days, and my skin has a gray, sallow look to it. It's not exactly the healthy glow of pregnancy women are supposed to get. But then, most pregnant women don't have to deal with what I'm going through.

When I walk back into the kitchen, I stop and gasp at what I see. I've left the sliding doors open.

How stupid can you be, Mal?

Closing them, I make sure they're locked. Twilight has set in. I plug in the kettle to make myself a cup of calming chamomile tea and take the entire box of chocolate-covered biscuits with me to the living room. I deserve a bit of a treat with all the stress I'm under. Not wanting to resort to medication for the anxiety that's been overwhelming since Jake's been gone, I settle on the couch with Nellie and the tea and biscuits, my phone on the coffee table in front of me. The nine o'clock movie is just beginning. It's a murder mystery. Someone's being killed.

It's fiction, I remind myself. None of it is real.

Chapter Twenty-Six

Halfway through the movie, my phone startles me. "Hello? Jake?"

"Mallory, it's Craig. Is everything okay there?"

"Oh, Craig. Yes, I'm fine. I'm watching a mystery movie. I thought it would take my mind off things, but it's not working."

"Do you want me to come back? I can be there in half an hour," he offers, and I'm tempted to say yes. Tempted, but no.

"I'm just going to bed when the movie's over. There's no need for you to be here." Part of me hopes he'll come anyway, but the last thing I need, after what happened Thursday night, is for Jake to come home to find Craig and me in bed, even if it's in separate beds, in separate rooms.

"Okay, I'll check with you in a bit, then."

A little later, the goosebumps on my arms tell me I'm not alone. Reassuring myself it's just the movie that's frightening me, I walk through the main level of the house. Yellow streaks flash through the sidelights as I return to the front door. Too afraid to open it, I peer through the living room curtains. Craig must have changed his mind. A vehicle coasts down our road. It stops in front of the house, then continues on. Not Craig.

I breathe a sigh of relief when it moves down the road, but it's short-lived. Minutes later, there's another flash through the curtain I've left open a crack. The vehicle is back, parked in front of our house. "Don't panic," I tell Nellie, who lies curled up on the couch. I grab my phone, ready to call for help if someone approaches. The vehicle sits without moving for a couple of minutes, then takes off in the direction of the Winstons' house.

I turn off the interior lights, leaving only the television on, and open the curtains wider. If someone's out there, I want to be alerted. The flash of the security lights will warn me if anyone comes near.

At eleven, when the movie's over, I tidy up the mess I've made on the coffee table and couch and head to bed, Nellie rushing past me on the stairs. No more headlights have illuminated my entrance; no security lights have so much as flickered.

When I get to our room, the door gapes open. I don't remember leaving it that way, but it's understandable that I'm extra forgetful. I have a lot on my mind. The bed is made, and the curtains were opened to allow the late afternoon sun into the room. Closing off the darkness now, I peek through the glass. No headlights flash by. Whoever was driving past has gone. Removing my clothes, I pull my white nightgown over my head, turn down the bed, and reach for the hairbrush on the dresser, forgetting my head is still bandaged. I freeze. The runner on the dresser is slightly scrunched up. My jewelry box is in its usual spot, but I can tell it's been touched, turned to the right a smidge. Someone's been in here. I open the jewelry box to see what's missing.

My diamond and pearl earrings and necklace are there. So is the zirconia bracelet. My gold studs, my birthstone necklace, my gold locket, my silver bracelet... As I go through the inventory in my head, I'm relieved to find it's all there. Is it possible I bumped the jewelry box at some point? Or has someone been in our bedroom?

There's a place for everything and everything in its place. Jake's voice zings through my head.

After straightening the top of the dresser, I head across the hall to Jake's office and flip the switch. It's just the way he left it that last morning when he was here, sorting through our bills and checking the bank accounts. The antique walnut desk is uncluttered, with the desktop computer and printer turned off, a letter tray sitting in one corner with unpaid bills on the top, paid on the bottom, waiting to be filed away in the cabinet next to the desk. The small floor safe is bolted down. All our important documents are securely tucked in behind the dual dial and key lock—Jake says you can never be too careful. Closing the office door, I stroll down the hall to the guest room.

Vicky has made the bed, but it still has a rumpled look, something I can fix tomorrow with freshly laundered sheets. Nothing else seems to be out of place. My walk through continues with a check of the main bathroom, where used towels are thrown over the bathtub, and a trace of toothpaste smudges the sink. Apart from that, the house appears to be in its normal state.

I relax, realizing my imagination is playing tricks on me. No one is in the house. It's just me and Nellie. Craig and Vicky are gone. As I glide through the hall back to my room, thinking I'll listen to my audio book to help me sleep, a clunk travels from downstairs. It sounds like something has fallen or been knocked down, not the usual creaking sounds the house makes.

Trying to convince myself there's a logical explanation, that no one is in the house because I've checked all the rooms, I tiptoe with care as I descend to the front entry. No lights. If someone *is* down there, I don't want to announce my presence. One hand firmly on the banister, feet feeling their way along the back of the steps, I take my time. *Creak.* I'd forgotten the stairs have a sound of their own. Funny how you don't take much notice of those kinds of things in the daylight during the normal course of events. *Creak.* At night, in the dark, all alone, the familiar sounds of the old house are anything but reassuring. If there is someone downstairs, there's a good chance they know I'm about to join them.

A flash of light through the frosted front door illuminates the bat on the floor. It's fallen from where Craig left it leaning in the corner next to the hall closet. I breathe a sigh of relief. Nellie probably rubbed against it and knocked it over. Opening the door, just a crack, I peer outside to see the tail lights of a vehicle slowly moving down the road toward Paul and Linda's place. Whether it's the same one as earlier, I'm not sure, but I wait for it to move on. Once the front door is locked again, I turn around and gasp, startled by what's on the top landing.

Nellie sits there, eyes aglow, peering down at me, no doubt wondering what I'm doing. Which means she wasn't downstairs knocking down the bat. That doesn't mean someone else knocked it down. It could have just fallen over.

I need to calm my nerves and get some sleep. Back in bed, Nellie and I snuggle, lights out, bedroom door slightly open, and I search for the last chapter I remember hearing on my audio book. As usual, I don't get far before I slip off into nightmare land, where I pay my dues.

Chapter Twenty-Seven

My finger on the trigger, the gun points at Jake's heart. The crack of the pistol startles me awake from a hazy dreamscape. My first thought is it's just some hunters in the bushes, going after rabbits or deer. It's posted as a 'No Hunting' area, but the signs don't deter everyone. We've called the police on a couple of occasions after hearing shots in the wooded area across from our farm. Jake's always reluctant to make those calls, but I insist. "What about when we have kids? It's not safe to have people shooting guns across the road from where they'll be playing."

The clock on the bedside table tells me it's past midnight. Why would hunters be out there this late? My mind groggy, my hand goes up to my head, and I remember the concussion. In the dark, I pull myself to a sitting position and listen. It's not the sound of a gun firing I've heard. The rumbling tells me the storm that was forecast has arrived, and it's the crack of thunder that I mistook for a gunshot. Outside my window, little is visible until a lightning bolt splits the sky, shadows of the trees and bushes forming an ominous backdrop for a lonely back road upon which is set a sole farmhouse next to fields of tall corn. The vastness of the space surrounding me is awe-inspiring during sun-up when I'm with Jake, and we're enjoying our solitude. Now, in the middle of the night, it closes in on me, the woods encroaching, the corn field swallowing up the house with me in it. Just me and Nellie. No Jake. A good setting for a horror movie.

I want to scream. I'm tempted to bawl, to wail, till someone comes. But no one will hear. As I turn to Nellie, stroking her head to settle my fear of the storm, a sudden deluge of hammers batters my home, my normally safe place. Hail pounds the roof, smacking the windows, the wind having picked up its fury from the previous calm. I wish I'd taken Craig up on his offer to stay another night. But, it would be silly to call him now and have him drive all the way here in a storm just because I'm afraid of the weather. I can handle this on my own.

What I need to do is shed some light on my situation. I'm perfectly safe in my own house, and I just need to prove that to myself. Moving off the bed, I switch on the overhead light, use the bathroom, then flick on all the upstairs lights. As a precaution, to prove to myself that everything is fine, I peer into closets, under the beds, through the windows. With the staircase lit, I descend to the entry hall. The bat leans up in the corner. Did *I* pick it up and set it there earlier?

My phone rings. Not bothering to check the caller ID, I answer. "Hello? Craig?" There's no reply on the other end. "Craig? Is that you? Hello?" No answer. Maybe it's a bad connection.

In the living room, I turn on the T.V., with the volume loud, because the sound of people talking is comforting. It's some Rom-Com. Maybe I'll sit and watch for a while, until the storm settles. My nose pressed against the frosted glass of the entry, complete darkness stares back. Confirming the door is still locked, I turn on the interior and outdoor lights, walk to the back of the house and do the same, illuminating the back yard. Through the locked kitchen patio doors, the hail has changed to rain, slapping the deck in torrents, the wind mercilessly whipping my hanging baskets, the wind chime swaying and tinkling with a vengeance.

Some warm milk would be comforting. I pour myself a large mug, add a couple spoonfuls of hot chocolate mix from the tin in the cupboard, and pop it into the microwave. The cup of steaming liquid sits on the counter as I do another walk through of the main level of the house to assure myself that I'm alone. The only disturbing thing I find is the basket of dirty clothes in the laundry room, which I've neglected to do because I've been worrying about Jake. Finding the back door secured, my shoulders relaxing, I turn to the right and scream at the sight of the wall-mounted coat rack and the mat sitting under it. Jake's rubber boots are below his black rain jacket, and for a moment, it seems he's standing right there. A chill runs through my spine, and I look closely to convince myself I'm not seeing his ghost. The boots taunt me, one upright but slightly askew, the other leaning against it.

It's not the haphazard way they're tossed there that spooks me; it's the fact that I could have sworn they weren't there earlier when I did my rounds of the house.

Chapter Twenty-Eight

O f *course*, the boots were there before. The boots must have been there all day and all day yesterday, and who knows how long before that. I just didn't notice them. It's only now, when I look directly at them, that I actually see them. Craig must have bumped into them, knocking them over, on his way out the door last night when he found me hovering in the back yard like a phantom.

Take a deep breath, Mallory.

The house is locked up tight—there's no one here except me and Nellie. And there's no one stupid enough to be out there in this weather. I grab my mug of hot cocoa off the kitchen counter, leaving on all the lights, inside and out. With both our cars parked in the driveway, the house lit up, and the television blaring, no one's going to try to break in. Settling myself on the couch, curled up under the cotton throw, I try to get involved in the movie, which is already halfway into the story.

It's the usual tale. Girl goes back to her hometown, meets or reconnects with the man of her dreams, runs into some snags in their relationship, then lives happily ever after with her soul mate. It's like our story—Jake's and mine. Except ours isn't going to have a happy ending. My eyes burn with an intensity that makes me want to pluck them out. No amount of rubbing stops the stinging tears from springing afresh.

We've certainly had more than our share of snags during our short marriage. This one, though, is beyond mending. The wind whistles through the front door, the rain pelts the living room window, and I wish more than anything that Jake was here with me. We'd be cuddled up together on the couch, his arms around me, keeping me safe in our sanctuary from the storm.

Just after one o'clock, the phone rings again. This time, the connection is clear. "Hey, everything okay?" Craig asks. "The storm's getting nasty."

I reassure him I'm fine. His constant checking up on me is fraying my nerves, though part of me wishes he were here. "It'll probably blow over quickly. Did you try to get me a little while ago?"

"No, not since I talked to you earlier. Why?"

"It's nothing. Probably someone dialed the wrong number. I'll talk to you tomorrow. Goodnight." I hang up before he has a chance to say more. Part of me blames him for what happened with Jake.

When the movie ends at 2 a.m. and the couple kiss, the storm still rages. I'm beginning to understand how improbable it is that Jake will come back. It's time for me to face reality. He's gone for good. Lying dead somewhere. With no one left to protect me, I need to fend for myself. Baseball bat in my right hand and left hand on the banister, I climb the stairs, tears clouding my vision as I face the empty bed.

Chapter Twenty-Nine

I wake in total darkness. How that's possible, I don't understand. I'd left on every light in the house before climbing back into bed with Nellie. "Nellie?" She doesn't respond. My hands grope around the bed. No Nellie, no iPad. Reaching out to grab my phone from the night table, I fumble with the lamp switch to no avail, knocking over my glass of water.

"Oh, shit!" I scramble to get out of bed, set the glass upright, and grab the Kleenex box, wiping up the spilled water in the dark as best I can.

Who turned off all the lights?

Moving toward the door, hands outstretched, one foot out at a time (I *do not* need another head injury), I find my way to the light switch. It's already in the up position. I flip it up and down anyway. Pulling the door wide open, I check the hall switch. Great—the power's been knocked out by the storm. Knowing I'm going to remain in the dark sets off an attack. Panic flows through me, from head to toe, and sweat breaks out under my crisp linen nightgown. A flashlight. A rational part of my brain still functions. Jake keeps a flashlight in the night table drawer just for times like this.

The bit of illumination allows me to breathe again. I'm fine. The power's out temporarily. They'll have it running again in no time. My iPad is partly hidden under the pillow next to me. I must have tucked it there before falling asleep. When I flip open the purple cover, the light brings a sense of relief until I remember there won't be internet if the power's out. Where is my phone? The strong need to connect to other human beings at 2:33 in the morning is overwhelming. The window rattles with the gale force of nature outside the double panes. Without the air conditioner, an oppressive atmosphere presses in, drowning me. Another crack of thunder prompts me to peer out the window. If anyone lurks out there, I can't see them. Only the dark, only the shadows. Wind and rain. I'm caught in a horror movie. Maybe a sci-fi movie. I inch away from the window.

As a child, I had an irrational fear of aliens landing in our front lawn during the middle of the night and whisking me away from the safety of my home. I shouldn't have snuck out of bed to watch those scary late-night movies while my parents slept. When Jake and I have kids, we'll...I'm not sure. My own parents were strict; there were rules for me to follow. I did my best to break them. Maybe Jake and I won't have rules. Then they won't be broken.

It doesn't seem implausible that aliens might prowl outside my house right now. Maybe they're after my unborn child.

Get it together, Mallory. That's what Jake would say if he were here.

Several booming cracks shake the house. A lightning show brightens the sky. Fireworks. Fire in the sky. It makes it all the more scary, actually seeing what's beyond my house. The dark woods, the empty road, the swaying branches of the maple trees, the expanse of lawn. The shadows.

The figure staggering past.

It vanishes beyond my line of sight, and the sky illuminates it for such a brief time that I'm sure my eyes are playing tricks on me. Russ? Would the Winstons' let their dog out for a run on a night like this? A stray cat? Some wild animal out of the woods? Or just a trick of the lightning against the black sky?

The safest place for me is my bed. Whatever's out there can't get inside. I turn off the flashlight and my iPad. The last thing I need is a dead battery. Lying on top of the covers, I concentrate on breathing. Deep breath in, then slowly exhale. Deep breath in, slowly—

Bang!

The front door slams shut. It's the familiar sound I hear when I go to bed early, and Jake comes home from work. My hands tremble as I grab the covers and pull them over my head. Any minute now, I'll hear the creak of the steps as he approaches. He'll stand in the doorway, see me cowering in bed, and—

NO! I'm not going to lie here and wait for someone to hurt me, not when I have the baby to think of. I roll out of bed, grab the bat and flashlight, and tiptoe to the open door, listening for any sign of an intruder.

If it's Jake and he's drunk, I won't say anything. Better to keep quiet and let him sober up.

The hand holding the flashlight also uses the banister as a guide. I'm not taking chances. I carry the bat in my right hand, ready to swing. No one could blame me for defending myself. It's like Brad said, "Self-defense isn't a crime, Mallory. You need to protect yourself."

I manage to get to the bottom of the stairs without bumping into anyone. The front door is closed, locked, with wind howling through gaps in the frame. Maybe I imagined hearing it slam. In the glow of the flashlight, the dining room and living room are empty, only shadows of the furniture haunting me. The furniture that was part of the home Jake and I created together, the furniture that doesn't matter now that he's gone.

In the kitchen, I twirl around, almost expecting Jake to be grabbing a beer, asking me how my day was. No one is in the den, laundry room, or bathrooms. Of course. What did I expect to find? Sweeping the flashlight toward the back door, I check the lock, find it secure, and turn back toward the stairway. What I need is sleep.

It's what I don't see that stops my heart for a few seconds.

On the floor mat is an empty space where Jake's boots sat just a couple of hours ago.

Chapter Thirty

alm down, calm down, calm down.

I'm just tired. Stressed out. I've got a head injury. I'm having trouble remembering. It's hard to know what's real and what's not. Then there's the baby on my mind. And I haven't been taking my medication properly for a long time. It's no wonder I can't think straight.

Back in my room, I lie down and try to understand what's happening to me. Is someone messing with my head? If Jake came back, he'd let me know he was home. We'd sit down and talk about it, we'd forgive and forget.

So, who would want to frighten me to death?

Does this have something to do with Jake's dad coming back into the picture? With his mom allowing him into her life again? Is Jake's dad behind this? What about Vicky and Craig, our best friends? They tried to convince me that Jake might have gone off with another woman. Why would they do that? Does Vicky want him back for herself? Have I missed something that's right under my nose? Is *Vicky* the other woman? Or is Craig trying to steal me away from Jake? We're just friends, Craig and I, nothing more. Craig knows that, doesn't he? And what about Brad? He's been out of the picture for years, ever since I first laid eyes on Jake.

I don't know what to think, who to trust. I'm tempted to get an impartial opinion from Heather or Sue. I need to hear another human voice, someone who can ground me, tell me my fears are unfounded, that there's a reasonable explanation for all of this.

A howling makes its way up the stairs, down the hall, and into my room. *Owww... owww....* As though someone is screaming in pain. Where is Nellie?

Why doesn't the power come back on?

Flashlight off to conserve the battery, I huddle underneath the covers, even though my skin is clammy. I open my iPad to check the time: 3:08. If I can get through three more hours, it will be sunrise.

I concentrate on Jake, willing him to come back. This has all been a mistake. He didn't leave me. He wouldn't let me go. We've never been apart this long. As I'm about to drift off to dreamland again, I hear the definite slamming of a door. Either I'm going completely batshit crazy this time, as Jake would say, or there actually is someone down there.

I am *not* crazy. I need to call Craig and tell him someone's in the house. Then I'll hide in the closet, with my bat ready, and wait 20 minutes while Craig races to get here.

It sounds like a good plan, but loses something in its execution. For one thing, I can't find my phone. I try to remember whether I left it on the coffee table. There's also the issue of my anxiety disorder. If I actually meet an intruder, will I be able to act and react, or will fear paralyze me? But if I sit in the closet waiting, there will be nowhere to run, even if I am able to move.

I won't be a sitting duck. I refuse to be a victim ever again. Not with the baby growing in me. I need to find out what's happening and who's responsible for the nightmare I've been living the past couple of days. This time, as I descend to the entry hall, I'm more mad than scared. I refuse to believe I'm losing my mind. There are no aliens outside trying to get in, no evil monsters lurking in the bricked-in fireplace, and my husband's ghost is not wandering through the house. Someone's trying to put a fright into me. And I won't allow it.

My phone sits on the coffee table. Thank God. Grabbing it, I click on Craig's name, and he answers after several rings. "Craig, I need..." I stop when I realize it's gone to voicemail. He must be fast asleep with the storm raging.

The realization that I'm alone to deal with whoever's in the house hits me full force as I walk toward the kitchen, flashlight lighting the way, my bat swinging.

The clatter from the kitchen startles me, and I can't suppress my scream. The loud meowing that follows my own cry tells me Nellie thinks it's feeding time. There she is, on the table. I move the flashlight around the room. The mug I used earlier for hot cocoa is knocked on its side, the spoon batted onto the floor. I'd been too tired to even make it to the sink.

That's what you get for being lazy.

"You scared me silly, girl." I scoop her up, setting my phone down, leaning the bat alongside a chair. "There's no one here but you and me. Let's go back to bed."

The flashlight sheds a glow over the countertop as I gaze through the kitchen window into the dark, out toward the shed.

Nothing to see here, folks. Jake's voice is in my head, an imitation of a police officer steering people away from an accident they really don't want to witness, but can't stop themselves from craning to get a glimpse.

But I've learned it's what you don't see that can terrify you more than what you do see. Reality is just too much sometimes. As the light lands on the knife block sitting in the corner, I stare in disbelief. There's an empty slot where the slicing knife should be.

When did it go missing? Was it there the last time I was in the kitchen? I can't recall. The realization that someone may have broken into the house and could be armed with a knife hits me like a lightning bolt, much like the ones flashing outside, and nearly knocks me to the ground.

Hold it together, Mal.

I can't let myself lose consciousness. I take action, fully armed, cat on left shoulder, flashlight in left hand, bat in the other. If I can knock the knife out of the intruder's hand, maybe I'll have a chance...

With Nellie as backup, I check the patio sliders, then the back door. All locked.

I've been foolish to think someone managed to break in, then locked the door after themselves. The missing knife can be easily explained. Vicky must have put it in the dishwasher yesterday. I just haven't noticed it was missing. I set the bat down by the back door.

When I shine the light on the mat, my mouth flies open. The boots are back, caked in mud. As I stumble backward across the mud room, I slip on something wet. My cry startles Nellie, and she jumps down, running toward the front entrance.

Water cools my feet, small puddles on the tiles, but there's something else, too. Something red. I stand frozen, staring down at the drops of blood, mixed with rain water and mud, a trail leading to the basement door.

Whirr. Whirr. Whirr. Gurgle. Gurgle. Gurgle. Noises travel through the wooden aperture.

The thought of what's down there paralyzes me. If I open the door, it'll drag me down to hell. I won't go down there. I won't.

Feeling myself start to slip away, I repeat Jake's words: *Hold it together, Mal. Hold it together. You'll be fine. You can do this.*

Shaking off my terror for the sake of our baby, I grab Jake's rain jacket, slip on his rubber boots, open the back door, and run.

Chapter Thirty-One

There's only one place I can think of to hide. The ground underneath slips and slides, Jake's boots several sizes too big. I move in slow motion, the soggy ground sucking me in. There's no time to think, no time to be afraid. I just need to get away. Once I'm hidden amongst the tall stalks, I keep going in what I hope is a straight line. As much as I want to lose myself to anyone who might be following me, I need to find my way out.

The cornfield.

If I had to choose the moment I began to doubt that Jake and I had the perfect marriage, it would be the day I stumbled into the cornfield. My discovery that day led to an unraveling of secrets my husband had been keeping from me.

Rows of dark stalks surround me, the hood on Jake's rain jacket over my head, his rubber boots sinking into fertilized ground, as I wonder how things got so out of control. I should be sitting comfortably in my home with my husband, talking about our future with our baby. My tears mix with the rain streaming down my face. I'm too frightened to move. The corn is tall and dense enough to hide me, even to provide shelter from the weather. I won't crouch down and risk falling over, although I'm too tired to stand. It's going to be a long wait until daybreak.

I find myself thinking it could be worse. I could be standing here in the middle of a full-blown blizzard. Jake and I have weathered some nasty storms out here over the last three years. So has our marriage.

* * *

Three years ago

It wasn't long after I discovered Jake was hiding his lottery tickets from me that I discovered what else he was hiding. The flower beds take a lot of tending during the spring and summer, which is good because it's something to keep me busy while Jake's at work and I'm off school. That particular afternoon, I was working in the side yard next to the cornfield when a stray cat caught my eye. I'm a softie for homeless creatures, especially cats, so I brought out a bowl of milk. As hungry as the kitty was, he was too frightened to come near me, and took off into the cornfield. Holding the bowl of milk and softly calling, I followed him.

I didn't even know what I'd found when I came across it, but I knew it wasn't corn. Leaving the bowl of milk on the edge of the cornfield, I sat down at the kitchen table with my iPad and did some research. It prompted me to call the police, and I got as far as dialing, then hung up, remembering Jake doesn't like me to make decisions without him.

That evening, running up to his car when he got home, the first thing I said was, "Honey, you won't believe what I found today!"

"What, honey? What did you find? You seem awfully excited about it, whatever it is." Placing his arm around me, Jake walked me to the front porch.

"There's something in the cornfield—I think it's marijuana. I was going to call the police, but I thought I'd better wait for you." By the glow of the security lights, his reaction appeared neutral, but it was the tensing of his muscles that told me he already knew.

Jake escorted me into the house, telling me to shush in case someone might be listening. Who'd be out there in the middle of the night, I didn't know, but I did as I was told.

"Do you want to call them?" I asked once we were behind closed doors.

He stared, open-mouthed, before speaking. "No, no police. I'm sorry, hon,

I should have told you."

"Told me what?" Surely, my husband wasn't growing cannabis next to our home, in the field he rented to corn farmers, whom I'd never personally met.

"The guys who rent the land—they grow a bit of weed for their own use amongst the corn. It's no big deal."

"No big deal? It's illegal, isn't it? Are they licensed? " I couldn't believe we were having this conversation. My husband was involved in drugs.

"There's more money to be made renting out a section of land for a bit of weed than there is for a whole field of corn," he said, justifying his decision to allow drugs to be grown on our property. "I don't want you worrying your pretty little head about it. It's just business. Stay out of it."

Who was this man I had married? And what had he done with my husband? "There's a lot more than just a bit. It's against the law," I repeated, in case he didn't quite understand that fact.

"Everybody does it, Mal. It's just the way it is out here on the farm. I don't want to talk about it anymore. These guys rent the field, they pay good money, we don't know anything about it. Got it?"

I knew better than to continue the discussion. From then on, I steered clear of the cornfield.

* * *

Until now. Now the cornfield is my sanctuary, as thunder rolls and booms around me.

I should have grabbed the car keys before running out of the house. And my phone. It's not realistic to stand in this field for hours waiting for someone to save me. Maybe I should make a run for it, over to Paul and Linda's place, and try to wake them. Unsure of how much time has passed, I turn and begin to walk in the direction I came from. At least, I'm hoping that's the direction I'm going.

Swoosh, swoosh, swish. Muck underneath my boots, the corn stalks smack me back in the face as I keep shoving them aside, wind and rain pelting me in spite of the shelter offered by the rows of crops. With each step, I sink and slip, slip and slide. Too much rain won't be good for the weed, I find myself thinking. Jake won't be happy.

I laugh out loud at the absurdity of it all.

I'm cowering in a cornfield with the drugs my husband is hiding while someone who shouldn't be here invades my home. Rainwater drips into my boots, slowing me down and making me more uncomfortable. An image of worms and creepy crawlies insinuates itself into my brain, and I imagine them covering my body. What about snakes? I need to get out. The scream that escapes me is involuntary, but once it's out, there's no stopping me.

Fear, shock, rage, sorrow—I can't even put a name to it. The night swallows me whole, the storm battering me, the corn closing in. There's no more Mallory. Because there's no Jake.

Just as I'm about to give in and sink to the ground, to let it consume me, a light flickers at the end of the cornfield. It moves in a sweeping motion, back and forth. Aliens? They're calling my name.

Earth to Mallory, Jake would say.

Shoving the stalks aside, I work my way toward the light.

"Mallory! Mallory! Where are you?"

Breaking out into the open grass, I stand still, not sure I can trust the light. When it lands on me, I'm caught like a deer in the headlights. I can't run.

"Mallory! What are you doing out here? I've been going crazy thinking something happened to you."

He runs to me, pulls me into his arms, cradling my head against his shoulder. I continue sobbing as he leads me to the back door, into the mudroom where I remove my wet boots and leave them on the mat. He helps me out of the rain jacket and hangs it on the hook.

"My God, you're sopping wet," Craig says. "Let's get you into some dry clothes."

"There's someone in the basement."

"What? Who's in the basement?"

"Water. Blood."

"Where? Where's the blood, Mallory?"

132

I point to the floor and inch toward the basement door, the flashlight guiding my way. The floor is perfectly dry and clean. "I don't…I don't understand. There were puddles of water, drops of blood, here on the floor. Noises coming from the basement. And Jake's boots were muddy."

"You were wearing Jake's boots, Mallory. They're muddy because you were out in the cornfield. There's no water here. No blood. No noise."

"Someone was in the house. I heard noises. I saw the boots, the mud. I saw the water, and blood. Then I ran outside."

Craig assures me I'm safe now and helps me upstairs to my room. "It's okay, I'm here now. Why don't you change and get back into bed?"

"What about you? You're wet through." I grab a couple of towels from the bathroom. "Here you go. I'll get you some of Jake's clothes, and you can put yours in the dryer when the power comes on. You can change in the bathroom." Craig hesitates, saying he'll dry eventually, but I insist, trying to focus on him and not my fear. "You can't sleep in those wet clothes."

I grab a pair of boxers, sweatpants, and a t-shirt from our closet and send him to the ensuite while I change in the bedroom. "You have no idea how relieved I am that you showed up when you did. I didn't have my phone or my car keys. I was too afraid to go back into the house, worried I might run into whoever broke in."

"If there was someone here, they're gone," he says through the partly open door. "I searched the whole house looking for you. When I got your voice message, I came as quickly as I could. You didn't answer the door, so I went to the back. It was wide open."

"I ran out when I heard the noise coming from the basement." I'm dryer and more comfortable now in one of Jake's t-shirts and my pajama bottoms instead of the flimsy nightie.

"There's nothing in the basement, Mallory. I checked it out. Just the sump pump running."

"The sump pump? But the power's out."

"There's a battery backup."

"And there's no blood?'

"No blood."

The water could have dried up, but the blood? "No one was here when you got here?"

"No. And it terrified me. I didn't know where you were. The cars were still in the driveway, but there was no sign of you. Just the open back door. Thank God I found you. What were you doing out in the cornfield?" Craig wraps me in his arms again.

"Hiding. I was scared." I allow myself to sink into him.

"There's nothing to be scared of. I've got you." It's comforting to be enveloped by him, but also uncomfortable. What I need is Jake. "I'm going to stay with you. Go get some sleep. Don't worry about getting up until at least noon."

He leaves me alone in my dark room and heads downstairs. Something crawls along my leg, making me holler. I shine my flashlight down while swatting away whatever's climbing on me. It's Nellie's tail.

"It's okay," I yell as Craig's footsteps pound up the stairs. "It's just Nellie."

His sigh of relief reaches my ears. "Good night, Mallory. Rest your head. Things will look better tomorrow."

Chapter Thirty-Two

Howling wakes me. I stagger out of bed to empty my bladder as wind wails outside the bathroom window. Except, it's not wind. The storm seems to have settled down. No more thunder cracks, no rain hitting the roof, no flashes of light. Just the howling.

An owl? No. A dog? Maybe. Or a pack of coyotes. I shudder, thinking I won't be running around alone outside in the middle of the night again anytime soon. No more slugging through the mud in the cornfield. My purse is in the closet, with my wallet and keys inside. If I need to run again, I'll be prepared next time. Putting it in bed next to me, I slip under the covers, my phone in one hand. The display is black when I swipe to check my messages. The battery has died.

I tackle the stairs one at a time, my flashlight sweeping the darkness ahead, to retrieve my charger from the kitchen so I'll have it when the power comes back on. And I freeze. Jake's lying on the couch, his back to me, snoring. "Jake! Jake!"

"What? Jake's back? Where is he?" Craig jolts off the couch.

My disappointment at seeing Craig must show as he shines his flashlight on me. "Oh, I thought you were Jake. I expected you to be in the den."

How stupid can you be, Mal?

"I'm sorry, Mallory. The couch seemed like a good spot to keep an eye out. I know you're hoping he'll just reappear, and everything will be back to normal. But I don't think that's going to happen."

"Why not?"

"You know why."

We're both quiet for the longest time as I sit down next to him. When I speak, I ask the question I already know the answer to. "This can't be happening, can it?"

He lays his head back against the top of the couch cushion and sighs. "Mallory. You're going to have to face it sooner or later. What we did to Jake—it's unforgivable."

"I know," I whisper. I need to stop burying my head in the sand.

* * *

The display beside my bed flashes. Right away, I sense something is different. The space on the other side of the bed, where I usually sleep, is empty. I'm not there because I'm in Jake's spot. As my mind clears, I realize the power has come back on sometime in the last couple of hours. Light filters through the curtains, a welcome respite from the dark that's enveloped me. I check my iPad. It's 10:49 a.m.

Nellie isn't on the bed. Maybe she's downstairs with Craig. I'm halfway down the steps when I notice something missing. Not something. Someone. As I peer over the banister, the living room couch is empty.

The front door, with the daylight shining through, is locked. The dining room is empty. I walk to the back of the house. "Craig? Where are you? Craig?"

There's no answer. No smell of morning coffee. He's not in the powder room or the bathroom off the mudroom. Not in the den. Jake's boots aren't on the mat by the back door. No water or blood on the floor. The basement is silent. Where could he possibly be? In the laundry room, checking to see if his clothes are dry? When I push on the half-open door to the laundry, Nellie comes out, meows a good morning, and indicates she'd like some food in her dish. Craig's not in there. Nor are his clothes in the dryer.

Panic courses through me as I run to the front of the house. How much of what happened last night did I imagine? When I swing open the door and look out at the driveway, I know it was a dream. It had all seemed so real. But Craig's not in the house, and his car isn't in the driveway.

136

Chapter Thirty-Three

T he ringing of the phone steals my attention. It'll be Craig, telling me he needed to get back home and didn't want to disturb my sleep.

"Hello?"

"Mrs. Shelton?" An unfamiliar voice.

"Yes? If you're trying to sell something, I don't have time for it." I'm about to hang up when I hear Jake's name. "What about Jake?"

"This is Detective Swarovski. I'm in charge of your husband's case." It finally registers. He has some news. But I don't want to hear it.

"Yes, yes, of course. Have you found something?" The hand holding my phone shakes, and I'm losing my grip.

"Could you come to the Grandview Hospital? A man was brought in early this morning, looks like he may have been the victim of a mugging. He's in a coma, no ID on him. We're not certain it's him, but he has a resemblance to your husband."

Oh my God! He's alive! Thank goodness. "It's Jake? He's okay?"

"You'll have to come identify him yourself. If it's him, the doctors will fill you in on his condition." He says he'll meet me there within the hour.

There's a good possibility it isn't Jake. I know that. No point in getting myself riled up until I find out it's him and know he's going to wake up, not until I see if he remembers what happened. I won't get my hopes up just yet. Still, my heart pounds, my pulse races, taking over my body. Could it be that Vicky got it wrong? Jake never meant to leave me? He was mugged in the parking lot at work? Maybe some guys he owes money to? Like Craig suggested? That could explain everything.

Making sure I have my phone, I head upstairs to dress as quickly as possible. The slamming of the front door startles me, and I stop midway through pulling on my jeans, listening for the sound of footsteps. Someone's in the house, heading down the hall to the kitchen. I do up the button on my jeans and grab my purse, ready to make a run for it, but it's too late. *Creak.* The step announces someone's presence on the stairs. As I begin to call 911 for emergency police assistance, my bedroom door swings fully open.

"You're awake." Craig stands in the doorway, assessing me. "I'm glad to see you're up and dressed. How'd you sleep?"

"I… Where were you? I was looking for you, but your car was gone." I'm about to ask if he was here last night when he explains.

"Sorry, I left a note on the coffee table. I went out to get us some breakfast. You were sleeping so soundly, I thought I'd leave you to rest a while longer."

"The door was locked. How'd you get back in?" I'm trying to sound calm, but part of me wonders if Craig is lying to me. It wouldn't be the first time I've been lied to by a man I trusted.

"The spare key in the holder. I wasn't about to leave the door unlocked after your scare last night. Let's eat while it's still warm. You'll feel better once you have some coffee in you." Craig's hand rests on my back as he leads me to the stairs.

The aroma of coffee fills my nostrils as I grab a cup from the entrance table, my hands cradling it. Craig unwraps a breakfast sandwich, tosses a piece of ham to Nellie, who sits by his feet, staring up expectantly.

My eyes drift to the wall-mounted key holder and the empty spot that usually holds the spare house key. What I can't remember is how long the extra key has been missing. Hard as I try to focus, I don't recall whether the key was there last night.

"I have to get to the hospital," I say, accepting the proffered sandwich. "The police called while you were gone. Someone matching Jake's description was brought in. He's in a coma."

Craig's mouth hangs open as he stares at me. "So they've found him?" He considers this for a moment, then adds, "That's good. He's going to be okay, isn't he? Then the two of you can work things out."

"I hope so." Part of me wants to put this off, or I would have already been out the door. "Do you want to come?"

"Of course, I'll come. Whatever happens between you and Jake, I'm a part of it."

I nod my head, regretting having brought Craig into this. One small mistake and everything changes. One big mistake, and nothing can ever be the same again.

Taking breakfast with us, we make the trip in silence, not knowing what we'll find at the hospital. The drive to the city takes forever, countryside giving way to the main highway, then to civilization. If Jake's not conscious, there's no point in wondering what he'll say. Maybe it's not even him. As we approach the turnoff to the hospital, following the blue H sign, Craig finally speaks.

"We should get your head injury checked out while we're here." He says it so casually, it's as though everything is normal. Mallory going to the hospital getting checked out. Not Mallory going to the hospital to see if the comatose man is her missing husband. "I'm worried about you."

"I'm fine," I say. But I agree my head needs to be examined.

At the front desk, I'm tempted to shove aside people in line waiting to talk to the receptionist. Now that this is actually happening, I'm anxious to see him, to know if it really is Jake. The elevator takes forever to open; once we get in, it seems like we're stopping at every single floor. "Come on, hurry up," I whisper, and Craig grabs hold of my hand in an attempt to calm my nerves.

There are three people in Room 634. One is a doctor or nurse, I'm not sure which. She's talking to a man in a suit, who looks to be in his forties. As I enter, he asks, "Mrs. Shelton?"

"Yes. I'm Mallory Shelton." My eyes shift to the third person, lying in the bed hooked up to tubes and machines. Bandages cover his head and parts of his face. It's obvious he's been beaten.

"Oh my God, Jake…." I approach the bed, leaving Craig in the doorway.

When I grab hold of his left hand, I notice he's not wearing his wedding ring. It takes a great deal of courage for me to look into the face of the man lying there, the man that I love, the man that I've hurt. My eyes scan his swollen face, hoping he'll open his blue-green eyes. A flood of relief and disappointment rushes through me as I realize I don't recognize this man. Turning to Craig, I say, "It's not Jake."

Craig joins me at the bedside of the beaten man and addresses the detective, confirming what I've said.

As we leave the hospital, Craig says, "It's just as well it wasn't him."

I know exactly what he means. The thought that the two of us could have been responsible for Jake lying there, beaten and comatose, is too much to handle.

"Your head. We forgot to have you checked out," Craig remembers as we pull out of the parking lot. "We should go back."

"No, I'm okay. It's just a little bump. I'm perfectly fine. I want to go home."

Again, we drive in silence. When we pull up in front of the house, Craig tells me he'll call in sick if I want him to stay. His shift is about to start in a couple of hours, and I don't want him to stop living his life because of me. "I'll be fine, don't worry."

"Okay. Call if you need anything." He hands over the spare house key and waits until I'm safely in the house.

There's an explanation for everything. Craig's clothes aren't in the dryer because he changed out of Jake's clothes, which are now in the laundry hamper. Jake's boots are just outside the back door, where Craig put them in the sun to dry up the mud. After I watch him drive off, Nellie by my feet, I find the note he left, under the couch, where it must have been swiped from the table by Nellie's tail. There's a reasonable explanation for everything. Just as I know there must be a logical explanation for why Jake hasn't come home. I just have to think of it.

Chapter Thirty-Four

J ake's the one who always has a logical explanation for everything, not me. He's had his share of making up reasons for things being the way they are. Me, I'm good at making things up, too; they're just not quite as logical.

* * *

Two years ago

The day he forgot to lock the safe, and I discovered another one of the secrets he was keeping from me, he had a good story ready. I was pulling weeds in the front flower beds one morning while Jake slept in. When I went upstairs to shower and change, he wasn't in bed. At first, I assumed he was in the bathroom, but he wasn't in the ensuite or in the main bath. As I walked by, I noticed the door to his office wasn't latched, and the safe stood partly open. Curiosity got the better of me. Kneeling, I flipped through the contents. Like Jake had told me, he stored important documents there. Our birth and marriage certificates, passports, investment statements, sealed wills, insurance papers... and something that shocked me. The folder holding our life insurance policy showed that Jake had insured me for a million dollars.

I sat staring at it till Jake entered the room carrying a cup of coffee. "What are you doing, Mal?"

"What am I doing? What are you doing? I think you're the one who has some explaining to do."

"I was just going through some of our bills, organizing statements," he said. I could tell from the way his eyes flicked toward the safe that he was wondering what exactly I'd found. "Why don't you take a nap? Get some rest. You look exhausted."

"Why do you have a million-dollar life insurance policy on me? Are you… are you… planning to kill me?" I stammered, thinking if this was a dream, I needed to wake up before I got myself murdered.

"What? No. No, are you crazy? Mallory, I would never do anything to hurt you. Never. How could you think that?" He set his cup on the desk and knelt next to me, cupping my face and gazing at me with those eyes, pleading for me to believe him. "I have a life insurance policy on both of us."

"A million dollars?"

"Yes. Look." He took out the policy on himself, naming me as the beneficiary. "I know it seems like a lot. But with the mortgage on this place… if anything were to happen to one of us, I want to be sure the other can stay here without worrying about money. The million dollars would take care of the house, the cars, the credit cards, the funeral—"

"The funeral? Oh my God! Are you dying?"

"Am I…. No! Why would you ask that, Mal?"

"You said it would take care of the funeral."

"Yes, but nothing's going to happen to either of us for a long time, trust me." He put his arms around me and told me it was just in case. "That's what insurance is for. Just in case something were to happen, *which it's not*, then I would want you to be able to stay here and not worry about the bills. I took the insurance policy out on myself first, but then I thought you'd probably want to be sure I was okay financially if something happened…." He released me from his grip and forced me to look into his eyes again. "I would never hurt you, you can't possibly think that."

"It's…it's just that it's a lot of money. Why so much?"

"It's perfectly normal for couples to have insurance on each other, Mallory." He ran a hand through his thick head of wavy dark brown hair. "The rates are low at our age, so it's not that big an expense. And I know we're young, not even 30 yet, but things happen." Seeing my eyes widen, he added, "But nothing's *going* to happen. To either of us."

"Then why do we need million-dollar life insurance policies?"

"Because…. Jesus, Mal, you know how much it costs to keep this place running. One of us can't pay the bills. Two of us barely manage, and that's with Mom's help. Do the math. With one paycheck gone and the expenses still coming in, the farm would have to go."

Something about what he said didn't ring true. I had inherited my parents' estate. It wasn't likely I would need the life insurance money to support myself. I reminded him of that. "And besides, I'm sure Gloria wouldn't kick me out if I couldn't pay the mortgage."

"No, no, of course she wouldn't. But I just want to be sure you'll be provided for. It's my job, as your husband, to take care of you."

So, it was all about his male ego. "But you don't need to have a policy on me. You'll inherit my parents' money when I'm gone. There's no point in wasting the premium payments when we're already having trouble paying the bills."

He was quiet for a while, considering what I'd said. "I didn't know," he said quietly.

"Know what?"

"That you were planning on leaving me your parents' money."

"Of course. Who else would I leave it to? You're my husband." I could have left it to my aunt and uncle and cousins, I suppose.

"Then why, for God's sake, don't you let me have some of that money now, when we could use it?" He raised his voice, towering above me. "What the hell, Mal? You've got enough to get us debt free."

We had talked about this before we got married. Jake knew I had money. Before the wedding, he was the one who insisted I keep it separate, in my own name. "I don't want anyone thinking I married you for the money. I can support my own wife."

After we got married, he asked for help with the bills, and I had no problem giving him money. Until I realized what he was doing with it. Then I put a stop to it.

"You know why," I had said then. And that seemed to be the end of his asking for my help financially.

Holding the insurance policy in my hands, I wondered if he had other ideas of how to get his hands on my money besides begging for it. Did my husband want me dead? Was I worth more to him that way?

"You know why," I said again. "I don't want you to squander it all. I want to make sure there's something left for the kids." Shoving the insurance folder back into the safe, I noticed something along the back wall, stopping it from going all the way in. My hand reached inside and pulled out a thick wad of bills.

"What…." I held the cash up to my husband, "is this?"

He swallowed hard, raised his hand to his temple, and shook his head. "Shit, Mallory. You have no fucking idea."

Chapter Thirty-Five

I'm about to hang the spare house key into the wooden holder when I see red. On the dining room table is a vase with three red roses. There is no way it was there when Craig and I left for the hospital. We stood in the entrance hall when he brought breakfast. Craig would have mentioned the roses. Someone was in the house while we were gone.

Armed with the baseball bat from the mudroom, I return to the dining room, open my laptop, and check our email to see if there's a reply to my question about who is sending the Tick Tock message. What I read makes me physically ill. My recently eaten breakfast splatters over the floor in the entry in my rush to the powder room. **They all ran after the farmer's wife. They cut off her ring finger with a carving knife.** The cut red roses, the missing slicer knife, the blood on the floor. If this is someone's idea of a joke, it's sick. This isn't a children's nursery rhyme. Someone seriously wants to hurt me.

In the bathroom, I wash my face and rinse out my mouth. The face staring at me in the mirror is a ghost. The white face, dull eyes, the bandage I haven't removed—I don't recognize the person I see. There is no Mallory without Jake. I'm fading away. The thought of taking the pills in our ensuite bathroom is tempting, just one to help me get through this. But I won't. I'm stronger than that.

When the doorbell rings, my first thought is it must be Vicky, dropping by to check if I'm okay. Without thinking, I open the door to usher her in.

Nick and Adam block out the sun as they stand in my doorway. "We're heading out of town and thought we'd stop in to see if Jake's home," Nick

145

says.

"No, he's not here." I shove the door, but Adam sticks his foot in, preventing it from closing. "He's not coming back."

"The car's here," Nick nods toward the driveway. "I'm sure he'll want to see his old chums. Tell him we're here." He smiles and adds, "Please."

I shake my head. "He's not here."

Adam strains to see past me into the house. "Let him know we don't plan to be in the area again for a while. We'd hate to miss him."

"No, you don't understand. He's not here. Jake's missing. He hasn't been home since Friday afternoon. I have no idea where he is. The police are looking for him."

"Police? Have the police been here?" Nick's composure falters.

"Yes. They could be back anytime." I want to make sure these guys know Jake isn't here, but I also want them to know I'm not alone. "And my friends will be back any minute now."

Adam backs away from the door, allowing me to close it and turn the lock. Through the curtains, their imposing figures stand on my lawn, turning 360 degrees, as though they expect Jake to materialize. I dial Craig, but end the call before it goes through. He's at work. So's Vicky, now that I think about it. I don't know who else to ring. Except... I click another contact.

"Gloria? I'm okay. Nothing about Jake yet. But there *are* a couple of guys who have been hanging around the house, asking about him, and I'm sure they're up to no good. Probably gambling buddies of his or someone he owes money. I was wondering if Steve could come by and help me get rid of them."

Steve already knows Jake's business because I've confided in him. And Steve holds the solution to Jake's money problems in the form of half a million dollars. Only Jake doesn't know that. Of course, if Jake ends up being gone for good, his problems become mine. So does his inheritance. Jake and Mallory—we're a team.

Calling the police again isn't an option. Having them snoop around, asking questions. I'm afraid of what they might find. The drugs and ill-gotten money. And who knows what else they might dig up? This house holds secrets that need to remain buried. They say the truth will set you free. If you tell the truth, you don't have to remember anything. But, truth is subjective. And...

It's not as though I've been lying to everyone, including myself, the whole time Jake's been gone.

Chapter Thirty-Six

Still alive. Hanging in. Things are getting less muddled. I'm not sure how much time has passed since I woke up here. Minutes? Hours? The light has become brighter, illuminating my grave. Stone walls enshroud me. Am I in prison? A dungeon? Mud on the ground underneath me, a soft covering of wet, rotting leaves. Above, the circle of light. Something hovering beyond, blocking some of the light. Something hanging down. And it hits me. I know where I am.

At the bottom of a well.

How the hell did I get here? Think. Am I in the old well on our farm property? It's closed up. Why would I jump in? I wouldn't. I must have fallen. Lifted the cover for some reason and toppled in. Mallory must be getting help. She'll be back soon.

In the meantime, I need to help myself. Get up off the ground. Sit up.

I'm lying on my side, curled up, like an unborn baby struggling to get out of the womb. I try ungluing myself from the muck that has me stuck like a pig on a spit. Pulling my knees to my chest, then out again, I grapple to find a way to hoist myself up. It's my upper body strength that does the job, allowing me to push myself to a sitting position. I sit and rest, everything spinning.

With my head in my hands and eyes closed, I try to settle the dizziness and focus on what to do. Phone. Call for help. That's it. My hands to my pockets, front then back, I feel for it and find nothing. No wallet, no keys, no phone. There's probably no reception down here anyway. I open my eyes and inspect my prison. It's about six feet in diameter, and actually not that far down, now that I take a good look at the opening. Maybe twelve feet? It doesn't matter. There's no way I can get to the top.

I cup my hands around my mouth and holler for help, but it comes out as a squeak. My throat's dry, but drinking this stale, muddy water mixed with leaves doesn't seem like an appealing option. I need to get up. Stretching my legs in front of me, I move my feet back and forth. All good. The ground beneath me is slick, no traction, and I slowly slide my bottom backward toward the stone wall. I'm going to have to climb out. Whether there's anything to grip onto, I don't know, but the walls seem like the only way. I sure as hell can't jump out.

My head hits something quicker than I expected, and I'm surprised by the feel of it. Not stone? Eyes closed, I focus my strength on what I need to do. Turn around, brace myself against the wall, grip hold of the blocks, pull myself up. Find a foothold, climb to the top. Piece of cake.

Inching myself around to face the rock wall behind me, my knees drawn up to my chest, I come face to face with a suspended wooden bucket. Still here, after all these years, although the well itself has been partly filled in. Hallelujah! There's some rainwater in it. I scoop a handful to my mouth; the cool liquid is a welcome relief to my dry lips and throat. My eyes follow the rope attached to the forgotten bucket. Reaching up and grabbing hold of the nylon rope, I give it a good tug, test it with my weight, one hand over the other, and pull my body to a standing position.

The rush of empowerment when I find I can stand on my own two feet drives me up the wall. Bracing one foot against the stone, I begin the climb, hand over hand, using my leg muscles to push against the wall for traction. I'm at the end of my rope, but I'm lucky to have a rope. Looks like I'm on a streak of good luck. When I get out of here, the first thing I'm going to do is buy a lottery ticket or two.

The first time I slip takes me down a couple of notches. The mud on my soles against the damp stone leaves a streak as my foot slides, and I hold on for dear life, my hands feeling the rope tear into them. But all the hours I spent digging up the ground to make new flower beds for Mallory and hauling topsoil have strengthened my muscles, and my will to survive for her is even stronger. Each movement of hand and foot brings me closer to the light. Closer to Mallory.

And then I fall.

Chapter Thirty-Seven

Three years ago

The first time Jake raised his hand to me would be the last. I made that promise to myself and that threat to him. I wasn't going to be one of those women whose husband hits her. I refused to be anyone's victim. The day Jake learned I went out for coffee with Brad was that first time.

It wasn't long after we were married.

"Did you have fun?" Jake asked when I came home on an August Saturday afternoon not long after our wedding, carrying a large shopping bag brimming with my purchases. "Looks like you bought the store out."

"I got all this for under a hundred dollars. There was a big end-of-season clearance sale at Clara's. You know I'm going to need some fresh outfits for the start of the school year," I said, justifying my expenditure.

I didn't dare point out that I earned enough to splurge a little now and then.

"That's good. Let's see what you got for your money."

I modeled the two new dress pants, the skirt, three tops, and the cardigan I purchased in the city that afternoon, and was pleased Jake liked them all. "Nice. Very appropriate, teacher," he drawled. "Now, take it all off."

Laying back on the bed, he watched as I did a striptease for him. Before I could get my new outfits on hangers, he pulled me down onto the bed with him.

It was my fault, really. If I had kept my mouth shut after we made love, he wouldn't have felt the need to slap me. As I got up and dressed, Jake, a big smile on his face, rolled over on his side, his elbow supporting him. "I'm going to make some coffee. Want one?"

"No, I'm okay. I had a couple of cups in town with Brad."

The curve of his mouth flattened as he stared at me. "You did what?"

"I ran into Brad at the mall. He suggested we get a coffee and a muffin at the food court."

"You're seeing Brad?" He sat up, pulling on his pants. "How long has this been going on?"

I turned away and headed for the open bedroom door. "Nothing's been going on, silly. We met in the mall and had coffee."

The door slammed shut in front of me before I got there, Jake's hand flat against it. I turned around, and his body pressed up tight against me.

"What...?" I didn't get to finish. He grabbed me, his hands on my upper arms. "You're hurting me, Jake."

He loosened his grip, but held me prisoner. "We're married now, Mal. You can't go out with other men."

"It was coffee with a friend from work. That's all. You know we broke up before the two of us started going out. It's not like we ever slept together or anything. Not like you and your exes."

"That was different. I planned on marrying them. It's not my fault my relationships didn't work out. But that's over now." His grip tightened again. "And you need to get over your jealousy."

"*My* jealousy? You're the one who goes ballistic every time another man looks at me."

"Maybe if you didn't dress like a slut...."

He held my arms pinned against the door, so I used my knee and punched him in the groin. Not hard enough. His right hand sprang up, and he was about to backhand me when he stopped midair.

"I'm sorry," he whimpered, backing away and falling to his knees, doubled over. "I'm so sorry, Mallory."

I grabbed my purse from the closet and sidestepped him on my way out, but I didn't get far. His arm entwined my ankle.

"Where are you going?" His face tilted to me as my hand reached for the door.

"I told you I would never stay with a man who hit me. How your mother put up with it, I don't know. But I won't. I'm leaving."

His eyes didn't have their usual spark. "Please, Mallory, don't. I wouldn't, you have to know that. I don't want to be my dad. I won't be him. Please don't leave me. I can't live without you."

And not for the first, nor the last time, I witnessed my strong husband cry. It was pitiful. What could I do?

I knelt next to him and put my arms around him. "You're not your dad, Jake. But sometimes you say and do things…"

I didn't know how to explain that he was hurtful in a different way, not in the physical way his dad had been. "You make me feel like I'm not capable of doing things on my own. Like I'm helpless. And sometimes, I feel like a prisoner. I should be able to go out for a coffee with a friend without you thinking I'm cheating on you."

I flinched and pulled away, thinking he was going to try to hit me again, but his arms encircled me, and he held me close. "I know. I just love you so much. It makes me crazy sometimes."

We sat on the floor together, with our arms around each other for a long time, then he helped me up, and we went back to bed to make up.

It was our first fight. It's always our *first* fight. Because we forgive and forget. Or at least, I do.

Chapter Thirty-Eight

They're sitting in their car now, behind Jake's Honda. Waiting patiently. I imagine they're discussing what to do next. Definitely not friends of Jake's. Arming myself with the bat, I sneak out the back and into the cornfield. It seems like the lesser of the two evils. If Nick and Adam are here to collect their weed, I don't have a problem with that. If, on the other hand, they're here for something else, they won't find it. And they won't be happy when I can't help them.

Steve's on his way. But, for extra insurance, just in case, as Jake would say, I give Brad a call. Like me, he's off work for the summer. When he answers, I fill him in on the situation and explain what I need.

Brad arrives before Steve, as he lives closer. His car drives up while I work my way to the edge of the cornfield. He has Nick and Adam blocked in. They exit their vehicle, and I jog across the lawn, shouting, "I told you the police would be back."

Brad flashes his police badge with an air of authority and introduces himself to the two men. "Detective Streicher. I'm investigating Jake Shelton's disappearance. I understand you're looking for him."

The fake badge he uses was purchased from the dollar store for a play his Grade 6 students performed for the spring assembly. It does the trick. When Brad suggests they accompany him to the station, Nick and Adam insist they know nothing about Jake's disappearance. They're just old school buddies who dropped by for a visit.

"We're following all leads," Brad says, playing his part. "When did you last see Jake?"

"Years ago," Nick answers, palms outstretched. "We have no idea where he is."

Brad records their license plate number in a little notebook and asks for their names. "Last names?" he asks when they give only their first. Brad doesn't ask for their IDs, and I'm relieved they don't ask for his. The College of Teachers ID card won't cut it.

When Steve pulls up next to Brad's vehicle, he and Gloria join Brad and me, encircling Nick and Adam.

"Where's my son? What have you done with him?" Steve raises his fists, ready to strike at the two men he believes have something to do with Jake's disappearance.

As I said, there are two things I'm hoping to accomplish. One is to let these guys know Jake truly is missing, and the other is to let them know I'm not alone. I have people looking out for me. If they *are* a threat to me, maybe they'll back off knowing that. If they really are Jake's old friends, I doubt they'll be paying us a visit ever again. "I think it's quite a coincidence that you show up at my door twice looking for my husband when he's gone missing."

"Have these guys been threatening you? We can bring them in for questioning, if that's the case," Brad says.

"That won't be necessary." Nick takes a step back. "Like we said, we just thought we'd look up an old friend. We should get home to our families. We've already overextended our weekend trip by a day."

"Hope you find Jake soon," Adam says. "If you don't mind moving your vehicle, we'll be on our way."

Steve and Brad defer to me, and I nod. "Maybe think about calling first next time you visit an old friend," I suggest.

Brad gets in his vehicle to move it as Steve glowers at the two men. Once Nick and Adam are gone, Steve asks Brad what he's doing to find his son. I intervene and explain the ruse. "Brad's a friend of mine from school. I called him because I knew he could play the role of a cop." To Brad, I say, "You were very convincing, by the way."

"No problem. If you need help again, you know who to call." Before leaving, Brad touches my shoulder, saying he hopes Jake turns up soon.

Gloria puts her arm around me. "Come stay with us. You shouldn't be alone."

I don't argue this time. "You're right. I'll go pack a few things. Why don't you come in and have a coffee while you're waiting?"

With the threatening emails and these two strangers showing up again, I need to think about the baby first. A threat to me is a threat to my baby. I'm willing to do whatever it takes to protect my unborn child.

Chapter Thirty-Nine

T he fall is only a couple of feet, but it jolts me as I hit the ground still grasping the rope, wondering whether it wasn't tethered to the windlass. If not, I'm shit out of luck. Giving it another test pull, I keep yanking till there's no slack, till it feels taut. One foot against the wall, hands tight on the rope, I give it another try, picturing Mallory waiting at the top.

My eyes focus on the light, my goal. As I climb, the metal cylinder across the top of the well, the rope attached, comes closer. Just a little farther. I grab hold of the metal, swing one arm over it, breathing heavily, and rest for a moment, taking in my surroundings. Trees. Something's not right. Our well's out in the open. What the...? Prioritize. Get out first, think later. I reach for the lip of the well and struggle up and over, tumbling onto the grass, and lying there for I don't know how long.

Mixed with relief is the pain shooting through my head, in my back muscles, my arms, and legs. I could use a good stiff drink. Forcing my battered body off the ground, hands against the stone wall, I brace myself. The wooden supports on the lip of the well sit splintered and broken next to the metal cylinder they supported till the weight of my body was too much for them. Lucky for me, both ends of the cylinder lodged onto the lip of the well when it dropped. I'm on a winning streak. What are the odds of falling into a well and surviving? The odds of there being a rope? The odds of the cylinder being heavy metal and falling just so? Not as good as the odds of winning at the roulette table. When I get home, I need to hit the casino before my lucky streak...

Then it dawns on me. The reason why I'm here. The reason the rope was left hanging. The reason I've survived. It's a warning. From Dom. He wants his money back, all of it, with interest, and he wants it now. I've been ignoring his requests for payment, trying to save up so I can pay back Mom and Mallory and build a nice nest egg for our future, with a bit on the side for myself. Turns out he wasn't kidding when he gave me that final warning last week. Guess I shouldn't have messed with this guy.

Chapter Forty

I feel safer already, being in Gloria's home. As she prepares a nice meal for the three of us, we discuss the possibility that Jake's gone on the run because of the money he owes. When I found out the trouble he was in, I confided in Gloria, who told Steve. The three of us know Jake's secrets, but only one of us knows the truth.

I text Vicky, Craig, Brad, Sue, Heather, John, as well as my aunt and uncle. **Staying at Gloria's**. **Still no sign of Jake.**

All of this stems from Jake's addiction; that's what Gloria and Steve believe. And maybe it does. The people he borrowed money from so he could keep gambling want their money back. Jake doesn't have it. What Gloria and Steve don't know is Jake was saving up to pay his debts. The money he made from renting out the land for the special crops growing in our corn fields was growing nicely in his locked safe.

Until I stole it.

* * *

Two years ago

"I owe a shit load of money to these guys, Mal. I'm sorry I lied to you." Jake had said the night I found the roll of cash tucked behind our documents.

"What guys?"

"Bad guys. Really bad. The kind that want their money back with a lot of

159

interest. Or else."

"I don't understand. Why do you owe them money? Who are these guys?"

That night, Jake told me the whole story, and I finally understood the full extent of his addiction. The lottery tickets were just the tip of the iceberg. Jake had been going to the casino regularly since his first visit when he turned twenty-one.

"I couldn't stop. I knew I was so close to the big win, the one that would have me and Mom set for life. My credit cards were maxed out, Mom stopped lending me money, I couldn't get any more loans from the bank. Then I met you."

"So you thought I could bail you out?" I gasped. "You married me for the money?"

"No, of course not! No, I married you because I love you. I told you to keep your inheritance in your own name. I knew if I had access to it, I'd be tempted to use it."

I gazed up at the man I loved but didn't know. "So you still owe all that money? Why didn't you tell me about it?" We were man and wife, Jake and Mallory. "We're not supposed to keep secrets from each other."

"I know. I should have told you the truth from the start. When I told Mom I was going to ask you to marry me, she was so happy. She paid off the debts for me so you and I could have a fresh start. It took a good chunk out of her investments, and I meant to pay her back, but my lucky streak petered out."

I unrolled the bills and counted. "There's a lot here. Is it to pay Gloria back? Where did you get it?" The fifties and one-hundred-dollar bills added up to over ten thousand dollars.

"No. Yes. In a way."

Staring at him, I tried to understand. "I want the truth, Jake."

"I've been going out to the casino once every couple of weeks since we got married, not drinking with the guys like I told you. Sometimes, yes, I was at the bar with the guys, but sometimes I went to the casino."

"Where did you get the money?"

"The pot you found growing in the field. A couple of old friends approached me just after we moved in and asked if I'd rent out the land to them. Like I told you, they pay good money, in cash, so there's no taxes to pay, and I don't bank it, so there's no record."

"This is your gambling money? For tickets and the casino?" I searched the eyes of the stranger I had married, trying to find the Jake I thought I knew so well. "Gambling with illegal money made from growing drugs in our cornfield? And lying about it to your wife and your mother?"

"If my wife would have lent me some of the money she's got stockpiled, then that wouldn't have been necessary, would it?" His tone was cold, like his crystal eyes.

"So this is my fault? The drugs, the money, the gambling? You want to blame me for it?"

"That's not what I'm saying."

He grabbed my arm and yanked me to a standing position. "It's not your fault. But you have the power to get me out of this situation, and as much as I hate to ask, I really need the money."

"For more gambling? No."

"To pay off the thugs I owe. The guys I met outside in the parking lot casino the night I went bust. It was just a bit at first, but I kept having a bad streak and borrowed more."

"Who are they?"

"Just some guys. I don't know them personally. They hang around the casino."

"How much?"

"Twenty grand, give or take, the interest keeps growing every minute."

My mouth flew open, and I looked at the bills in my hand. "So you only have half. That's a start, though."

"It's not enough. And I don't know what they're capable of doing if I don't come up with rest. If I don't have a big win soon, I don't know…." My big, strong husband broke down. His bottom lip quivered, his shoulders heaved, and the tears flowed. "I don't know… what they'll do… to me… to you… to us."

A good wife supports her husband. I'm a good wife. "It's okay. We'll pay them off and be done with them." I took him in my arms and patted his back.

He stopped crying abruptly. "Really? We can do that? You *will* do that? For me?"

"For us. I'll get the money tomorrow morning."

I thought that was the end of it. If we paid off the money Jake owed, then we wouldn't need to grow marijuana in our fields, and we wouldn't need to worry about the thugs or the police. As an added bonus, I gave Jake the money to pay back his mom what he owed her as well. I was fifty thousand dollars poorer, but my marriage was richer for it.

That's what I told myself.

When I found out he didn't pay Gloria back, I was furious. "I can't believe you! You owe your mom and me! What did you do with the money?"

One of the things I like about Jake is his honesty. He can lie through his teeth, but when I confront him and want a direct answer, I get it.

"I spent it on tickets and the casino. I was so sure I was due to win," he said sheepishly, with a boyish grin on his face. "Next time will be the big one."

I hit the roof that time. The smack across the face left a red welt for the rest of the day. "Next time?" I screamed. "There's no next time, Jake. No more loans, no more gambling, no second chances to get out of debt free cards."

I raised my hand to him again, and he grabbed it in midair.

He stared down at me, his other hand touching his red cheek and his mouth agape. When he composed himself, he spoke in a cold voice I didn't recognize.

"Don't ever. Ever do that again, Mal." His eyes bore into mine, and I regretted striking him, but only for a moment. Then I was angry again.

"Or what?" I taunted him. "You'll leave me? And my money?"

"No. I'll kill you."

My jaw dropped. So did his. I backed away as he apologized, telling me he didn't mean it, he would never hurt me. "It's just the trauma I went through as a child. And you, you reminded me of my dad just now and how I got him to stop hurting us. I'm so sorry, Mal."

162

It was my fault, apparently. Like everything else.

"I'm sorry, too, Jake. But you won't be getting any more money out of me. It's your problem. You need to deal with it. It's a vicious circle, borrowing money, gambling, borrowing more money. You're the only one who can end it." I was done being an enabler.

We didn't discuss the gambling or the debts after that. He never mentioned my slapping his face. The first year of marriage can be tough, getting to know each other. After that, it's smoother sailing. Especially if you learn to ignore the problems. Then it can be perfect.

* * *

I didn't doubt Jake was still gambling and borrowing money beyond what the illegal crops brought in. When Steve came back into Gloria's life, eager to be part of Jake's life, that turned out to be a stroke of luck. Steve, having just inherited his father's estate, wanted to share it with his sons and his wife. When he told me about it two weeks ago, I knew it would be the answer to Jake's problems. No more borrowing from his mom or his wife. No more high-interest loans from thugs in the casino parking lot. No more illegal crops growing in our field. Steve's dad had spent conservatively and invested wisely over the course of his 84 years. The money would be Jake's, his to do with as he pleased, no freeloading off his wife. It would be more than enough to cover Jake's debts and for us to start a family. All Jake had to do was quit gambling. All I had to do was convince him to forgive his father.

As if reading my mind, Steve says, "All we need to do is wait for Jake to get in touch. Once he hears about his inheritance, he can pay off the guys he owes and get rid of the drug-op."

Gloria agrees. "When he comes home, the two of you can start a family."

Neither of them knows that the family has already been started and I'm going to be a single Mom.

163

Chapter Forty-One

I stumbled upon the key to the safe by chance last week. Until then, both Jake and I pretended I didn't know about the illegal money he kept there, just like we pretended I didn't know what was growing in the cornfield. And our biggest game of 'let's pretend' was that he'd given up gambling.

I was carrying a load of dirty laundry through the mudroom when I noticed Nellie scratching around her litter box, seeming agitated. Setting down the basket, I crouched and asked, "What's the matter, sweetie?"

The sight of red streaks on the side of the box frightened me, and upon closer inspection, I discovered blood in Nellie's stool. Panicking, I phoned the vet and made an emergency appointment.

Jake's usually the one to take Nellie to the vet. She's not easy to get into the cat carrier. In fact, she puts up such a struggle, Jake has to wear gloves and trap her in the mudroom. Since Jake was at work, it was up to me to figure out a way to get her in. Armed with Jake's work gloves, a tin of Nellie's favorite food, and a bag of treats, I lured Nellie into the mudroom, closed all the doors, and gave her a good meal before sending the poor thing off to her least favorite place. As she ate, I slipped the cat carrier out of the laundry room. The minute she saw it, she scrambled for an exit.

Finding none, she ran from door to door, meowing pitifully, begging me not to do it, not to send her off to her execution. My normally calm, loving kitty cat transformed into a vicious wild beast, claws out. I should have thought ahead and changed out of my shorts and t-shirt into jeans and a long-sleeved sweatshirt. By the time I'd made four or five attempts to stuff her into the cage, my arms and legs were covered in scratches. Just as I was about to give up, an idea came to me. Maybe I was going about it all wrong. Sitting down on the tiles, I waited. Patience. If Nellie and I could calm down enough, we'd find a way to solve the problem of getting her into the box without my eyes getting scratched out.

Twenty minutes later, Nellie sprawled on the tiles with me, feigning sleep, one eye open. One of the towels in the laundry basket was just what I needed. With the carrier tipped on its end, I gently but firmly placed the towel over and around Nellie, scooped her up, and dropped her in the box, feet first, before she knew what hit her. Cage door slammed shut, job done, I set about gently turning the box back onto its bottom.

As Nellie protested my betrayal, my eyes focused on a piece of duct tape at the bottom of the cat carrier. Using my nails to scrape it off, I uncovered a small silver key. It sat in the palm of my hand as I tried to process why it was there. Pocketing the key in my shorts, I lifted the carrier, grabbed my purse from the living room, and headed out to my car, Nellie yowling the entire time.

"It's probably just constipation," the vet said after giving Nellie a checkup. "Keep an eye on her the next few days, and if it continues to happen, then bring her in again, and we'll do some tests."

As soon as I got Nellie settled at home, hiding under our bed, I went into Jake's office. To open the safe, I needed a key and the combination. With the key in the lock, I turned it, pushed the numbers on the keypad, and watched as the green light came on. Our wedding date—the same numbers Jake uses for his passwords. Fortunately for me, he's a creature of habit.

I expected to find a roll of cash in there. Same old Jake, I thought. What would I do when I found the money? Confront him? Start an argument? Pretend there was no problem? I hate it when we fight. The documents were all neatly placed in their spot. I pulled them out and ran my hand against the back of the safe. No money.

As I returned the documents, I noticed something on the lowest level, pushed to the back. A dish towel was wrapped around a tin chocolate box.

When Jake came home from work that night, I didn't tell him about the trip to the vet. Nellie wasn't talking either. I had cleaned out the litter box, so there was no trace of any problem. The key I found under the cat carrier was tucked behind the frame of our wedding photo on the living room bookcase. When Jake noticed the key was missing, I knew he'd be fuming, and he'd either find it or get it out of me somehow.

I got lucky. He never mentioned it. When he asked what happened to me, referring to the scratches on my limbs, I explained I'd had a run-in with the rose bushes in the back flowerbed.

"I was trimming them, hoping they'd bloom once more. And I used the gardening gloves you bought me so I wouldn't get thorns on my hands. But I lost my balance and fell right into the bushes, so I got a little scraped up."

"A *little* scraped up? Did you put antibiotic cream on those cuts? Some of them look pretty nasty."

"Yes, I did, but I'm fine." Jake was used to me getting bruised and gashed. Between the insect bites and the gardening, bumping into things, and tripping, I was often covered in bandages. Long pants and long sleeves in public for me most of the time.

* * *

Gloria and Steve don't know what Jake keeps in his safe. They also don't know what lies buried beside the shed, in my back flower bed, next to the red roses.

Chapter Forty-Two

T he sun shining through trees, lighting up the paths, brings with it a warmth that's comforting, as is the birdsong from their branches. Above me, the sky is blue, below the ground is green, mixed with brown. Yellow, blue, green, brown. Nature's colors surround me, but what I'm looking for is some sign of civilization. Where there's a well, there's people. Somewhere in this forest, there must be buildings where people live. I turn 360 degrees, taking the time to look for a sign to guide me in the right direction.

With my back to the well, I glimpse a structure several hundred yards ahead, almost hidden by evergreens. Following the once-worn path, I hobble toward it, my legs and back sore and my left ankle twisted from the fall into the well. At least nothing seems to be broken.

The sight of the dilapidated wooden structure brings me to my knees as I climb its sagging front porch. Not much chance of finding help here, but I force myself back on my feet and try the door, just in case. An empty room greets me, sunlight coming through the door and the gaps in the boards on the windows.

It's one big room, with what used to be the kitchen to the right and an open door leading to the bedroom on the left. Removing my socks, I wrap them around my sore ankle for support. A few minutes to rest on the worn floorboards, and I push myself up and head back out.

Hold on—what do we have here? A small lean-to shed is attached to the shack. I pull open the door and get a whiff of... Shit! I don't know when I've seen one of these before, but I recognize it for what it is. A bench with a hole in it. An old department store catalog next to it. Not exactly The Ritz, but at least it's private, and it beats pulling my pants down in the bush.

After using the facilities, I keep hobbling through the forest. A broken limb across my path comes in handy as a cane. Old man Jake. I'd laugh out loud, but Mallory's not here to laugh with me. After a short stroll through the trees, the outline of a larger building stands out amongst the greenery—it really is my lucky day. Hope and adrenaline keep me going till I reach the front door of a log cabin, more than twice the size of the one I just left, and in a hell of a lot better condition. I knock several times, wait, then knock on the wooden door again, with more force, shouting, "Hello! Is there anyone there? Hello?"

I try the handle and lean my weight into the door, with no success, then slump into one of the two Adirondack chairs on the front porch, partially shaded by maple and birch trees. As I sink back, I regret it, knowing how difficult it's going to be to get myself up and going again. But for now, I'll rest. Maybe someone will come. I close my eyes, shade them from the filtered sunlight, and let myself relax in the warmth. There are worse places to be—like at the bottom of a well.

When I open my eyes, the sun has shifted to the other side of the house, and the porch is fully shaded. Shit! I've wasted time. My mind's clearer, though. I fight to disentangle myself from the chair and peer inside one of the windows through the open curtains. Cozy, cottage-like. This must be someone's retreat, not their principal residence, being way out here in the woods. The thought of vandalizing it makes me uneasy. I could throw a rock through the window... But how would Mallory feel if someone did that to our home, our retreat from the world? On the other hand, if it was a matter of life and death, I'm sure she wouldn't mind providing refuge to a stranger. Mallory's always thinking of others. I'm just about to look for a rock when a thought crosses my mind. A spare key. Mallory and I keep one hidden in case we get locked out of the house. The car remote and the keypad let us into the garage, where a house key hangs on a hook, hidden behind a shelf.

There's no garage here, but a garden shed sits to the right of the cabin at the back. Like the cabin itself, it's locked. So much for that idea. On the back deck is a patio set with four chairs arranged around a table. The sliding glass doors are locked, the curtains drawn. Back on the front porch, I'm tempted to sit down again, but I know it's getting late in the day, and if I have any chance of getting home to Mallory today, I need to keep moving. She must be out of her mind with worry. I'm about to leave my refuge, but first, I take a look under the doormat. And there it is—the spare key. I'm on a roll.

Chapter Forty-Three

The door opens to a large living space, fireplace in the middle, a big screen T.V. mounted above, cushy sofas and chairs arranged around it. Bookcases flank the fireplace, filled with reading material. The kitchen, in the back, has a center island with a couple of stools, as well as a separate eating area with a round table and chairs for four. In the fridge, a twelve-pack sits unopened on the shelf, along with two bottles of wine. I've hit the jackpot. There are also bottles of water, and the freezer is well-stocked, as are the cupboards. Off the kitchen is a bathroom, along with laundry facilities. There's hot running water. Well, Saints be praised! A wooden staircase to the right of the living area leads to the three bedrooms and bathroom. What I don't find are personal items, like photos or knick-knacks or a full closet of clothing, which confirms my initial thought that this is a vacation home. I consider myself a guest, so I take full advantage of the amenities and make myself comfortable. If the owners of the cabin show up, I'll explain my situation. I'm sure they'll understand.

After a long shower to wash the mud and smell of the well from my skin and hair and brushing my teeth, I crack open a beer and down a couple of pain pills from a bottle in the medicine cabinet above the toilet. Lying on the comfortable sofa in front of the television in a white terry robe, I watch the evening news, eating my way through a whole pizza with a couple more beers, a bag of frozen peas on my sore ankle, and a microwavable heat bag under my aching back. My clothes are in the washing machine, and I've wiped my shoes clean. I feel like Goldilocks. Anytime now, the front door will swing open wide, and the owners will say, "Somebody's been eating our pizza and drinking our beer. And they're still here, half asleep on our sofa."

Mallory will die laughing when she hears about this. As soon as I get my strength back, I'll be home where I belong.

I wish there was some way I could let her know I'm okay. But there's no phone, no computer. It's a damn good thing the T.V. works, or I'd be stuck with a bookcase full of books for entertainment. Mal would like that, but then, she's the smart one. When the newscast ends at 7 o'clock with no mention of me, I wonder why she hasn't reported me missing. I saw Mallory last night after Craig dropped me off after a night out with the boys. I was way over the limit, right out of it. It's Friday evening. I should be at work now. Why isn't anyone looking for me? I guess it's too early to make the news just yet.

* * *

When I wake up, it's dark, except for the T.V. screen, which is tuned to some crime drama. The clock on the fireplace mantel indicates it's 10:56 p.m. There's still no one home except me. Struggling to my feet, I limp to the kitchen counter and tune the radio to the local station. The eleven o'clock news has no mention of a missing person.

It's time for me to go home. It's not a good time to be heading out, in the middle of the night, but no one's looking for me, no one's likely to show up here tonight, and I need to know Mallory is safe. If Dom's guys are capable of dumping me in a well, who knows what they might do to my wife, just to make a point. I toss my newly laundered clothes in the dryer, tidy up the mess I've made downstairs, leaving a note to thank my hosts for their hospitality. In the upstairs bathroom, I open the medicine cabinet and stuff a handful of pain pills into a plastic baggie. The first aid kit contains an elastic support bandage, which I wrap around my ankle. Rummaging through drawers in the master bedroom, I find a flashlight, then scoop up the handful of change from the dresser. Once I've downed a couple more pain pills, I stuff a bottle of water and a granola bar for the road into a plastic bag, get dressed, and head out into the night, being sure to lock up and place

171

the key back in its hiding spot.

Chapter Forty-Four

From the side of the house, a gravel driveway leads to a narrow road. No traffic. To the right, my flashlight illuminates a yellow sign against a backdrop of dead trees: **Dead End**. In spite of, or maybe because of, my bleak situation, I find that laugh-out-loud funny. With my cane in my right hand, bag of water, granola bar, and pills slung over my left shoulder, looking like a fine old hobo, I shuffle off in the opposite direction, down the dark road bordered by trees.

It's a never-ending gravel back road, and when I finally reach the crossroads, a *paved* back road, I shout out to the uninhabited darkness, "Jeezus! It's about fucking time!" I keep walking, choosing to turn left and face any oncoming traffic should there happen to be any.

Headlights in the distance flash bright, and I'm determined to make the vehicle stop. Stupid as it is, standing in the middle of the road seems like the best option if I want to get the driver's attention. With my flashlight pointed directly at the oncoming vehicle, I swing it back and forth, up and down, making myself a sitting duck, hopeful I can get out of the way fast enough if this guy doesn't slow down.

"Hey," he shouts through the open window, the car stopped a couple feet short of where I'm standing. "You got a problem?"

No shit. "Yeah, can I hitch a ride?"

He looks me over, head to toe, and seems to conclude I'm not a threat. "Sure, hop in."

"Thanks, man. I appreciate it. I've had a rough day."

He's about my age, muscled shoulders, scruffy beard. As the car heads down the road, he asks where I want to be dropped off.

Clueless as to my whereabouts and how the hell I got here, I ask, "Where exactly are we?"

"Just off the cottage area of Heart Lake, in the woods. How'd you get here, anyway?"

So I'm not too far from home. About a fifteen-minute drive. "Like I said, I've had a rough day. I drove to the lake and set off for a short hike through the woods, but I got disoriented. Next thing I knew, it started getting dark. To top things off, I fell over a fallen tree trunk and twisted my ankle. By the time I found my way out of the woods, it was pitch dark."

"Why didn't you call for help? On your cell."

"I would have," I say, thinking on the fly, "It smashed when I fell."

"That's tough luck."

You have no idea. "Lucky for me, though," I grin, "you showed up. Where are you heading?"

"Into the city."

"Perfect. Can you drop me off at the corner of Grand and River Road?" I need to let Dom know I got his message before something else happens. To me, or worse yet, to Mallory.

"Sure, no problem."

The guy's not much of a talker, and that's fine by me. I'm in no mood for chit-chat. I thank him when he drops me off and offer five dollars of the change I stole.

"No, that's all right. Keep it. You look like you need it more than me."

Not sure what he meant by that. Sure, I look a little roughed up, but who wouldn't after being thrown down a well? At the corner of Grand and River, I cross at the green light, amble across the huge parking lot, and pass through the main entrance of River Grand Casino.

Once inside, I inquire at the cashier's booth. "I'm looking for Dom."

When she shakes her head, I add, "He's looking for me." That prompts her to ask for my name and pick up the phone.

"He's in the back room," she says, her head indicating the right of the gaming floor, as though I might not know where the high roller room is.

Dom sits in one of the plush chairs at a blackjack table, under a crystal chandelier, tossing back a drink. I don't dare disturb him till he's ready to speak to me, so I stand by the doorway like an idiot, taking in the ambiance. Subdued, quiet. A hell of a lot classier, more glamorous than the main casino. Not for your average Joe like me. The night view of the city through the floor-to-ceiling glass is pretty damn cool if you're into that sort of thing.

After Dom lets me sweat for a respectable amount of time, he nods in my direction to let me know he's ready to talk. I join him at the bar, and he slaps me on the shoulder. "I hope you've got something for me."

A quick motion to the bartender and a couple of drinks appear in front of us. I wait for him to tip his glass back, then do the same. Looking directly at me, Dom remarks, "You look like shit. What the hell happened to you?"

"I tripped and fell into a well. You wouldn't happen to know anything about that, would you?"

The corners of Dom's mouth turn up in amusement. Rubbing the growth on his chin, he says, "These things happen. You're lucky to be alive. You should be more careful. Your luck might run out one of these days. It'd be a shame to lose a good customer like you."

Dom owns the casino. I'm sure he has customers who provide him with a better profit margin than I do, but I guess every bit helps.

"I'll have the money for you. I just need a little more time."

"That sounds like the same old song and dance, Jake. I'm getting tired of hearing it." Dom's glass hits the counter with enough force to get the attention of several patrons. They quickly go back to their business when they see where the sound comes from.

"Just a few days, and I'll have a substantial payment," I promise, knowing I'm going to have to use the money I set aside to pay back Mallory and Mom. They can wait. Dom won't.

"A few days? The interest rates are increasing every day, my friend. I'd hate to see you get in over your head," Dom smirks.

"I'll pay you back. As soon as I get home, I'll put together the money and give you a call. It won't be long. You'll have your money, all of it, with interest." If I can appease Dom temporarily, it'll give me more of a chance to convince Mal to hand over some of that cash she's got stashed in the bank.

"A few more days." Dom signals the bartender for another drink as he watches me squirm. Taking his glass and heading toward the card table, he waves his hand in the air, dismissing me. "I'll send you another reminder tomorrow."

"Just one more thing," I say before he's back in the game. "Is there any chance I could get a ride home? And I seem to have lost my wallet and phone when I fell into the well. I'd really like them back."

"Can't help you there. And I don't run a fucking chauffeur service for bums off the street. But seeing as you're really down on your luck, I'll get someone to run you home. We'll just add it to your tab."

He pulls out his phone and arranges my ride. "Nick? I got a client here needs a lift. Make sure he gets home safe. He'll meet you out front."

I'm escorted out of the room by a couple of goons and deposited on the walkway bordering the entrance of the casino. A few minutes later, a dark vehicle pulls up.

"Looking for a ride? Courtesy of Dom?"

Tall guy, about my age, dark hair, man of few words. After I give him directions, there's no further conversation. As we turn onto my road, I'm excited at the idea of seeing Mallory's expression when I come home. She'll be so relieved. I don't know what's been going through her head the last 24 hours, but one thing I'm sure of is she'll be beyond thrilled to see me. I can't wait to get into bed with my loving wife and have her show me how worried she's been.

The house comes into view, set back from the road, the interior lights on in the front windows, our vehicles parked in the driveway. But something in this picture isn't right.

"Keep driving," I direct Nick as he slows down in front of my driveway. "Turn around at the end of the road and head back the way we came."

Nick turns to me briefly, raising his eyebrows, but does as he's instructed. Once we've turned off my road, I tell him to pull over and thank him for the lift. "This is good. I'll walk home from here. I want to surprise my wife."

It takes a bit of effort for me to stagger to the farmhouse, and when I get there, I walk along the right side of the property, next to the evergreens, away from the house and the security lights. It's going to be a surprise, all right. What the hell is my best friend's car doing in my driveway in the middle of the night? What the hell is he doing with my wife?

The sight of Craig's car in my driveway, blocking mine in, brings it all back and sends a flurry of emotions through me. Yesterday was the worst day of my life. If I could go back and erase one day, Thursday would be it.

Yep, it all comes back to me as I see Craig's car. I know he's in there. Are the two of them in our bed right now? I've barely been gone one night, and there's another man in my bed. The sheets can't even be cold yet. How could she do this to me? I thought she loved me as much as I love her.

I know I didn't show it Thursday morning. Or afternoon. I sure as hell didn't show it Thursday night. I should have taken her in my arms and told her everything was going to be all right.

But I didn't. I fucked things up royally. Which is why Craig's with Mallory, and I'm not. His car's here. He's in there. Please, God, don't let him take her from me.

Chapter Forty-Five

Through the gap in the curtains, I get a glimpse of movement. My first thought is to confront them, catch them at it, but I know my marriage won't survive that, and I'd never get the image of Craig and Mallory having sex in my house out of my head. No, it's better if I get Mallory alone, and we have a chance to talk things over, without Craig sticking his nose in our business. Should I ring the doorbell to my own house? Demand he leave?

I limp up the side of the driveway, next to the Toyota, trying to decide how to handle this, when the front door opens. Crouching down between the evergreens, I listen as Craig tells Mal to be strong. Once his car backs down the driveway, the front door closes, and the living room lights go out. He's not staying the night. That's gotta be a good sign.

Still, I'm not sure how to approach her. I don't want to get into it again about Craig and the baby. If she's still pissed off about what I did to the shed and what I said about the baby and about her.... What the hell was wrong with me? We've never had a fight before yesterday. Not like that. I've never spent a night away from home until now. How am I going to get her to forgive me? I can't lose her.

Things will look better tomorrow. I just need to get some rest and think things over. The best place for me is in the dog house. Since we don't have one, the shed it is. Following the line of trees, I stumble to the back of the property, a couple hundred feet. Upon opening the door and flashing the light in, I'm relieved that I took the time to clean up the mess I'd made yesterday morning. Nothing like coming home to a tidy house. Our tent and sleeping bags lie in one corner, unused the last couple of years.

* * *

Three years ago

The summer we got married, we camped out at the lake a few times. Mallory had never gone camping, so I wanted to give her a taste of what it's like to be out in the fresh open air. She thought the idea of sleeping under the stars was romantic, until the night she unzipped her sleeping bag and found a garter snake in it. It took weeks for her to get over the shock. I should have known better. When I'd set it in there, I meant it to be a joke. Jake the Snake, our new pet, I was going to say when she found it. It was only a little one, a baby, for God's sake.

But she wouldn't stop screaming. She ran out of the tent, her arms brushing imaginary snakes off her body, while our fellow campers rushed outside to see what the commotion was all about. I assured them my wife was fine, just overreacting to a little snake in her sleeping bag. My words had the opposite of their intended effect. A number of the other women, and some of the men as well, let out a holler or two, waking any kids who had managed to sleep through Mallory's blood-curdling shriek, resulting in a complete shaking out of sleeping bags and cleaning out of tents. To make matters worse, some nut job in the park, hearing all the screaming, must have thought someone was being murdered. By the time the police showed up, a large group of us were sitting around a campfire, slinging back beer and getting to know each other. Mallory was in the Honda, with the seat reclined, still shaking from her encounter with Jake the Snake.

* * *

Shaking out one of the sleeping bags to check for stray snakes, I lay it on the wooden floor of the shed and zip myself in. It beats the bottom of a well.

After a good night's sleep, Mal and I will talk. I'll apologize, and everything will be back to normal. I close my eyes for a few seconds, then they pop wide open, as I remember. Nothing's going to be normal ever again.

Chapter Forty-Six

The sun's shining through the shed window when I wake. My head's throbbing, my body aches, and I try to figure out where the hell I am. Camping? The riding lawn mower next to me brings it back. I need to talk to Mallory, tell her everything's going to be okay. We'll get through this, whatever *this* is. I'll pay back Dom somehow—all of it. Get him off my back. I'm sure Mallory will give me the money when she hears about the well and finds out what Dom's capable of doing. Then she'll explain again there's nothing going on between her and Craig, that I was seeing something that wasn't there, that she loves me, only me. And she'll get an abortion. Women do it all the time; it's not that big a deal. It'll be Jake and Mallory again, the way it's meant to be.

The back door to the mudroom is locked. Same with the patio doors off the kitchen. She's probably still asleep. I'm walking along the side of the garage when I notice Craig's car behind the Honda again. He *has* spent the night, after all. I'll kill him. The sound of another vehicle coming down the road stops me in my tracks, and I duck down amongst the evergreens. When it turns down our driveway, Craig dashes across the lawn toward the vehicle, and I'm just about to emerge and put my fist to his nose when Vicky and Mallory step out of the vehicle. I'm shocked by what I see. Mallory has a bandage around her head. Did I do that? I don't remember. Oh God, please, don't let it be my fault. I hit my pregnant wife. Have I become my father? What kind of monster am I?

Craig mentions my name as he leads Mallory toward the house. So it *is* me. I've done this to her. Thursday night? I thought I'd hit Craig. Did I hit

Mallory, too? And what is Vicky doing here? Did she tell Mallory about the time I raised my hand to *her*? I didn't touch her, but it was enough for Vicky to break off our relationship.

* * *

Nearly four years ago

"You want to hit me, Jake? Go ahead, try it. I'll have you in jail so fast it'll make your head spin," she had said as I restrained myself and lowered my arm. I had just found out she had a lunch date with an old boyfriend. My dad would have said I was within my rights to give her a slap, to keep my woman in her place. It was my dad's voice in my head that stopped me in time.

"No, no, of course not. I'm so sorry, Vick," I apologized. "I would never." I sobbed like a baby, begging her to forgive me. "I don't want to be like my dad. I don't."

She did forgive me, but she also broke off our relationship. As devastating as that was, it was for the best, because it left me free to be with the woman I was meant to be with—Mallory.

* * *

If I've hurt Mallory, I'll never forgive myself. It's back to the doghouse. I can't face her now, especially with our two best friends here to judge me. I'll wait till they're gone and give her some time to cool down before I apologize.

My stomach tells me it's time for brunch. Not much chance of getting Mal's French toast and scrambled eggs with a side of bacon. I'd kill for a strong cup of coffee, but the granola bar, pain pills, and water in the plastic bag will have to do. As ridiculous as it seems, I'm the outsider, the intruder here. This is Mallory's home. Mallory and her supportive best friends have the right to be here. Not a wife-beater like me. I don't deserve anything.

Hunkering down in the shed seems like the best option for now. Not much in the way of entertainment, though. No T.V., no internet, no phone. There's some sort of plant reference book on the work table. It doesn't make for very interesting reading, but the pictures are nice to look at. Hopefully, Craig and Vicky will leave soon, and Mallory and I can sort things out.

Time passes slowly, and with the sun coming through the window, it's hard to breathe in the stuffy space, so every once in a while, I slip out and wander through the trees alongside the lawn for some fresh air. I'm taking a chance on being seen, but it *is* my house, for Christ's sake. I shouldn't have to sneak around like a fugitive. If they wonder what I'm doing, I'll just cite amnesia as the reason I'm wandering around my own yard.

When the police cruiser drives up, I know they've reported me. Whether they've reported me missing or reported me as a wife abuser, I'm not sure, but walking up to the cops doesn't seem like a wise choice, so I hide deep within the rows of trees. If I can just talk to Mallory alone, she'll drop the charges. Craig and Vicky are probably the ones who've convinced her to report me. And I can't really blame them. If I've hit Mallory, I deserve to be locked up.

I'm relieved to see the cops drive off a short while later, but Craig and Vicky seem to have no intention of leaving. A couple of hours later, a dark sedan pulls in the driveway. We've had more company today than we've had for months. The sight of Nick exiting the vehicle with that sidekick goon of his makes me physically sick. Dom's changed his mind about giving me more time. They're here to start cutting my fingers. I need to get Dom his money, and I need to get it fast.

Chapter Forty-Seven

Darkness settles in as I watch the house. My stomach's grumbling, my water bottle's empty, and the treed area doesn't make for the most sanitary bathroom. I need to get into my own house and be in the comfort of my wife's arms. God, I wish I could do that! Before that can happen, I need to sort out my problem with Dom, make sure we're safe from his threats. There's only one way I can think of to do that, but I don't dare ask Mal for help. The last thing I need is to piss her off even more.

I wait. The interior house lights come on. Some time passes, then the interior lights go off. I wait some more. At some point, she'll fall asleep, and I'll slip in and do what needs to be done. Why are Craig and Vicky's vehicles still in the driveway? Have they never heard of overstaying your welcome?

Time to make a move anyway. Like a thief, I prowl the length of the treed border to the front of the garage and enter my code into the keypad. The security light comes on. Hoping to high heaven that the buzzing of the garage door and the lights don't wake anyone, I grab the spare key from behind the shelf, close the garage door, and stumble toward our bedroom window. Is he in there with her? With Vicky, too? The three of them? In my sudden rage, I pick up a stone and aim it up toward the glass. But as I limp up to it, another security light flashes on. Shit! Mallory and her insecurities. The damn lights. I back off, sliding around to the side of the house. There's a smarter course of action for me to follow.

Patience. I've got the key. I can get in, check on Mallory, do my business, and get the hell out.

When the security light at the front door flashes, I peer around the corner to see what's set it off. Mal's standing on the porch, swinging my bat around. Deciding it's probably not the best time to say, "Hi, honey, I'm home," I skulk off to the rear of the house, along the tree line. The next thing I know Mallory and Craig are in the back yard. Not a good time for me to wander through the house if I want to remain undetected. I slink back to the doghouse.

Later that night, I use the spare key, enter my home, and creep around the mud room area, searching. It's not here. I'm screwed.

Chapter Forty-Eight

In the morning, the cars are gone. It's just me and Mallory. But I'm not ready to talk yet. I haven't solved my Dom problem. I need more time. Time to find the key. Time to get the money. More time to think about how I'm going to get Mallory to forgive me for hitting her and to think about what I'm going to say about the baby. More time to think about how I'm going to convince her to pay off the rest of my debts.

I'm a little bolder now that she's alone, going up to the windows to see if I can get a peek. There she is, in the dining room. I don't dare enter the house while she's awake. She'll take an afternoon nap. If not, I'll wait till nighttime.

The key wasn't where I'd hidden it. It should have taken a minute to get the key, another five to get the money out of the safe, five more to book a cab online, and then a half hour or so to get to the casino and hand over the cash to Dom. Not all that I owe, but a good start. Enough to stop him from being a threat to me and Mal.

But when I turned over Nellie's carrier last night, I found only the duct tape, peeled back to reveal the plastic. No key.

As far as weekends go, this one tops the list for the shittiest on record. And I can't even remember all of it. I run through what I do know. A pregnant cheating wife, a best friend who's betrayed me, and an ex-girlfriend who's likely convinced my wife I'm abusive and that I cheated on her. Then there's my memory lapse. What happened after Craig left Thursday night? How did Mallory injure her head? How did I get to the bottom of the well? But of immediate concern is Dom and the issue of my fingers. I need to pay him to save myself. To save my wife. And now, to save Mallory's baby. Because she'd never get over losing it. It's time for me to man up. I need to get my shit together and save my marriage. Before I can save my marriage, I need to find the key so I can get the money.

It's late afternoon by the time she's asleep on the sofa. I enter through the back, do a sweep of the house, trying not to disturb anything, careful not to wake her. The drawer of the T.V. stand is where I'm looking when I hear her stir. She makes one of her cute little snorting sounds, then rolls around to face the back of the sofa. A quick bathroom stop off the mudroom, then back to the kitchen, where I grab a beer and bottle of water from the fridge along with a block of cheese, an apple, a Tupperware container of days-old leftover cooked ham, and the quarter loaf of bread. From the knife block, I pick up the slicer. My hands full, I hold tight, unfasten the door latch on the patio doors, and skulk off like a thief into the night, bumping into the blasted wind chimes I bought Mallory as I make my way off the deck. At least I'll have a decent supper. Keep up my strength for tonight's search.

Chapter Forty-Nine

The dinging of hail on the shed's metal roof wakes me in the middle of the night. I sit upright, wondering how I let myself fall asleep. There's so much I need to get done before morning. I remove my wet shoes before setting foot inside the front door, then set them on the tray inside the front entry closet and grab the flashlight off the shelf. My fingers explore the top shelf, coat pockets, and inside shoes. I check the entrance table and bench. Nothing. The clang catches me by surprise as the baseball bat sitting in the corner crashes to the floor, and I rush to get to the basement before Mal investigates. If she calls the police and I'm arrested for abuse, I won't be able to protect her—not from inside a jail cell. If Dom can't collect my fingers, what's to stop him from going after Mal's?

The creak on the stairs tells me she's heading back to bed. Opening the basement door a crack, I check if the coast is clear. My eyes spot the coat hanging by the back door, and I root through its pockets. In the mudroom closet, I search the shelves, rifle through more pockets and shoes, including my rubber boots. They could come in handy with the rain. I toss them onto the backdoor mat and keep searching as rain pellets the windows and the wind howls through the doors.

I'm in the laundry room going through the dirty washing when the sound of the television in between cracks of thunder spooks me. She's up again. This game of cat and mouse is getting too dangerous. I barely have time to make it to the basement to hide. While I'm there, I take the opportunity to look along the shelves and the tool bench, although I know it's not a logical hiding place for Mallory. Where could she have put it?

I come up the stairs empty-handed, open the basement door, and listen for the sound of the television. Hearing nothing, I venture out and continue my search of the laundry room. Once I've worked my way through the shelves of detergent and fabric softener, I sneak back to the kitchen for a second look.

Everything goes black.

The familiar sounds of the house are eerily silent. I stumble through the dark, pull on my rubber boots, and slip out the back door. Bolts of lightning light my way. Halfway around the side of the house, I realize I should have grabbed my coat on my way out. The wind and rain batter my body as I slug through the soggy yard.

The generator sits alongside the house, facing the cornfield, and it should have automatically kicked in. Mallory will be an absolute basket case if she wakes up in the dark alone. I need to get the generator working. What the hell's wrong with it? Once I pull the door open and push the fuel button, I see the problem. Out of gas. By the time I get to the garage door and enter the code, I'm sopping wet. The gas can's tucked in the corner by the door, so I'm able to grab it quickly, but the ease with which I pick it up tells me it's empty. Just great. I used the last of the gas for the mower Wednesday morning. I meant to tank up the Honda Friday after work and bring along the gas can, but then my life went to shit Thursday morning because of the baby...

There's no point in dwelling on that. Right now, with rainwater flowing down the driveway and the yard getting soggier by the minute, I've got other problems to worry about. I work my way to the back door, leave my boots on the mat, and descend to the basement, my flashlight focused on the steps. Without power, the sump pump won't work, but the battery backup should have kicked in by now. I'm not hearing any noise. Just my luck. When I lift the lid and look in the hole, the water level is dangerously high.

I lift the battery box and shine the light inside. The terminals look corroded. I should have been on top of this and made sure it was in working order. I've been sloppy lately with too much on my mind. Removing the cables, I take some fine sandpaper and brush off the corrosion from the

189

clamps and terminals. Then I reconnect the cables tightly, and it springs to life, immediately lowering the water level in the hole. One less thing to worry about.

While it's still nighttime, I might as well take another look around the kitchen, although it's hard to see much. I'm sifting through the wooden flour canister when I notice the mess Mallory has left. Bowl, spoons, knife, plate, pot, ladle, empty can—all her filthy supper dishes just sitting there on the counter. When I open the dishwasher, I find it full. If she was too tired to empty it, the least she could have done is put her supper dishes in the sink. I lower them in there now, wipe down the counter with the wet dishcloth, and come in contact with the soup lid. How many times have I told her not to leave lids lying around? There's no excuse for this. It's just laziness.

I grab the lid with the intention of wrapping it in a paper towel. The sharp metal slices through my hand, and it hurts like a mother…. "Fuck, Mallory!" The words fly out of my mouth, mixed with a scream, and I know she's bound to hear. With a paper towel wrapped around my left hand, I pick up the lid between my thumb and forefinger and push it into the bottom of the garbage can. I don't want Mallory to hurt herself.

The steps creak with her descent as I retreat to the basement. It's only when I look down at my left hand that I notice the blood. It's more than a little nick. The first aid kit sits on the shelf next to my workbench, and I disinfect the gashes, wrapping several layers of gauze around the palm of my hand. Satisfied Mallory's gone back to bed, I head back upstairs. The light guiding my way illuminates the rainwater that dripped from my clothing when I came in, the blood from my hand mixing with it. In the kitchen, I pull off a handful of paper towels, pour some hot water over a few, and clean the mess before Mallory sees it and freaks out. The sight of blood makes her queasy. Once the floor's wiped, I dispose of the paper towels in the bottom of the garbage can. I've turned the house upside down, and I can't find the blasted key. I'm going to have to confront Mal in the morning and beg for her forgiveness, beg her to give me the key, beg her to lend me more money.

At the back door, I stand and stare for a minute, trying to understand what I see. Or what I don't see. My boots are gone.

Chapter Fifty

My memory loss must be getting the better of me. I could have sworn I left my boots on the mat. Scratching my head, I slink to the front of the house, stop at the stairway to listen for Mallory, and hear nothing. Good, she's asleep. I remove my shoes from the closet, slip them on, and I'm just about to open the front door when yellow flashes shine through the sidelights. In the slit between the curtains, I watch Craig's car pull up. What the hell is he doing? Has he been out looking for me? Is he going to turn me in to the cops? If he touches Mallory, I'll kill him.

I run to the back door, flinging it open and make a mad dash to the far corner of the yard. By the time I'm back in the shed, I'm so drenched I peel off all my clothing, hang it to dry on the hooks lining the wall, and crawl into the sleeping bag. My last thought is I hope Mallory still loves me.

It's the same thought I have when the sun wakes me. My clothes are still damp, which leaves me in my boxers as I wander through the trees to check out the driveway. His car's gone. So he didn't spend the night, after all. Thank God.

This is my chance to make it up to Mallory, to plead for forgiveness for insisting she get rid of the baby, even though I was drunk out of my mind at the time and shouldn't be held accountable for my actions. It's my chance to apologize for striking her by accident during a moment of drunken rage at my best friend, who deserves a broken jaw for the way he looks at my wife. I need Mallory to understand that wasn't me Thursday night—it was the booze. Just like the night of her birthday party.

CHAPTER FIFTY

* * *

Six weeks ago

We came so close to blowing it all that night. My life, my marriage, our friendship. It was all on the line. And so was Vicky's relationship with Craig. I could see what was going on between the two of them, even though they were being all secretive about it. Vicky and I shared a cab after waiting what seemed like a long time for Craig to call after taking Mallory home. By the time he did text, we'd given up waiting and were sitting in front of Vicky's house.

"Do you want to come in?" Vicky giggled, her hands all over me, in the back seat of the cab, the meter still running as the driver's eyes focused straight ahead. "Make sure I get tucked in safely?"

The image of Craig doing exactly that with Mallory popped into my head. I needed to get home. I gave Vicky a hug, with every intention of saying goodnight right there and then, but she grabbed me and planted a big, sloppy kiss on my neck. What could it hurt to see Vicky in? I opened the door, slid out of the back seat, my mind on getting into bed with her.

But the words that came out of my mouth as I gave Vicky my arm to assist her out of the cab were surprisingly sensible. "I can't. I love Mallory. I need to get home."

"Mallory's a lucky woman. You're more of a man than I thought you were." Vicky kissed my cheek. I waited until she stumbled out of the cab and got to her door. As it closed, I gave the driver my address and told him to take me home to my wife.

The taxi driver turned around and said, "That's a smart move."

* * *

All that matters now is that Mallory loves me, that she'll take me back. I don't care if she did sleep with Craig… well, I do care, I sure as hell care…but

I love her. I can't live without her. Once I prove to her that I'm serious about giving up the gambling and that our family means everything to me, she'll take me back. I'll do whatever it takes to keep her.

The red roses in the flowerbed catch my attention. They're her favorite. From the shed, I take the gardening shears and cut 3 stems, then carry the roses to the house. One for each of us—me, Mallory, and the baby.

"Honey? I'm home," I call, standing in the mudroom in my underwear. "Sorry, I'm late." More than three days, but I'm sure she'll see the humor in my comment once all this is behind us.

No answer. Maybe she's still sleeping. She did spend all night wandering around the house. She must be exhausted. Removing my shoes, I lay the roses on the dryer, and head to the bathroom for a nice, warm shower. With a towel wrapped around my waist, I find a narrow vase in the laundry room cupboard and place the roses on the dining room table. I plug in the kettle to make myself a cup of instant coffee, then settle myself on the living room sofa with the television turned on low, giving Mallory a chance to sleep in.

The sight of Craig's car turning into the driveway turns my stomach. I take my cup to the kitchen sink, rinse it out, and place it in the dishwasher. Grabbing my boxers out of the bathroom, I head to the basement for temporary refuge.

The old clock radio on my workbench tells me about half an hour has passed before the doorbell rings. The police again? I may as well give myself up and hope Mallory will drop the charges. I open the basement door a crack and listen. It's worse than the police. Nick's asking for me.

Mallory gets rid of him by mentioning the police are after me. As she closes the front door, I head to the cornfield to watch them leave. Craig's car is nowhere to be seen. From behind the tall stalks, I observe Nick and his buddy standing in the driveway as though they're waiting for me to show my face. That's not going to happen unless Mallory's in danger. A rustling in the cornfield, several rows ahead, startles me. An animal?

When a car pulls up behind Nick's sedan a short while later, Mallory runs out from the cornfield, across the lawn, to the driveway, shouting about the police coming back. I don't believe this. Brad, the ex-boyfriend, the work husband, gets out of his car and talks to these goons. How does he know them? Is he working with them?

While I'm trying to figure out what's going on, another car pulls in beside Brad's. It's a regular hub of social activity here since I've been gone. At the sight of Mom getting out of the car, I'm about to exit the cornfield and demand these guys get the fuck off my property, regardless of whether they take one of my fingers with them. Before I get the chance, I see good old Dad joining Mallory and Mom, waving his fist in the air, yelling at the top of his lungs, "Where's my son? What have you done with him?"

This is a whole new ball game. My abusive dad is looking for his abusive son, threatening the abusive goons who are also looking for me. It's a regular three-ring circus. I back up into the cornfield and wait for things to play out so I can have a better understanding of what the hell this is about.

First, the goons leave. Then Brad leaves. Mom and Dad go into the house with Mallory. When they get in the car together fifteen minutes later, Mallory's got a duffel bag with her and Nellie in the cat carrier.

Did she just leave me? Of course, she did. I've been such an ass.

Chapter Fifty-One

Mallory had a meltdown Thursday morning in the garden shed. Completely snapped. Because of me. It's been four days since my world fell apart. And now she's gone.

When I woke up Thursday, all I wanted was some sweet lovin' from my wife. A man's got a right to that. And it started out nice, with her being all kissy and cuddly. But then she opened her mouth. To talk.

"There's something I need to tell you," she said in that tone she uses when she wants me to be serious. "It's important."

I nuzzled her neck and nibbled her ear, giving her my full attention. "We've got something really important going on already. I'm sure it can wait."

I tried to listen to what she had to say, but she tensed up as my mouth moved lower. "Come on, relax. Whatever it is, we can talk about it later."

She responded with her teacher's voice. "Jake. Stop. We need to talk. That's enough."

I rolled over, propped myself up on my elbow, and gazed down at her. "Okay, Mal. What is it?"

She sat up. "I know you said we should wait until the time is perfect, but sometimes things happen for a reason. The time's perfect now." Her blue eyes searched mine for my reaction. I had a bad feeling about what she was going to say next. "We're pregnant."

I felt like I'd been sucker punched. This couldn't be happening. Literally, it couldn't. "We're what?"

"We're going to have a baby. It's a bit sooner than we planned, but you know how much I've wanted to start a family ever since we got married. It's been three years, Jake. I know the money's tight, and I'll be off work for a while, but I know we can make this work. Isn't it exciting, honey?"

I couldn't look at her, the betrayal in her eyes. Hopping out of bed, I put on some work clothes. "I'm going out to the shed. It needs cleaning out."

"Jake, honey? I love you."

I knew what I should say. But I couldn't. So I pulled myself together and did the best I could. "We'll need more space once the baby's here, hon. I'm going to make room in the garden shed for an office, and we'll get an electrician in for lighting and heat. That way, we can turn the office into a nursery."

I hightailed it out of there before I did something I knew I would regret. The garden shed got cleaned out real good. By the time I was done, I wasn't sure if anything was left in one piece, but I didn't give a shit. I was so pissed off I needed to unwind. I met Mal in the kitchen when I went to get a beer. She asked if I was okay and wondered what I wanted for brunch.

"I'm good," I responded, showing her the beer as I passed by on my way back out. "Got lots of work to do."

After chugging the beer, I took a good long look at my handiwork. Mal's gardening tools cluttered the floor, having bounced off the walls I had thrown them against. Her empty ceramic flower pots lay smashed, sharp edges facing up. The riding mower, push mower, and weed wacker were saved from attack because they're my babies. But the contents of the bags of grass seed, potting soil, and fertilizer littered the wooden floor. Even the seed Mal puts in the bird feeder spread out in a furious pattern. But I'd only begun. There was still plenty to be done. It occurred to me to take the shears to her precious roses and give them a pruning they'd never forget, but I stopped myself in time.

I was holding the shears in my hand, my attention turned to the new gardening gloves I'd bought as part of her birthday present, when she walked in. Her mouth fell open, she stared at me like she didn't know me, then she slid down the side of the wall into the pile of soil, seed, and fertilizer, her hands covering her face. And she sobbed. Then she wailed.

"I...I...I...thought..." she blubbered. "You'd be...." Her shoulders shook, she choked and sputtered, and when her hands slid off her face, she stared at me and said, "Happy."

Happy? She thought I'd be happy she was pregnant? What the hell gave her that idea? I'd made no secret of the fact I didn't want to become my dad. What kind of father would I make, having been raised by that man? An abusive one, that's what kind.

But I didn't tell her that as she sat there, all snotty-nosed with tears pouring from her eyes. No, I didn't say I had no intention of ever being anyone's father. What I did was take her in my arms and apologize.

"I'm so sorry, honey. You know I need to let off a bit of steam now and then. This was just one of those times. It's been a rough week at work, and I was looking forward to the two of us spending the weekend together alone, and you took me by surprise. I wasn't expecting there to be three of us."

She stopped crying and sat staring, without moving. It was like she was comatose or something. Seeing her like that, I knew I'd hurt her beyond repair, and I didn't know what to do about it. I couldn't lose her. She's mine. If she ever left me...I don't know what I'd do. I'm nothing without her. Jake and Mallory. Without Mallory, there is no Jake. I'd die without her.

"I'll clean this up. You go on inside and get some rest. I'm so sorry, Mal. So sorry I lost my temper. It's not you. It's me. I've had a lot to cope with lately. This..." I swept my hands across the mess I'd made, "it's not about you. Or us. Or the..."

I couldn't say the word, so I just pointed at her stomach. "It's something else entirely."

I helped her back into the house, laid her on the couch with a cup of calming tea, slipped her a benzo, pulled the throw over her, and went back to the shed to clean up. As I swept up the pieces of pots into garbage bags and hauled the dirt off the floor into the flower beds, I wondered how I was going to pick up the pieces of my marriage. How the hell did she get pregnant? She took birth control pills. I used a condom.

Hanging the gardening tools back into their spot, I thought back to when I gave Mallory her first baby. Nellie.

The farmer who gave her to me warned she was too young to take from her mother, but I paid him to let her go. I knew Mallory would make a good mom for the kitten. I dumped her into the crawlspace under the front porch before work that day while Mal was at school. I figured if she ran off before I got home, it was no big loss. If she stayed, maybe she'd get Mallory's mind off having a baby. It worked like a charm. Granted, I wasn't too keen on being a cat dad, but the darn little thing got to me.

But now, I could see another pet wasn't going to be the answer to keeping us childless. Mallory managed to get herself pregnant. What good is birth control, anyway, if it doesn't even fucking work? I refuse to become my father. If she got herself pregnant, could she get herself unpregnant?

Chapter Fifty-Two

Mallory was asleep on the couch when I left for work Thursday afternoon. I called Craig and asked him to pick me up. "I've got a lot of drinking to do after work. I'll need a ride home."

Somehow, I managed to get through the workday. For the first time in nearly four years, I didn't text Mal during work or call her at break, and there were no messages from her, either. At the bar, I started drinking hard and fast the minute my ass hit the bar stool. Not only did I have a pregnant wife whom I loved in spite of that fact, I owed more money than I'd be able to pay back in three lifetimes. How was I going to afford a kid? If I didn't start paying it off, with interest that never quit, my lender was going to start chopping fingers, one inch at a time. Not personally. Dom would never resort to something like that. But I knew damn well he had people who'd take great pleasure in making me pay my debt. I was going to be a fingerless father.

Craig's no dummy. He sensed something was bothering me. "Is everything okay between you and Mallory?"

Me and Mallory. Fuckin' great. Except now it was going to be Jake and Mallory and the baby. "We're fine. We're just having some financial difficulties. Every married couple has them. You'd know what it's like if you were married," I snapped.

Craig inched away. "That's a low blow. I'm sorry to hear you're having problems."

He was sorry. *He* wasn't about to become a father. What did he have to be sorry about? *He* was going to keep all his fingers. He didn't have a care in the world.

The more I drank, the more I wondered about the timing. How did she end up pregnant at all, much less now? By the time my best friend drove me home, I was spinning in more ways than one. The sight of my pregnant wife at the door, holding Nellie like a baby, spun me out of control.

I should have taken her in my arms, told her I loved her, and everything was going to be okay. Instead, the first words I blurted were, "We can get rid of it. It's still early months, right?"

I wasn't drunk enough. Not drunk enough to misinterpret the look on her face. It was as though I'd punched her in the stomach and knocked that baby clear out of her. But I didn't stop there.

"My wife's managed to get herself with child," I said to Craig as he stood next to me awkwardly. "But I know it's not mine. She's carrying somebody else's brat."

It was the drink talking, not me.

The look Mallory and Craig exchanged was so brief I might have imagined it, but the whiskey had cleared my mind, and I was seeing things I hadn't seen before. Craig and Mallory.

"You!" I shouted, pointing an accusing finger at my best friend. "You and Mallory! You fucked my wife! My cheating…." The words I used to describe Mallory are words I won't repeat, even to myself.

I didn't get a chance to see Mallory's reaction to my barrage of expletives and derogatory insults. Craig slugged me and knocked me to my knees. I tried to get up and punch the best friend who betrayed me with my wife, but I couldn't keep my balance long enough to get to my feet. I would have liked to say I gave as good as I got, but I only managed one good swing that missed its target as he extended his hand and bent down to help me up.

"Don't you dare talk about Mallory like that. She's the sweetest woman I know. She loves you, only you," he berated me.

I smacked him good because I knew that wasn't true. She loved the baby. She loved the baby that wasn't mine.

"The night of Mallory's birthday party. You took her home early. You were gone for a long time." It was more than a statement—it was an accusation.

201

WHERE IS MY HUSBAND?

We'd all had too much to drink. Craig, as usual, was the most sober of us all. Mallory had gotten one of her headaches partway through the night and wanted to go home. Vicky and I weren't ready to call it a night. But Craig...Craig offered to take Mallory home and come back to get us. "What took you so long to text me before heading back, Craig?"

My best buddy was speechless. Mallory spoke for him. "He made sure I got up to bed safely and stayed with me till I fell asleep. That's all. Nothing happened. I wouldn't cheat on you."

She added, "Like you did on me."

She had to bring that up. One time, before we got engaged. One time with Vicky. Mallory didn't know it was Vicky. She thought it was another of my exes. I figured what she didn't know couldn't hurt her.

When Craig responded to Mallory's words about me cheating with another blow to my jaw, Mallory screamed and told Craig to leave. "You're making it worse. He'll settle down. Just go home."

That was the last I saw of Craig till I stumbled home Friday night and found his car in my driveway, the sight of it bringing back the memory of Thursday, the worst day ever.

Chapter Fifty-Three

I 'm left alone in the cornfield, bath towel covering my privates, boxers in my hand. If I had my phone, I'd take a photo and post it on social media with some silly caption. At least I have the key to my own house. No wife, no cat. I've still got all my fingers. No money. The money's the key. If I can get the goons off my back, I can save my fingers. Then I can concentrate on saving my marriage and the home Mal and I have made for the two of us. Three. Shit.

In our ensuite, I rinse off the corn silk and bugs, shave the four day's growth off my face, and brush my teeth. In our bedroom, I pull on some fresh clothes, look around for any sign Craig's been here—something left behind, maybe a smell.

I need to give the house a thorough search to find the key to the safety deposit box. There must be some square inch in the place I haven't looked yet.

As I roam through the empty house, I notice Mallory's computer open to our email. What I read sends a chill down my spine. These guys mean business. If they can't get to me, they'll get to Mallory. Mallory and her baby. I'm not going to put them in danger. My reply is meant to be threatening. **If you want to ever see your money, leave my wife out of this. That's the way the money goes. Or else, POP, goes the weasel.** I'm not sure how tough that sounds, but it's the only nursery rhyme I can think of.

After I click send, I note that Mallory has been opening the emails from Dom. Just how much does she know? It's time for me to get back what's mine—Mallory and the money. With no phone in the house, I type a message, hoping she'll check her mail. **I'm home, Mal. I love you. We need to talk. Please come back.**

My stomach rumbles in protest to a missed breakfast and lunch. I take eggs, bacon, cheese, and sliced mushrooms out of the refrigerator, figuring I can throw together an omelet. When I reach down to take out the frying pan from the cupboard, it hits me. I remember exactly what happened Thursday night after the fight.

The question is—what am I going to do about it?

Chapter Fifty-Four

I t's Jake! I read the message again and check the sender to ensure it's coming from our joint email address. He's come back. He loves me. That's all that matters. We can work things out.

"He's home!" I shout. "I just got an email. Can you give me a ride?"

"Why doesn't he call?" Gloria grabs her phone. We all wait for Jake to pick up. "No answer."

I type a message telling Jake I'm on my way, grab Nellie, and ask Steve to help put her in the carrier. Gloria's partway out the door when I stop her.

With my hand on her shoulder, I say, "I just want to talk to Jake on my own first. We need some alone time to sort things out. He has a lot of explaining to do."

For a minute, I think she's not going to back off seeing Jake. "I just want to know that he's okay. But you're right, the two of you have to work through your problems."

I'm about to tell her we don't have any problems, but I bite my lip. "Maybe you can just say hello, then leave us to talk," I concede, meeting her halfway. She *is* his mother.

We pull into our driveway half an hour later, but Jake's nowhere to be seen. Steve hangs back on the front lawn as Gloria and I walk to the entrance. "Jake, honey? I'm here."

Nellie runs out as soon as I open the door to the cat carrier, rubbing against Jake as he saunters into the entranceway carrying a fry pan.

"Hi, honey," he greets me with a stupid grin on his face. "I'm sorry I'm late getting home. I've had a bad few days, a bit of a run-in with some guys I

205

owe money to, but I've got everything worked out. It's going to be okay. If you can forgive me, that is."

Setting the pan down on the bench, he hugs and kisses me like he hasn't seen me for four days.

I know he's very conscious of his mother standing there, listening. Would he have reacted differently if she wasn't with me?

"I'm just glad you're back." Tears stream down from my eyes, my arms enveloping him. "Oh, Jake, I thought you'd gone for good."

"I would never leave you. Not while I'm still breathing. You know that, Mal."

Gloria hugs Jake once we release each other. "What's important is that you're okay. You had us out of our minds with worry."

She glances at the dirty skillet and tilts her head toward it. "Since when do you cook?"

"Mallory's been teaching me lots of things to do with a frying pan, haven't you, hon? I made myself an omelet and was just about to put this in the dishwasher when I heard the door. As long as I have it out, would you like me to make you one, Mal?"

He picks up the cooking utensil and takes a couple of playful swings in the air, telling Gloria that he and I have a lot to talk about. "I'll see you later, Mom."

The sight of Steve standing on our front lawn turns Jake's grin into a scowl. "What the hell is he doing here?"

Pan in hand, he advances, as his dad backs away toward his vehicle. Jake's face reddens by the second as his fury builds.

"No!" Gloria runs after Jake, with me on her heels. "Don't hurt him!"

Jake comes to his senses and lowers the arm holding the skillet. "You need to leave."

He ushers me back into the house, and we watch his parents pull out of our driveway.

"So. You have some explaining to do." His eyes lock on mine, wide as the deep blue sea.

Bits of gooey cheese and egg stuck to the surface of the skillet as he waves it in the air. I'm nauseous, with an image of fresh blood dripping off the bottom of it swimming through my head.

He stares at me for the longest time, and I'm sure he, too, remembers everything. The sight of the frying pan brings forth a vivid memory of our last night together.

Chapter Fifty-Five

As Jake swings the frying pan, he asks a question, but it's not the one I'm expecting. "Where is it?"

"Where's what?"

"You know what. The key."

The muscles in my face relax. He wants the key, that's all. "The key? What key?"

"The key to the safety deposit box, that's what key. Where'd you hide it?"

"I don't know. You're the one who keeps it hidden."

"Don't play dumb with me, Mal. I know you took it. I need the money." The frying pan stops swinging. "It's important. Let's sit down and talk this out, honey."

His left hand, covered in gauze, gestures toward the couch.

"What happened to your hand?" I ask, sitting down.

"Soup can lid. Somebody left it lying on the counter. What happened to your head?"

"Armoire. Somebody put it in the wrong place."

A laugh escapes him, and it makes me think my Jake is back. The moment passes as he puts his hand to his forehead and shakes his head. "All this time... all this time, I've been thinking it was me. That I'd lost control and hit you. That you went to the hospital because of me, that you called the police to press charges. But that's not what happened, is it?"

His eyes search mine for answers, but I look away. "No, it was the armoire. Not you."

"I've had a tough few days, Mal. Thank God it wasn't me. I'd never forgive myself."

He sighs, then tells me where he's been for the last several days. "I woke up at the bottom of a dry well Friday morning."

I gasp. "Friday? A well? What well? How did you get there?" He must be mixed up. A fall into a well can mess with a person's memory.

"Nick and Adam, I assume. They work for Dom. He sent the threatening emails. I owe him a huge gambling debt." He stops to gauge my reaction. "Dom wants his money. Now."

"They threw you into a well? How's that going to get them their money?"

"It was a warning, I guess. I spoke to Dom after I got out." He explains how he climbed out and found a cabin in the woods, then went to see Dom at the casino Friday night. I don't mention anything about the fact that he couldn't have woken up in the well Friday morning because I dropped him off at work Friday afternoon. At least, that's what I told everyone.

"So, where have you been since you saw Dom? Why didn't you let me know you were okay? I've been going out of my mind, Jake, thinking you weren't coming back. Why didn't you come home when you got out of the well? Why didn't you call? How could you let me think you'd left me? How could you let me think you were dead or something? How could you do that to me, Jake? How could you?" My voice rises with each word. My blood pressure must be going through the roof.

"I'm sorry, Mal. I had some things to work through."

"Things to work through? What things?" If he mentions the frying pan incident, what will I say?

"I was going to let you know I was okay, but then I saw you with Craig. It brought back the fight we had Thursday night."

Thursday night. The fight. The day my world ended.

"I was afraid." His brow furrows, as if he's puzzled. "Afraid of losing you to Craig. Afraid I'd hit you. Afraid Craig called the police."

I keep quiet. Maybe he'll keep talking, apologizing.

"I'm sorry. About the fight," he says.

I nod, acknowledging that I know what he's referring to. The baby.

"And I was afraid that if I didn't clear up this shit with Dom, I'd lose you forever. That's why I've been hanging around the house, keeping an eye on you. I didn't want Nick and Adam to find me before I had a chance to pay back Dom some of what I owe and hopefully come to an agreement."

"Hanging around the house? You've been here this whole time?" I don't believe this. He's been spying on me while I've been going out of my mind. "Where?"

"In the shed, the basement. I've been watching out for you, making sure you're safe, waiting for the right moment to talk to you alone. And I've been trying to find the key. So I can pay off Dom and not end up at the bottom of a well again. So you and I can have a fresh start."

He explains everything that's happened the last few days. But I know he's leaving something out. I can tell by the way he watches me, waiting for me to say something.

"You should have let me know you were back. Right away. We're not supposed to keep secrets from each other, Jake. We're supposed to face things together."

"We are, you're right." He runs his right hand through his thick brown hair and stands up. "That's why I need you to work with me, Mallory. We need to get these guys off my back, off *our* backs. You read the emails. You know how dangerous they are. If they can't get to me, they'll come after you. I sent a message to Dom telling him that's not an option. I won't let him hurt you. I'll do anything to keep you safe."

My protective husband. Lucky me. "What are you going to do? I mean, we, what are *we* going to do?"

"You're going to give me the key. I'm going to give Dom the money. Then, I need you to pay off the rest of the debt. I'll pay you back."

"No."

"No?"

"No, I won't pay off your debt. Because I know you, Jake. As soon as it's paid off, you'll gamble some more, and we'll end up in the same boat again."

We've had this argument so many times it makes my head spin every time. Again and again. Same old. I need him to quit. Period. Until he takes a genuine step in that direction, I'm not about to hand over my money.

Not my parents' money, not the money in the safe that's owed to me and Gloria, not the hard-earned money I use to pay the mortgage and bills. I could mention that he's inherited his grandfather's money, but first, I need a commitment from him. A promise that he'll never gamble again. I don't believe he's ready to make that promise and follow through, and I tell him so.

"Do you have any idea what these guys will do to us if we don't pay up?" His jaw is set, his eyes are cold, and his tone is threatening.

"That's your problem," I state, hanging tough. "Take care of it."

"Hand over the key, Mallory. Or else."

"Or else what?" I probably shouldn't provoke him, but I can't help myself. He picks up the frying pan and blocks my escape. "I think you know."

Chapter Fifty-Six

"The next time you try to kill someone, Mal, you really should check to make sure they're dead before disposing of the body."

"I...I.... What are you talking about?"

I know exactly what he's talking about. As soon as I entered our home and saw him with the frying pan, I knew what happened was real and not something I could pretend away.

"Give me the key, or everyone's going to know what I'm talking about."

"Don't threaten me. I'm tired of your abuse."

"*My* abuse? Jeezus, Mal. I've never laid a hand on you. But, you? You fuckin' tried to kill me with a frying pan."

The events of Thursday night run through my mind.

* * *

Craig left after Jake accused him of sleeping with me and lost the fistfight. What happened next might not have happened if I'd kept quiet.

"Really, Jake?" I'd said. "You come home drunk, swearing and calling me names? Then you make crazy accusations and hit your best friend? The very day you find out you're going to be a father, you become your dad. Our baby deserves better than this."

"Our baby?" He raised his hand as I picked up the frying pan I'd left sitting on the stove, too distraught from our fight that morning to put it away. "How many guys have you been sleeping with, Mal? Craig. Brad. Who else?" He pushed me against the table with one hand, the other still in the air, ready to strike. "We're getting rid of it. Tomorrow. Bye-bye, baby."

As he lowered the flat of his palm, I raised and lowered my skillet, bonking his head. Jake fell down and broke his crown. I thought he was dead. The sight of his blood on the bottom of the pan brought on the heaves and the tea I'd had for supper mixed with the red liquid. Jake lay motionless as I screamed for him to get up.

I picked up my phone to call Emergency. I even punched in the first two numbers. Then I thought of the baby. I couldn't have our baby born in prison. I made a call for help, but it wasn't for an ambulance.

* * *

"What I don't understand," Jake says now, gripping the attempted murder weapon, "is how I ended up in the well. I didn't go willingly. Someone had to help you. Craig?"

"There was no one else. Just me. It was an accident."

"The frying pan accidentally flew out of your hand? And by accident, you threw me down a well?" Jake enunciates each word, his voice eerily calm.

"You were going to hit me!" I shriek. "I just put up my hand to stop you. I didn't mean to hurt you."

It's the truth. I never meant to kill my baby's father. In that moment of fear and anger, I reacted without thinking. "But it just happened. And then...." My arms fold around my waist, protecting our child from this domestic violence. Our home is supposed to be a safe place. "And then... when you didn't move, I panicked. I didn't want to go to jail."

"So you had Craig throw me down a well?"

"No! Craig doesn't know anything about this."

"Then who? You didn't drag me into the well yourself. How'd you get me there?" His quiet tone prompts me to back away.

"You'd...be surprised...what I can do...when I need to." My blubbering belies my tough girl act.

Jake hands me the box of tissues. After a few good nose blows, I give him the explanation he deserves. "I was scared, for me and the baby. I drove the car up to the porch and dragged you into the trunk. Then I drove to the woods and dumped you by the side of the road. I thought maybe you'd sober up by morning and hitch a ride home. When you didn't come back, I was out of my mind with worry. I thought maybe you'd left me or you were dead…You must have fallen down the well. I have no idea how you got there, I swear. I'm just relieved you found a way to get out."

Jake forces me to look at him, his hand holding my chin, his voice showing none of the fury he must be fighting. "You dragged me to the car? I don't think so, Mal. You and Craig tried to kill me. I'm calling the police."

"No! No police! Please!" I slide to the floor, wrapping my arms around his legs.

"You tried to *kill* me. Then you disposed of my body."

It sounds worse than it is. "I didn't try to kill you. And I… I love you, Jake."

"I know you do, Mal. I love you, too."

"Please…don't call…the police." My body shakes as I hyperventilate. *Breathe, just breathe.*

I'm terrified at the thought of prison and petrified I'll lose my baby. "I'm pregnant. I don't want to go to jail. Please, Jake."

"I'm not going to call the police." He extends his hand to help me off the floor.

"You're not?"

"No, but you're going to give me that key. Where is it?"

My loving husband is blackmailing me. Through my sobs, I point to our wedding photo. He sets down the frying pan on the coffee table and walks to the bookcase. "Where?"

"I hid it behind the picture frame."

The frame holds our happiest moment, and it holds the key to Jake's money problems. As soon as he removes it from the backing, he's up the stairs in a flash. In a couple of minutes, he stands in front of me, his face red with fury, his voice menacing. "What did you do with it, Mal? Where's the money?"

He leaves me no choice. "I'll show you." I lead him outside and grab the shovel leaning next to the shed.

Chapter Fifty-Seven

"What are you doing with the shovel, Mallory?" Jake backs away. So, this is what our marriage has come to. When did my husband begin to lose trust in me?

"It's buried. Beside the red rose bushes." I point to the location and hand over the shovel. And run.

"Mallory!"

Back in the house, I lock the door and arm myself with the frying pan in case he comes after me with the shovel. From the kitchen window, his shadow digs as dusk falls over the expanse of lawn and flower gardens.

The doorbell rings. I approach the front door, frying pan in hand.

Nick and Adam. Judging from their tight lips and furrowed brows, they're not here for a friendly catch-up time with Jake. I need to get them off our property before they discover Jake digging up a small fortune.

"Jake's not here." I open the door a crack, bracing it with my body. "He's not coming back. He left me for another woman."

"Sorry to hear that, lady." The lack of sympathy in Nick's voice doesn't match his words. "Nice looking girl like you dumped." Nodding to Adam, he shrugs. "Whatever."

The door flies open and I'm manhandled by his big oaf friend.

"Get your hands off me!" I scream, swinging the frying pan while backing into the hallway. But these guys are neither drunk nor unsuspecting. It flies out of my hand as they duct tape my mouth, hands, and feet. The ease with which they do this tells me: a) they're no friends of Jake's, b) this isn't the first time they've done this, and c) I'm in a lot of trouble.

Adam hoists me over his shoulder like a sack of potatoes and hauls me to the trunk of the black sedan. As the lid slams, panic swells, and I can't breathe. Literally. I can't get air. With my mouth duct taped, I suck oxygen through my nose, but my breaths come quick and shallow, and my heart is about to explode.

Curled up in a fetal position, I think of our baby. He needs me to survive. In the pitch dark, I try to focus. Feel my fingers. They're still all there. Listen to the sound of the car engine. Close my eyes. Breathe in, breathe out. Concentrate on the car turning left off our driveway, right at the corner of our road, picking up speed. Slow down the breathing. Try to stay conscious.

Think about the good things. Jake's back, and he loves me. We're having a baby. I know he'll come around eventually and accept that. I've made mistakes, and so has he, but we'll work through it together. He'll forgive me for bopping him with the frying pan in a moment of panic. But will he forgive me for Craig?

* * *

My 28th birthday six weeks ago didn't go quite as I'd planned. I wanted a quiet night at home with Jake. But he booked a fancy dinner at an expensive restaurant. And he invited our best friends along to celebrate. So really, it was Jake's fault.

"Wear that little black strapless dress," Jake had said. "And your heels. It's a special occasion. I want to show off my sexy young wife." He watched me dress, straighten my hair, put on makeup, then stood back to appraise me. "Perfect. I'm a lucky guy."

Jake loves to take me out, parading his wife on his arm. But when he's not with me, he expects me to tone down the makeup and dress conservatively. That's not a problem because the only place I go on my own is to school and the local grocery store. But that Saturday night, I went all out to doll myself up, as Jake would call it. I wanted him to be proud of me. Especially since I had something important to tell him.

Craig picked us up, and we drove to the city, where we stopped at Vicky's before going to Michael's Steakhouse. I felt almost as glamorous as Vicky looked. It's hard not to be jealous of your best friend when she's drop-dead gorgeous. Especially when you know your husband has slept with her. Especially when you wonder if you were his second choice after she broke up with him. Maybe that's why I compromised my marriage.

We enjoyed the prime rib while we talked about work and what we'd been up to lately. Jake ordered an expensive bottle of wine. I had the feeling he was trying to impress our friends with the supposed success of our married life.

"We've done quite a few renos on the house. They don't come cheap, but whatever my beautiful wife wants, my wife gets." He gave me a wink.

"The house is looking good." Craig directed his smile at me. "You know how to put things together, Mallory. You should drop by my place, give me a few pointers."

I met his deep brown eyes, then looked away when Jake squeezed my hand.

"Speaking of looking good, you're looking amazing, Vick. Anyone in particular responsible for that glow?" Jake asked.

I had decided one glass of wine for the night wouldn't hurt, but that quickly turned into two when my husband's attention was diverted by his ex.

"Well, actually, there is someone. I'm hoping it'll work out." Vicky turned to Craig. "What about you, Craig? Any girl lucky enough to get you to think about settling down?"

Craig laughed and said he was happy being single for now. "Maybe someday. I'm not ready for the old ball and chain just yet."

"You don't know what you're missing. Getting married is the best thing that ever happened to me." Jake kissed me in a way that should have been reserved for a more private moment. "I've got everything I ever wanted."

When our waiter brought a small birthday cake for dessert, Jake, Craig, and Vicky sang 'Happy Birthday' while I was instructed to make a wish and blow out the candles. My wish was that Jake and I would soon be a happy little family of three, but I couldn't tell them that. If you tell your wish, it doesn't come true.

If the evening had ended there, Jake and I would have gone home and made love, and maybe everything would have worked out perfectly. But instead, Jake insisted we go out dancing. "The night's young. Let's head to The Starlight. I want to get my beautiful wife out on the dance floor."

He nuzzled my neck and whispered in my ear how sexy I was. I guess I was supposed to be flattered, but all I wanted was to go home.

To keep my husband happy, I said, "Sounds like fun. And since we're all here and dressed for it, let's go party!"

Vicky seconded my party idea, and half an hour later, we were at the nightclub, under the ceiling of stars, the four of us slow dancing to the country and western band. When the music switched to a faster tempo, we sat it out. Jake ordered drinks before I could say I'd had enough. The Singapore Sling sat untouched in front of me, and when Jake and Craig excused themselves to go to the men's room, I asked our waiter to exchange it for a non-alcoholic version. Vicky raised her eyebrows, grabbed my drink before it could be taken away, saying, "If you don't want it, I'll take it."

When the waiter left, Vicky asked, "What's going on? Giving up drinking all of a sudden?"

"I feel a migraine coming on. Probably the loud music. I don't want to say anything to Jake and ruin the night for everybody. I'll be fine. I took a couple of pills."

"You're sure? We can call it an early night."

"It's not that bad." Out of the corner of my eye, I spotted the guys heading our way. "Let's just have fun."

I steered Jake back to the floor for a couple of fast dances. When we returned to our table, Vicky took me by the arm, saying Craig wasn't up for the fast pace, and the two of us took over the floor, giggling and gyrating in our tight dresses. Plenty of eyes followed us, including Jake's and Craig's.

Jake came to claim me when the music segued back into slow mode, and Vicky, left standing on her own, grabbed hold of some other guy passing by.

"You look like you're having a good time," Jake said, nibbling my ear. "Can't wait to get home and rip that dress off you."

And it would have worked out perfectly if we'd gone home right then.

"I think we're going to call it a night," Jake said when we returned to the table where Craig sat, his eyes glued to Vicky, who'd gone to another table with her new dance partner. "It's getting late."

"It's only 11," Craig noted, his hand on his half-full glass. "Lots of time yet to have fun. Unless you're too old and married for it." He downed the rest of his drink, eyes still on Vicky.

She must have felt Craig staring because she came back, slid into the booth next to him, and slung her arm over his shoulder. "How about we go to the Karaoke Bar? Craig can entertain us."

Craig was the one with the voice. That's what I'd been told, but I'd never actually heard him sing. "I'd love to hear you, Craig," I said. "Vicky says you're really good."

"No, no…she's exaggerating. I like to sing, but I think I'm best confined to the shower," he laughed.

"He's being modest," Vicky said. "Come on, Craig. Do it for Mallory. For her birthday."

"Yes, Craig. Do it for me."

I shouldn't have asked. Craig grinned at me and said if that's what I wanted for my birthday, then that's exactly what he'd give me. He turned to Jake and added, "If that's okay with you, buddy."

Jake narrowed his eyes at Craig, then laughed. "Whatever Mallory wants, Mallory gets."

The Karaoke Lounge was packed when we got there. Vicky and Craig chose a song from the playlist and submitted it to the DJ. As we listened to the other participants, Vicky and Jake had a couple more drinks. Craig said he wanted to stay sober so he wouldn't fall off the stage. I said I was on a high already, having the night of my life.

Vicky was right. Craig has a great voice. He sang 'Jessie's Girl,' belting out the words about how he wished he had his best friend's girl. Vicky and I swayed to the music while Jake downed another drink. When Craig motioned for us to come onstage, the four of us finished the show to a round of applause and nearly fell over each other, giggling, on our way back to the table.

We didn't stop there, though. Vicky knew a spot nearby that had an all-night rooftop bar. "You've got to see it, Mallory. The view, the sky, it's beautiful. So romantic."

It was busy, even that late. As we pushed through the crowd, searching for a table, someone shouted, "Hey Jake! Over here!"

"Terry!" Jake led us to a booth occupied by a man and a woman. "Hey, man! It's been a while!" Jake hadn't seen his best friend from high school for months.

"Vicky? Wow! How long has it been?" Terry's wife, Becky, had been in the same year at high school as Vicky and I, but I wasn't much of a social butterfly back then. "Oh, and you're Jake's wife, um, Melanie, right?"

"Mallory. My wife, Mallory," Jake corrected her. "And I don't know if you guys remember Craig? He was a couple years ahead of us."

"Sorry, I don't recall…" Terry said, "That was such a long time ago. What a coincidence meeting you here tonight. Have a seat."

The four of us squished into the booth with them, me between Jake and Craig, Vicky sitting next to Becky and across from Craig.

"We don't get out much." Becky's voice competed with the babel and the beat of pop music. "We're home visiting our parents for a week's holidays, and Mom offered to watch the kids so we could have a night out on the town."

"Reliving our youth, like the good old days." Terry tried to retract his words when Becky nudged him. "Not that these aren't good days. They're the best. You should try having kids, you guys. We've never been happier."

"Some day," Jake promised. "But I'm way ahead of my buddy, Craig. He hasn't even got a steady girl yet. Still playing the field."

"You lucky dog."

Terry and Jake gave Craig a wistful look, as if they'd forgotten their wives sat next to them. Becky punched her husband's arm, and I emitted a nervous chuckle, while Vicky stared down at her hands. Next to me, Craig shifted uncomfortably. Terry signaled for the server once more, and we toasted to 'the good old days of high school.'

And so, we ended up in the open air, the six of us, talking, listening to music, dancing, and drinking. Except, I let my drink sit. Jake and I danced, kissed, and generally stumbled around the dance floor. Vicky managed to convince Craig to get up and shake his booty after he downed one more drink. We switched partners at some point, and when the tempo changed to a slow love song, Jake's arms encircled Vicky's bare lower back. I moved in closer to Craig. Just a group of friends, laughing and having the time of our lives.

A sudden rush of nausea hit me, and I slapped a hand over my mouth as I indicated I wanted to sit down. Craig led me to the table.

Jake noticed and followed us. "Are you okay, honey? Did you have too much to drink?"

"I don't feel so good. My head hurts."

I felt them hovering over me, a cold, wet napkin against my forehead, the glass of water brought to my lips. "Mallory?" Jake's voice sounded distant. "I think we'd better get you home."

"No, I'm okay. It's just a bit of a headache. Let's not spoil the night because of it. You and Terry have lots of catching up to do. Don't worry about me."

Craig offered a solution to make everybody happy. "Why don't I take Mallory home while you two stay and visit with your friends? It wouldn't hurt for you to get some coffee into you, either, sober up a bit. I've only had a few drinks. I'm good to drive and can be back in an hour to pick you up."

"I don't know…" Jake protested.

But I stopped him. "I wouldn't forgive myself if you missed out on seeing your friend just because of my stupid little headache."

"You're sure?"

"Yes, I'm sure. I'll just go home with Craig."

Vicky sidled up to Jake and asked if the party was over.

Craig slapped Jake on the back. "You guys stay with your friends. I'll be back in no time. I'll text when I'm ready to head out from your place."

Jake hesitated, then said, "Okay, if you're sure, Mal." He kissed me, and said, "I'll see you in a couple of hours. Get some rest."

Craig guided me to the elevator.

"I'm going to be...." I said as the elevator moved, "sick." Along with the words, the contents of my stomach spilled out onto the elevator floor. "Oh no, no, no—"

"It's okay," Craig said. "Wait right here." He had me sit in the lobby while he told the clerk at the desk about the mess in the elevator.

During the ride home, I thought about Jake and Vicky together at the bar.

I recall Craig giving me a glass of water and crackers. My dress was unzipped, and he led me to the ensuite bathroom. As he tucked me into bed, said goodnight, and was about to leave, I wrapped my arms around his neck.

"Stay with me," I whispered. I kissed him, remembering Jake's hand on Vicky's naked back, imagining his lips there.

"No, Mallory," he said. "We can't." Then he kissed me back.

The next morning, I woke up next to Jake with memories of being in bed with Craig. The knowledge that I'd cheated on my husband brought on another round of nausea. I convinced myself I'd either dreamt it or it was Jake I had sex with the previous night.

"Ohhh...my head," I said as Jake stirred beside me. "What happened last night?"

"You had a little too much, Mal. That's okay. It happens. We all overdid it."

We didn't talk about it anymore. But I knew I'd betrayed my husband. And I had the feeling he knew it, too.

When I emptied out the laundry hamper that afternoon, I understood why Jake didn't question what might have happened between Craig and me. His white button-down shirt, the one he wore the previous night, had lipstick on the collar. Not my shade. Ruby Red.

* * *

As the car slows down now, I think about the baby growing inside me. Please, let her be safe. Or him. Please. The trunk opens, and I'm lifted out and carried down a flight of stairs. The near darkness outside contrasts with the bright fluorescent lights that assault my eyes as we enter the back of the building and descend to the lower level. Nick knocks on a door at the end of a hallway, and Adam carries me through and deposits me on a chair.

A man sits behind a massive desk. He's probably around 40, attractive, with dark hair and stubble on his chin. After giving me a good look over, he says, "Take it off."

Nick removes the duct tape from my mouth, hands, and legs. Bolting out of the chair, I run to the locked door, screaming.

"Sit down," the man commands. "No one's going to hear you."

Adam escorts me back to the chair, kicking and screaming. The roll of duct tape materializes again, causing me to go silent. "I'll be quiet," I promise, sitting as still as I can. "Please, don't."

The man waves away Adam and the duct tape. "I'm Dom, a business acquaintance of your husband's. Mallory, is it?"

I nod.

"It's nice to meet you. What happened to your head?"

My hand touches the gauze I haven't bothered to remove. "A fight. You should see the other guy."

"Did you guys do this? You weren't supposed to hurt her." He stands, leans over, with his hands spread out on the desktop.

"She was like this when we found her," Nick explains. "We didn't lay a hand on her."

"She, on the other hand, threatened us and took a few good swings in our direction," Adam adds.

Dom grins. "I have heard your weapon of choice is a bat."

"That and a frying pan," I say, my tough guy act not fooling anyone.

He roars with laughter. "I want you to understand. I don't like to involve my clients' families, but I've got a bit of a problem here, and I'm thinking you might be able to help."

I'm not sure how to respond to that.

"Jake hasn't been keeping up with his payments on the loans I've been generous enough to extend, with him being such a good customer at the casino. I've been sending him late payment reminders, and he's ignoring them. I'm sure you can see the dilemma this poses for me."

"How much?" I sputter.

"With interest, we're closing in on a hundred grand. Growing by the minute, I might add. So, you see, the sooner he shows his face, the quicker we can stop the interest and fees from accumulating. It's in his best interest to come forward and pay his debt." Dom sits and places his elbows on the desk, hands clasped together. "Since he's too much of a coward to come around and deal with this himself, I wonder if he might be open to discussing payment terms when he finds out we're holding his lovely wife as collateral."

"Are you... going to... cut my fingers off?" I swallow the big lump in my throat.

Another roar of laughter. "Whatever gave you that idea?" Giving me an admiring look, he states, "A beautiful woman like you? It would be a real shame to damage the goods."

I'm about to offer to pay off the debt myself, but Dom has more to add. "I've sent a message to Jake, letting him know you'll be my guest until he can make arrangements for payment."

He walks up to me, looks down, and comments, "So, I guess we'll find out just how much Jake loves you." As Dom runs his fingers through my blond waves, I recoil from his touch. "I would think a woman like you would be worth a lot. To her husband."

He smiles, but it doesn't reach his cold blue eyes. Sweat beads on my forehead.

The ringing of a phone takes his attention from me. Dom pulls the cell out of his pocket to take the call. "Bring him down."

Turning to me, he raises his eyebrows and comments, "That was fast. Looks like you've got a husband who gives a damn about you. He's already here."

A few minutes later, Jake is brought into the room, an escort on either side of him. He's filthy, his clothes caked in mud, hands and face smeared with dirt, and the smell of sheep manure emanating from him. My knight in shining armor. He sets the chocolate box he dug up from the flower bed on Dom's desk and drops to his knees on the floor in front me, checking my fingers, asking if I'm okay. I sink to his level and put my arms around him, assuring him I'm fine. As he cups my face in his filthy hands, kissing my forehead, my body heaves, and I can't hold back the sobs any longer.

"What happened to you? You look like you're back from the dead," Dom remarks, then focuses on the box full of bills. "This is such a touching little family reunion. I'm glad to see it all worked out."

Jake and I sit on the floor, waiting for Dom to count the money.

"Forty-two thousand. Not bad. You know this unpleasantness could have been avoided if you'd just made your payments. Now, how do I know you're not going to renege on our agreement in the future? I'm afraid I'm going to need collateral this time, Jake. In case you end up on another losing streak. What guarantee do I have that you'll keep up with your payments?" Dom closes the box and towers over the two of us. "What have you got, besides your lovely wife?"

"There won't be any more losing streaks," Jake says.

Dom raises his eyebrows.

"I'll sign something, whatever you want. You can garnish my wages. Take my car, my house. I don't care. Take it all. Just leave my wife out of this."

Dom nods. "I can work with that. Let me get my lawyers to draw something up. In the meantime, your wife will be staying here as our guest. I'll contact you when the paperwork is ready." He indicates it's time for Jake to leave.

As Jake is pulled to his feet, he shrugs off Adam. "No. No deal. Let her go. Take me. Do whatever you want to me, but leave her out of it. This has nothing to do with Mallory. You'll get everything I owe you. But I do have another condition. I want you to bar me from the casino. No more gambling."

Dom strokes his stubble as he considers his next course of action. After a couple of minutes, he speaks. "What makes you think *you're* in a position to set forth conditions?"

"I don't think... I just want to settle things up," Jake answers, lifting me to my feet and easing me back onto the chair. "We're expecting a baby. I want a fresh start. Come on, Dom, please. I'll sell my car. I'll make the payments.

No more gambling."

Jake turns to me. "Honest, Mal, I'll get help. Go to meetings, whatever you want me to do."

"You're pregnant?" Dom points to my stomach. "I've got a couple of little ones myself."

He leans against his desk, tells Nick and Adam to wait outside the door, then sits on the edge of his desk, with one leg on and one off. "You're lucky I'm such a nice, understanding guy. I'm going to give you a break here, Jake, considering you're a family man now. I *will* garnish your wages, make sure you're barred from here and every other casino within the area, and you and your lovely wife can leave now. But just so you understand, *I* make the conditions, Jake. *I* choose whether to let you off the hook. And if for some reason I don't get paid on time and in full, I won't be so generous the next time I send my guys to look for you."

"I can pay." The words come out of my mouth. "I have the money."

"No, Mallory. Not your parents' money. It's my problem, like you said, and I have to deal with it." Jake tells Dom he'll make arrangements to take money out of his paycheck and sign his car over as collateral first thing in the morning.

Dom slaps Jake on the back, saying, "You've impressed me today. You're more of a man than I thought you were, taking responsibility for your actions. You're a lucky man to have a woman like this." Dom smiles at me and adds, "But don't push your luck, Jakey boy."

Dom opens the door and tells Nick to make sure we get out of the building safely. As Jake pulls away from the casino, I turn to him and expose one of the secrets he still doesn't know.

Chapter Fifty-Eight

"You have more than enough money to pay back Dom yourself and get him off your back permanently."

"What? What are you talking about, Mal?"

"Your grandfather left you quite a bit."

"I barely saw him the last dozen years or so. I just showed up at the funeral out of respect. Why would he leave me his money?"

It's understandable Jake would question his inheritance. He blamed his grandfather for taking his dad in as much as he blamed his dad for leaving his family, in spite of the fact that Jake forced him to leave.

"Well, he didn't directly. But your *dad* inherited it, and he wants to share it with you and John."

As Jake concentrates on the road, the muscles around his mouth twitch. I tell him what happened to his dad the last twelve years. "I really think you should talk to him. Give him a second chance."

"I don't want anything to do with that man. You had no right to go see him without telling me."

We continue home in silence. When he parks in the driveway, I try again. "Everyone deserves a second chance, Jake."

I knew he would be hard to convince, but I honestly thought the money would be a good incentive to let bygones be bygones.

"Not him. He doesn't." He puts his arm around my waist as he walks me to the front door of our home. "We'll get through this, the two of us."

"Three," I remind him, but he ignores my comment.

Jake trudges up the stairs, and I follow, hoping to continue our conversa-

227

tion. "We need to talk."

"I'm just tired, Mal. I need a shower and bed."

I'd almost prefer a fight to the avoidance of our problems, but I'm afraid if I goad him into a discussion, we'll both say and do things we'll regret. As much as I hate to tiptoe around him, the last thing I want is a recurrence of the events that led to this.

Leaving him alone, I go downstairs and begin the taxing job of letting everyone know Jake is home, safe and sound. I call the police to explain he's back. They were right. It was just a little argument between husband and wife, and he needed time to cool off.

Jake came home. All's good. The phone rings immediately after I send the text. Craig's first words convey his relief. "He's back? So he's okay? Thank God!"

"He's fine. You were right. He had a run-in with some guys he owes money. It's all straightened out."

"What about our fight? Did he mention that?"

"We haven't talked about it yet. I'll call you later. I have other calls to make."

When I contact Vicky, she expels enough air that I know she's been holding her breath waiting for this news, just as I have. "Oh, wow! I'm so relieved. Thank goodness! I've been going nuts worrying."

Then she suggests I should get rid of him. "But you're not taking him back? You know he'll just screw around again if he gets away with it that easily."

I assure Vicky he wasn't with another woman. "It had nothing to do with us and our marriage."

I work my way through the long list of people needing to be notified, leaving Brad till the end. Before making that call, I check on Jake. The snoring assails my ears before I reach the top of the stairs. Downstairs, I lock myself in the back bathroom. If there's one conversation I don't want Jake to walk in on, it's this one.

Brad answers on the second ring, sounding groggy. "Mallory? Are you okay? It's after midnight."

"Yes, I'm fine. I just wanted to let you know Jake's back."

"Jake? He's back? When? How?" It sounds like he's sitting up, fully awake now.

I explain that Jake thought he'd been roughed up by some goons to whom he owed money, and they threw him down a well as a warning to pay up. I leave out the part about me being kidnapped as collateral.

"That's what he thinks happened?" He exhales, whooshing into my ear. "Well, that's lucky."

"Not quite. When he saw the frying pan, he remembered I hit him. And now he thinks Craig helped drag him into the well. I'm trying to convince him *I* dragged him out of the house and dumped him off to sober up."

"And he believes you? Now what? What's he going to do?"

"I don't know."

Brad's quiet on his end. I chew my fingernails, lost in the memory of Thursday night.

* * *

When I slugged Jake with the skillet, he dropped to the floor like a sack of potatoes, bleeding on the new hardwood. I panicked, thinking that I'd killed him and he was going to be really upset if I didn't clean up the bloody mess. Somehow, I managed to call Brad. He ran through the unlocked front door as I knelt next to Jake, trying to wake him, the blood-smeared skillet evidence of my crime.

But he *wouldn't* wake up. I wailed, "Is he...is he...he's not dead, is he? Oh, my God, he's dead, isn't he? Jake, Jake, I'm so sorry. I love you. Wake up, Jake."

"It's okay." Brad knelt next to me, checking Jake's vital signs. "He's just knocked out. Head wounds bleed a lot. And he's drunk as a skunk. But maybe we should call an ambulance." Brad wrapped a kitchen towel around Jake's head.

"No. Oh no, no, no...Jake, please wake up."

Brad touched my bruised arms. "What happened, Mallory? Did he hurt you? Should I call the police?"

"We had a fight."

"Self-defense isn't a crime, Mallory. He'll be the one charged." He pulled out his phone. "If he hit you…"

"No! No police!" The phone smacked the floor as I struck it out of his hand. "Just help him. Please!"

His eyes widened. "I was going to call for an ambulance."

"What if he tells them I tried to kill him? What if they believe him? I don't want to go to jail." My arms wrapped around my knees, I rocked back and forth. "Is he going to be okay? Please be okay." One hand stroked Jake's bloody forehead, as I begged him to open his blue-green eyes.

Brad looked from his phone to me as though he wasn't sure he should make the call. "I'll handle it. But first, let's take care of you. You need to settle down. Come with me, Mallory."

He helped me upstairs to bed. From the ensuite bathroom, he brought a glass of water and a couple of pills. "Take these. They'll calm you."

After swallowing, I realized I shouldn't have taken them. But it was too late. As I drifted off to sleep, Brad said, "None of this happened. Do you understand me, Mallory? I need you to forget about it. Everything will be fine."

The last thing I heard Brad say was, "I'll call you tomorrow. Don't worry about Jake. I'll take care of him."

When I woke up Friday morning with a fuzzy head, Jake wasn't in bed. He wasn't in the kitchen. Neither was the blood. The frying pan sat in the cupboard, all clean. *Thank God. It was a nightmare.* From room to room, I walked, searching for him.

My phone rang. "Mallory? Are you okay?"

"I'm fine, but I can't find Jake."

After an extended silence, Brad reminded me what happened. "The two of you had a fight last night. You didn't want to involve the police. I thought you needed some time apart. Don't worry. Everything's going to be fine."

"Where is he, Brad? Is he alive?" My voice shook, as did my hands.

"He'll be sleeping it off or hitching a ride. I left him in the woods, not far from the road, figured it would sober him up and give him a chance to think things over. Keep him away from you till he simmered down."

"He's okay? Not dead?"

"He was starting to wake up. He'll likely have a concussion, but he was very much alive. Listen, Mallory, I've been thinking. In most cases of domestic abuse, it's the husband that gets blamed. But if Jake decides to press charges, it could be your word against his. He's the one with the head injury. And it's going to look strange that you didn't want to call the police. Is there something you're not telling me?"

The illegal drugs in the cornfield. The proceeds from the grow-op in the ground. The money my husband owes the loan shark. Money that I stole and buried in the ground. The night I slept with Craig. The baby whose father I tricked into getting pregnant. The fist-fight with his best friend. Jake's fear that he could have inherited his father's abusive nature. The crack as I brought down the frying pan on his head….

"No, there's nothing. I just don't want to involve the police in our private business."

"Let me know when Jake comes home. Maybe he won't remember, given the head injury and the booze. But if he causes more trouble, call me."

When it was nearly time for Jake to go to work, and he still hadn't returned, I called Brad back.

"He hasn't come home. What if he's dead?" I knew I had killed him. And Brad was covering for me.

Brad remained silent, and I thought we'd lost our connection. When he spoke, he instructed me to remain calm and pretend everything was normal. "We need to stall for now. Listen carefully. Have Jake go to work as usual, but extra early, when there's no activity in the parking lot. Put his backpack on the front seat of the Honda and drape your shirt and a hoodie over the back of the seat so it looks like you're on the passenger side. Wear his shirt over your own and a ball cap with your hair tucked in. Drive to work, like you and Jake do every Friday. Anyone who glances at your car passing by will think he's driving. In the parking lot, make sure no one sees you, duck down, take off the cap and shirt, throw all the stuff in the back seat, and drive off. Make it look like Jake went to work and took off from there. When you pick him up at the end of the day, act surprised he's not there. Make sure someone sees you. It's important you do that. You need an alibi, just in case he doesn't come home. And don't mention my involvement to anyone. Do you understand what I'm telling you, Mallory?"

"Yes, yes, I think so. Drive Jake to work like normal. Wear his clothes."

I followed Brad's instructions and even convinced myself that I was dropping off Jake as usual. I couldn't face the reality of what I had done to him. So I pretended. Just like I've pretended so many times before. My marriage is perfect. Jake is perfect. We're the perfect couple.

By the time I sat in the parking lot Friday night, I almost believed he would be there. That he'd picked himself off from the side of the road where Brad dumped him and went to work as though nothing had happened. I hoped he'd be there. I truly did.

* * *

Brad finally breaks the silence between us. "Well, I'm glad he's back. Glad he's okay. And I hope it all works out for you, Mallory. But the question is: Do you really *want* him back? Or do you want him back at the bottom of the well?"

Chapter Fifty-Nine

"Of course, I want him back. He's my husband. I love him."
I wonder whether he expected another answer. If I gave Brad the impression I would be free to be with him if Jake was out of my life, I need to make my feelings clearer.

"So now what? If he finds out I'm connected to his disappearance, the police are going to question me. I could be an accessory."

"I'm not going to involve you, Brad. I was the one who asked you for help. I told Jake I didn't mean to hurt him, that I was defending myself. That I dragged him into the trunk of the car and dropped him off by a wooded area to let him sober up and cool down. I'm going to stick to that story."

I won't point the finger at Brad because it points back at me. I could be charged with attempted murder. So, it's best to forget the truth. "Jake and I just had a little domestic dispute. I'm sure this sort of thing happens with couples all the time."

"Okay, Mallory. You take care of yourself. But I want you to know that if you ever need anything, anything at all, I'm here for you."

"Thanks, Brad. You're a good friend."

All the loose ends are tied up. Except for one.

"I've been waiting for you to call back," Craig says after the first ring. "I didn't want to say anything before, not while you were so worried about Jake being gone. But now that he's back, we need to talk. Can you meet me somewhere?"

"Whatever it is, Craig, you can tell me over the phone." I really don't want to have this conversation face-to-face.

Craig hesitates. "Is...is the baby mine?"

"No. It's Jake's baby."

"You're sure?"

"Positive."

"Because if it's mine, I'll take responsibility. You must know how much I care about you. But I hate myself for what I've done to Jake. Taking advantage of you like that—I'm ashamed of myself. I hope you can forgive me."

"It's not your fault." I recall enough to know I was the one who instigated what happened between us. "I kissed *you*. Don't blame yourself. I think I was just jealous of Vicky. She had Jake, and she had you. And seeing them together having fun... I just thought how easily she could take him away from me if she wanted to."

"Jake loves you, Mallory. Not Vicky."

"I know. I just get so insecure sometimes."

"Trust me, you have nothing to be insecure about."

There's silence for the longest time. I'm not sure what else to say. "You won't tell him?"

"No. Will you?"

"No."

Another long silence, neither of us quite ready to hang up. "That's good, it's for the best," he finally says. "If no one knows, no one gets hurt. I've always had a bit of a crush on you, Mallory. Not that it's any excuse for my behavior."

"I love Jake."

"I know. And he loves you. I was going to say I've always had a crush on you, but I understand now that's all it ever was. It could never be more than that. Jake's my best friend. And I think I've finally found the right woman for me. Someone I love enough to spend the rest of my life with."

My jaw drops, and I'm glad this conversation is taking place over the phone where he can't see my reaction. All this time, I thought he was secretly in love with me.

"I'd better get to bed. Jake's waiting for me."

"You're sure? About the baby?"

"Yes, it's Jake's."

"Well, in that case, I'm happy for both of you. Jake will be a great dad, he just doesn't realize it yet. I want you to know you can always count on me. Just let me know what you need, and I'll be there."

"You're a good friend, Craig." I end the call, hoping Craig will never again mention what happened between us. My marriage is too important to put at risk over a stupid mistake.

Chapter Sixty

"We need to talk." At eight in the morning, Jake is snoring when I nudge him. "Wake up, Jake. It's important."

He grunts and rolls over, moving farther away. "Need to sleep."

A few more minutes of sleep will be good for him and give me a chance to call his boss. The last thing Jake needs is to lose his job.

Down in the kitchen, I brew a pot of coffee and make toast, then make the call.

"Hello, Bob. It's Mallory Shelton, Jake's wife." When Bob asks if there's news about Jake, I tell him he's back. "He's had a rough time the last few days. Some guys mugged him, beat him up, and threw him down a well. It's a miracle he survived and managed to get out. He could use a few days to recuperate."

"Oh, wow! That's awful. Of course, whatever Jake needs. Glad to hear he's okay. Tell him not to worry about coming in till next week."

As I end the call, the aroma of coffee fills the kitchen. I bring a tray upstairs and set it on the dresser while I try once more to wake Jake. "Honey, I brought you toast and coffee." My gentle shoulder shaking causes him to open his eyes. "Bob says you can take the rest of the week off."

"Mallory? Is that you? Thank God." His arms wrap around me, and he pulls me down with him until we're lying side by side. "I thought I'd never see you again."

His lips find mine, and he slowly undoes the buttons of my nightie. "I've missed you, honey." His kisses trail along my neck and down the length of my body. Gently, asking me if it's okay with the baby. Smiling, when I tell him it's perfectly fine.

By the time he's ready for coffee, it's lukewarm. "I'll get you another cup. And some fresh toast."

"No, it's good the way it is, Mal. Just stay with me."

We eat our cold toast with jam and drink our lukewarm coffee, sitting up side by side on the bed, the tray between us. And we talk.

"How did you know I was at the casino?"

"I saw them. When I was digging up the money. I heard the car and saw Nick and his buddy, Adam, pull up. I figured they'd come around the house looking for me, so I hid in the trees."

"I told them you were gone. You left me for another woman."

"I'd never do that, Mallory." He kisses me again, his hands exploring my body. "When I heard them drive off, I ran back to the house to make sure you were okay. The front door was wide open, and you were gone. I knew I'd need the money to get you back, so I finished digging it up and drove as fast as I could to the casino. Thank God I got there in time." He caresses my fingers.

Once I remind Jake he needs to make arrangements to pay off the rest of his debt, he's ready to face the day. "I'll call work. Get HR to set up payments directly to Dom."

"What about collateral? You know we owe more on the cars than they're worth."

"Well, maybe you could just cut me a check, and we'd be done with Dom completely."

So we're back to this again. He expects me to bail him out, and then he can just keep on gambling and wasting more money. "Last night, you said you wouldn't take my money."

"I didn't want Dom to think I need to beg my wife for a bit of cash. How would that look? But just between you and me, what's mine is yours, and what's yours is mine. Right, Mal?"

I'm in no mood to argue. So, I change the subject. "We're going to need money for the nursery. Babies cost a lot of money, Jake."

Jake stops buttoning his shirt and gawks at me with his mouth open. "I don't think I can raise another man's baby, Mallory."

The words catch in my throat. "It's your baby, Jake. Nobody else's."

"You and I both know that's not possible."

So once again, I have no choice but to let him in on another secret I've been keeping. "Actually, it is."

"98% effective. That's pretty slim odds." Jake always insists on using a condom.

Until we're absolutely sure we're ready to start a family, he's been telling me for the past three years.

The condoms appeared in our bedroom the day after our honeymoon when he discovered I hadn't been taking my birth control pills regularly. I kept forgetting. I can't be expected to remember everything.

"They're a lot less effective when they have holes in them," I confess. "I poked the packages with pins for three months before I found out I was pregnant."

"You did what? How pregnant are you?" I can see the wheels turning in his head as he calculates.

"Ten weeks. I was going to tell you on my birthday. I did a pregnancy test in the morning, and I was going to tell you that night, but then we did the party thing and..."

"Why didn't you tell me the next day?"

Because I felt guilty about Craig? Because I was jealous of Vicky? Because I was worried how Jake would react? Or maybe once the initial moment of excitement wore off, I thought it might be better to wait till I was showing so he'd have no choice but to accept the fact that we were going to have a baby.

"I guess I got worried you might not be happy."

Jake puts his hand over his mouth, closes his eyes, and lowers his face. I'm afraid he's going to blow his cool.

When he speaks, his voice is quiet. "Are you happy, Mallory? About the baby?"

I slowly nod.

"Then that's all that's important." He walks out the door, and a minute later, the car starts up.

He's leaving me.

Chapter Sixty-One

The car's gone. He grabbed the spare keys from the holder and took off without saying goodbye. But he'll be back once he has a chance to cool off and think things over. His wallet, keys, and phone are missing. Without them, he won't get far. About as far as a quarter tank of gas can get him. Maybe he's gone home to his Mom's. I'm not sure he'd do that, knowing his dad is back. And he's definitely not going to Craig's unless...

I ring Craig to warn him Jake might be on his way to kill him. Or at least give him a good thrashing. Jake needs to blame someone for the situation he's in, and if it's not me, then Craig seems like the most likely candidate.

"Mallory? Is everything okay?" The alarm comes through in his voice. "Between you and Jake?"

"I don't know. We were talking about the baby, and then he left. I'm worried he might be coming to see you. I don't want you guys to fight again."

"Does he know about us, Mallory?"

"No, I told you I'm not going to tell him. It was a mistake. My mistake. Let's not talk about it anymore."

"How can you be so sure?"

"Sure of what?"

I can sense Craig shaking his head in frustration. "We can't pretend, Mallory. You and I both know this could be my baby."

The silence is uncomfortable as I consider how this could have gone so differently if I had told Jake he was going to be a father before we went out to celebrate my birthday. There wouldn't have been any doubt in Craig's mind then. Or in Jake's, even on the off chance that he found out that I slept with Craig. The four of us could have celebrated my birthday and my pregnancy. If we were a normal couple, in a normal marriage, that's what would have happened. Instead, I withheld the pregnancy from my husband until after I slept with his best friend. Instead, my husband destroyed our garden shed and demanded I get rid of the baby. And the image of a happily pregnant husband and wife eagerly awaiting their first child is just a fantasy I've concocted in my crazy head.

"It's Jake's. I'm sure. I was going to tell him the night of my birthday. I thought we were going to have a nice, quiet evening at home, and I would tell him. I did a pregnancy test that morning. I was late by more than a week already, and I suspected. The test confirmed I was pregnant."

"Oh, that's good." His sigh of relief flows into my ear.

"Just let me know if he shows up. And send him directly home. He's driving without his license and wallet. No phone. If he gets pulled over, he'll get ticketed. That'll make him madder than he already is."

Our conversation ends, and we both wait to hear from Jake. Nellie reminds me her food bowl needs filling. The litter box also needs changing, and that load of laundry sitting on the floor needs to go into the washing machine. Upstairs, I make our bed, change the sheets in the guest room, and take the breakfast tray downstairs. I empty the dishwasher, place the dirty dishes in, and wipe the counter. If I sit around waiting, I'll drive myself crazy. When Jake comes home, he'll be in a better mood if things are tidy.

The phone remains silent. No calls, no texts. No word from Craig. After a quick shower, I change into a sundress. Jake likes to see me in the flowery, feminine dress he bought for me last summer. I carefully remove the gauze from my head and fluff out my waves. I need to look my best. I need to be patient. He'll be back before I know it.

Time has a way of slowing down when you're waiting. It has a way of getting away from you when you're busy. I need to get busy. But I can't think of anything I want to do. Not without Jake here.

I grab my laptop, get comfortable on the couch with Nellie curled up beside me, and type in the search engine. **Baby furniture.** I can begin to design the nursery, pick out some furniture, have a look at the baby essentials we're going to need to purchase in the upcoming months. Maybe Jake can set up a spot in the basement for his office. He could finish the basement, make it more practical. It would be a good project for him—the basement and the nursery. We're going to need room for all the baby stuff. Baby names—something else I need to consider. I'll make a list. What about Jake Jr.? Jakey. Jay. Jacob. Jack. Jacklyn, Jackie, Jacoba. Jayna. Everything's going to be perfect.

My stomach grumbles, telling me it's past lunchtime. I root through the fridge and the pantry, looking for something quick and easy. Thinking of what Jake will want for supper when he gets home, I spread peanut butter on a bagel and grab a yogurt and a bottle of water. Maybe I'll make lasagna. His favorite.

With the laptop on the kitchen table next to my lunch, I search for nursery colors. The email folder indicates I have a message. In the subject line, I read: Just a friendly reminder. Clicking on it, I understand who has sent it. Dom. **Rock a bye baby if daddy don't pay, down will come wifey cradle and all.** Not exactly what I'd call friendly.

Nothing is worth this constant threat over our heads. Whether Jake follows through on what he promised Dom or not, it will take years to pay him back, and the interest will keep accruing. My family is most important. Not money. I log into one of my two personal bank accounts, the ones Jake can't access. The money my parents left me is spread between a variety of investments and accounts. If I put together another sixty thousand, maybe it will satisfy Dom, and he'll leave us alone. A few clicks of the keys later, my checking account looks a lot richer. Now, all I have to do is wait for Jake and ask how we should go about transferring the money to Dom.

All our problems will be solved. With the gambling debts gone and our baby on the way, everything is going to be perfect. Jake, Mallory, and baby Jakey. I like the sound of that. Jake will be home anytime now, and he'll be so grateful to hear I've decided to take care of his money problem.

After cleaning up my lunch dishes, I take my laptop to the front porch to wait for Jake and search online for baby clothes. I'm not ready to buy yet, but in a few weeks, I'll go for an ultrasound, and we'll find out the gender. Pink for a girl and blue for a boy. Jake's very traditional. He'll love dressing up our baby girl in dresses or our little boy in cute outfits that make him look all grown up, like daddy. They'll be like twins—Jake and Jakey, in their jeans and button-down shirts. I might just pick out a few neutral-colored sleepers, though. We can use them for our second baby that way.

I won't worry about the cost. What good is money if you can't spend it? Things will be a bit tight while I'm off work with Jakey, but maternity benefits will take up the slack. And if I have to dip into my parents' investments some more, I will. Whatever it takes for my family.

The sound of a vehicle coming down the road prompts me to close my laptop. I don't want Jake to find me looking at baby stuff just yet, not until I tell him I'm going to 'cut a check' for him. He'll be a lot more relaxed once that's dealt with. Then, we can concentrate on the nursery.

When the vehicle comes into view, my heart skips a beat. It's not the Honda. It's a police car. It can't be coming here. Please, God, don't let it come here. Drive on by. Just keep going down the road. Don't stop. Please, don't stop.

It slows down and pulls into our driveway. Two uniformed officers advance toward me, their expressions somber. They're going to arrest me. Jake has driven to the city and gone to the station to report me. The wife who hit her husband with a frying pan and dragged him to the woods—it's enough for a charge of aggravated assault if nothing else. I can't believe he actually did it. How could he turn me in? I need to call our lawyer. Or maybe she's just Jake's lawyer now. I'm going to need all the money I just transferred to bail myself out of jail. Maybe more. They won't keep me there, will they? If they kept every woman who went after her husband with a frying pan, the jails wouldn't be able to hold them.

"Mrs. Shelton? Mallory Shelton?" In my mind, I see the faces of the officers who came to my apartment to tell me my parents were dead. This isn't as bad as that, I tell myself. Going to jail is better than being told you won't be seeing your parents again. I brace myself and nearly hold out my wrists for the handcuffs.

"Yes, I'm Mallory Shelton. Is there a problem?"

"I'm Officer Glencoe. This is Officer Chen. Is Jake Shelton your husband?" I try to focus on the officer asking the questions. Not the same officer who told me about my parents. Of course, it couldn't be. He's older, gray flecks through dirty blond hair, brown eyes.

"Yes. He's not here right now."

"When was the last time you saw him?"

"A few hours ago, I guess. He drove off and didn't say when he'd be back. Why?"

"He's the owner of a 2022 Honda Civic?" I'm not sure what that has to do with me hitting him with a frying pan, but I nod. "Do you know where he was headed?"

"Maybe to the city, to his Mom's. Or maybe to his friend's in Bushwater? I'm not sure. We had a disagreement." Best not to mention the frying pan. It was just a little tiff between husband and wife. That's what I'll say if they ask for particulars.

"We're sorry. We have some bad news. Can we talk to you inside?"

Why do they need to come inside to arrest me? Maybe they want to hear my side, make sure I'm okay, see if Jake's twisting the story around. Who's going to believe a wife beat her husband?

"Yes, yes. Come in." I lead them into the living room. "So, what is this about?"

"There's been a car accident. The car involved was registered to your husband."

"Oh my God! Is he okay? What hospital is he in?" This can't be happening. Please let him be all right.

"I'm afraid the driver didn't survive."

A tsunami comes over me, dragging me under, my feet being pulled downward, my head struggling to get above water. But I'm not sure I want to surface. It's so much easier to let myself sink deep into the depths. Everything is murky. There's nothing to hang onto. There's no Jake. There's no Mallory. There's no baby. Without Jake, there's nothing. Only darkness.

Chapter Sixty-Two

Something cold on my forehead and the back of my neck forces me to the surface. I emerge shivering, my heart racing. A far-off voice asks if I'm okay.

"Is there someone we can call for you?" The voice of the female officer intrudes on my drowning. I just want to slip back under. "A family member or a friend?"

"Jake."

"Yes, is there someone we can call for you to talk to about what happened to Jake?" Her voice is gentle, soft, and kind. The words themselves are terrifying.

What happened to Jake can't have happened. I won't believe it. Jake is fine. Jake is going to come back. The wet paper towel on my forehead slides off as I sit up straighter, trying to clear my head. "It can't be Jake. It must be someone else."

"There is that possibility. The Honda is registered to Jake Shelton at this address. But we'll have to ID the driver through dental records. The car was destroyed by the fire."

"Fire?" The image of my parents burning in our house mixes with the image of Jake burning in our Honda. *None of this is real. This isn't happening. It's just a nightmare.* If I repeat it enough, I'll believe it.

"The Honda was hit by an oil tanker." Officer Chen places her hand on mine. "Is there someone else we should notify?"

Someone else? There's only Jake. "His mom, Gloria." The words find their way out of my mouth as I picture her face when she finds out Jake is really gone this time, not just missing. There is no way I can tell Gloria myself. I don't want to be the one responsible for bringing her world to an end. I give Officer Chen her name and address.

"Are you sure we can't call someone to be with you?" Her brown eyes brim with understanding. She's not much older than me, but I have the impression she, too, has lost someone near to her. "You shouldn't be alone right now."

"I'll call someone. Thank you."

Officer Chen gives me a number where I can reach her if I have further questions and tells me they'll be in touch when they have more information. "And if Jake shows up, call us immediately."

And just like when my parents died, I'm left alone again.

I stare at the wall Jake filled in—where the fireplace used to be. He had it removed when I told him about my nightmares, but getting rid of the fireplace didn't make the monsters disappear. My parents burned in a fire. Jake burned in a fire. The evil creatures living in the fireplace are real. They crackle and spit. They sizzle and hiss. Their ghostly yellow forms flicker and flare as they eat away at the flesh of the deadwood. Orange arms reach out to grab me and drag me in. Red eyes glow in the black coals, beckoning me to join them.

But I have the baby to think about. Jake's baby. I call Dr. Falcon and ask for help, then curl up on the sofa, the pain so unbearable I want to die. My chest aches with the pressure; I'm not sure how my heart keeps beating and how I carry on breathing. I'm shaking, heaving, so sick to my stomach, it feels like I need to expel my stomach along with its contents. Maybe the baby and I should meet up with Jake in heaven right now. The pills wait in the bathroom ensuite. Are there enough to do the job? Or will I survive and end up killing the baby?

The doorbell rings before I can make any decisions. Dr. Falcon enters through the unlocked door. "I came as soon as I could get away. Oh, Mallory, I'm so sorry."

She hugs me. Dr. Falcon reminds me of my dad, in a female form. Competent, caring, good at talking people down from their anxieties. But talking is not going to get me through this.

"I can't believe he's gone." My tears spill, although I should have been dry as a prune by now, after everything I've been through. They spring forth from some bottomless pool. "What am I going to do without him?"

She tells me to get it all out. Get what out? The tears? The words? The pain? There's no getting it out. This time, he's gone and not coming back. It was different before. When I couldn't bring myself to accept what I'd done to him. When I thought maybe he was letting me worry because of it. When I thought for one second, he was with another woman. When I convinced myself he'd gotten into trouble because of his gambling debt. When I believed there was a good chance he was alive. When I kept feeling his presence. I had hope then. Now, there's nothing.

"I'm pregnant. A couple of months." She's the first person I've told besides Jake and Craig. "I didn't know if my medications were safe. I haven't been taking them."

I don't mention the couple of times I've relapsed, through no fault of my own.

"Let me prescribe something different for you, Mallory. Just to be on the safe side. There is a slight risk with some of these meds, but there are safer choices. You should take something to get you through the next few weeks. The stress won't be good for the baby. Let's get you looked after. I'll order the prescription online and have it delivered."

After taking care of the meds, she settles back into therapy mode and tells me it's best to talk.

What is there to say? "I can't live without Jake."

"I know it seems like that now, Mallory, and I won't lie to you. Things will be tough. You don't have your parents for emotional support, and that's going to make it harder. But things will get better. You *will* get through this. For yourself and for the baby."

The baby is the only thing that's going to get me through this. It's all I have left of Jake. It's final now. Jake isn't coming back.

"You shouldn't be alone. I'm going to call someone for you." Holding out her hand, Dr. Falcon asks for my phone and a name.

Whose name? Gloria? She'll be in no better condition than I am. Vicky? Craig? Brad? No, not Brad. Not Craig. Maybe Vicky.

Dr. Falcon makes the call and instructs me on how to properly take the medicine once it arrives. "I'll wait for your friend." She gets me to talk about the baby.

Vicky arrives before my meds do. "Oh no, Mallory!" She swallows me in a hug. "I'm so sorry."

My first thought is that she should be sorry. For what she's done. He's my husband. She's my friend. And we both love Jake. The two of us sit on the couch, arms around each other, and the tears flow.

After Dr. Falcon leaves, the pharmacy van pulls up. Vicky brings a glass of water and gives me one of the pills from the new vial. "This should help you relax. I'm going to call Craig."

I want to protest, but he *is* Jake's friend and deserves to know. Vicky goes into the kitchen to make the call and my cell rings.

Gloria's first words, through sobs, stab my heart. "Oh, Mallory."

The rest of the conversation consists of more sobbing on both ends. She ends the call, saying she'll call tomorrow to discuss arrangements.

When Vicky returns, I tell her Gloria rang. "We're going to talk about arrangements tomorrow."

Vicky nods, saying not to worry about that right now. "Craig's coming over. We're here for you. You should lie down and rest."

I do as I'm told because I don't know what else to do. "I'm pregnant."

"Pregnant?" Her jaw drops. Vicky covers me with the throw and places her hand on my feet in an attempt to soothe me. "You need to take care of yourself. And the baby."

How am I going to go on? Nellie jumps next to me, rubbing her head against mine. She must sense that he's gone, and it's just the two of us now. Three. I need to stay strong for the baby. If Jake were here, he'd tell me I'm going to be okay.

I glance at the wedding photo on the bookcase. We were so happy. The afternoon shines brightly into the room, bringing warmth. My eyelids grow heavy as the meds kick in. I'm still thinking of Jake, still aware he's gone, but calmer, almost resigned. I'll get through this. Jake will always be with me. Never gone completely.

Through the window, birds appear as an omen, flocking to the feeder/bath combo Jake installed on the lawn weeks after we moved in, and he noticed my interest in bird watching.

A car drives up the driveway. Is Jake home? It's all been a big misunderstanding. It wasn't *his* Honda, after all.

I pull myself to a sitting position as Craig gets out of the driver's side and comes toward the door. For a moment, I wish it would have been Craig in the accident instead of Jake, but I know that's not fair. Nothing about this is fair.

I'm enveloped by Craig's arms, and he kisses my head. "Oh, Mallory, I'm so sorry. So sorry." Tears well in his eyes as he pulls away and sits opposite Vicky and me.

And I have this extraordinary sense of deja vu. Jake was missing before. Jake came back. Jake's gone again. But this time, Jake's not coming back.

Chapter Sixty-Three

The quiet is deafening. Why doesn't someone say something?

"He was going to give up gambling." I interrupt the silence only to have them stare at me. "After everything he went through, now he's gone. I guess his luck finally ran out."

Craig looks out the window as though he expects Jake might drive up and tell us this is just his idea of a joke. Then we can all have a good laugh. "I can't believe he's gone."

A huge sigh escapes Vicky, and I feel her body quiver. She's trying to hold back from breaking down. "How could this happen?"

I know she had strong feelings for Jake once. This can't be easy for her. Watching her work through her pain brings back the memory I've tried to suppress for more than three years.

* * *

Three and a half years ago

It was after Vicky broke up with him, but before we were engaged. Jake and I had been going out for a couple of months. We usually spent the weekends at my apartment. But that weekend in January, he went to Montreal for a work conference. I spent the weekend missing him, catching up on my reading. He only texted once, when he arrived at the hotel, to let me know he got there safely.

When he returned home Sunday evening, he called. "Hey. How was your weekend?"

"Lonely. How was your conference?"

"Boring."

I didn't see him all week. Just a couple of texts. When we got together at my place Friday after work, we fell into each other's arms and went straight to bed. "I missed you so much, Mallory."

"I missed you, too. I tried to make the time go faster by reading, but all I could think about was you. So, what did you do at the conference?"

"Meetings. Listening to speakers. Nothing exciting."

"Maybe next time I could come along. Make it more exciting." I didn't know why he hadn't asked me in the first place. We'd never been away together. A weekend at a posh hotel would have been nice. "I could shop and see the sights while you're at meetings. And at night, we could have dinner and spend a romantic evening in the hotel room."

"Sure, okay." Then he changed the subject. "Are you hungry? I could go for a pizza."

He ordered online, switched on the T.V., and searched for a movie. "How about this one? You like this kind of thing."

A romantic comedy. "They all live happily ever after. Just like you and me." We curled up on the couch and watched the film.

The doorbell rang twenty minutes later. Jake grabbed a credit card out of his wallet and answered the door, not noticing the slip of paper that fell out. As he stood in the doorway, I picked it up and unfolded it. It was a receipt for the Niagara Casino Hotel, dated the past weekend. Jake told me he was in Montreal, not Niagara. I returned the receipt to his wallet and didn't mention it. We ate our pizza along with a couple glasses of wine, and I tried to put the Casino Hotel out of my mind.

But I couldn't forget it. When Jake fell asleep, I rifled through his wallet. Taking a closer look at the hotel receipt, I found it listed a couple bottles of wine, room service for two, and spa service for two. More receipts were folded in his wallet, dated the same weekend. Dinner for two at an expensive restaurant. Two tickets for a concert at the entertainment center. Cash receipts from the casino.

He had lied to me. Cheated on me. I woke Jake and threw the receipts at him. "So, you had a boring work weekend? In Niagara? At the Casino Hotel?"

Jake pushed himself to a sitting position. My arms flew out and struck him across the chest repeatedly. "How could you cheat on me? And lie to me? Get out! Out of my bed!"

He dressed and started to leave the bedroom. At the door, he turned around. "I'm sorry, Mallory. It was just the one time. Honest. But you're right. I should have told you. It was one last fling. With one of my exes. I wanted to be sure she was out of my system before taking the next step with you."

I threw the pillows at him. "Get out!"

I received flowers every day the following week. The delivery man brought chocolates, stuffed animals, books, candles, and bath bombs. Jake called several times a day, but I didn't answer. He texted a dozen times a day, sending cute emojis and apologies, telling me how sorry he was that he had lied, that no one compared to me. He was sure I was the only one for him. No doubt in his mind. He told me it would never happen again and begged me to take him back. **Just one more chance. Please, Mallory.**

There was no way I was going to take him back. But when he showed up at my place the next weekend with a big bouquet of flowers and a sheepish grin on his face, I opened the door a crack. "Can I come in? Can we talk?"

I opened the door further. "We don't have anything to talk about."

"You know that's not true. Please, Mallory, don't let it end this way."

I let him in. And I never once regretted it. We talked more than we'd ever talked before. He was honest and straightforward, telling me he had trouble with relationships.

"When things start to get serious, I always do something stupid to mess it up. I get scared. When you started talking about how you wanted children someday, it spooked me. I wasn't sure I was ready for that kind of commitment, so I talked to one of my exes about it. One thing led to another, and...I'm so sorry I hurt you. We never really said we were seeing each other exclusively, but I shouldn't have hidden it from you. It was just that one time, honest. But I want you to know there's no question in my mind that you're the one I want to spend the rest of my life with. I love you, Mallory."

The crystal tears flowing from his blue-green eyes got to me. He was truly sorry. And he was right—we never once said we were dating each other exclusively. I had only assumed that. It was my fault for thinking I was the only woman Jake could possibly be interested in. A man like him could have his pick of women. I was lucky to be one of them.

A month later, he got down on one knee and proposed. "I love you, Mallory. More than I ever thought I could love anyone. Please tell me you feel the same."

Of course, I did. I couldn't imagine living without him.

A year after I caught him cheating on me, I found something that brought back all the pain of his betrayal and more. We had been invited to the wedding of one of Jake's co-workers at the warehouse. Weeks before the wedding, I chose the outfits we would wear, and prepared to send them to the dry cleaners—my little black dress and his black pinstripe suit. They'd been sitting in the back of the closet all year. I wasn't snooping. I'm not that kind of wife. But his pockets needed to be cleaned out. As I checked through them, I noticed a couple of long hairs on one shoulder. They weren't blond. I picked them off his jacket before continuing to check his inside pockets, where I found a parking receipt for the Niagara Hotel Casino. I left the suit and the dress in the closet and set the receipt on our dresser for Jake to find.

It was Saturday morning, and Jake was cleaning up the heated garage. When he came in for a beer, I didn't mention the receipt or the hairs. I asked if he would go to the hardware store and buy parts to fix the pesky toilet leak. When he left, I called Heather and asked if I could come for a visit. I didn't bother to pack, even though I didn't plan on coming home that night. I wanted to leave before Jake got back and tried to stop me.

I drove for three hours without crying. When Heather opened the door, it all burst like a flood. "He cheated on me," I blubbered.

Heather suggested we go for lunch, and we sat in the booth all afternoon, talking about my farce of a marriage. "So, this was before you were married? Before you were engaged?" She did her best to see my point of view and Jake's as well. "Has he cheated on you since then?"

"I don't think so. We're hardly ever apart, except for work. He goes out with the guys for drinks after work sometimes."

"Maybe you should talk to Jake about it; tell him you're still upset about what happened last year. But you're welcome to stay with me for a couple of days; let him suffer for a bit."

With the snow coming down heavily, I had a good excuse for staying overnight. I decided I would do exactly as Heather suggested—let Jake suffer. I didn't text to let him know I was safe. When he found me the next day, he was out of his mind with worry. We talked about the parking receipt, and he apologized again. He was so distraught I didn't mention the auburn hairs on the jacket's shoulder.

* * *

As Vicky and I sit side by side mourning the loss of my husband, I can't help but think she's responsible for the problems in our marriage. She pats my back and asks if I'd like some tea. I search her swollen red eyes. Straight auburn hair falls perfectly alongside her beautiful face, her lips Ruby Red.

Is she still in love with Jake?

Chapter Sixty-Four

"You should get some rest." Craig touches my arm as I attempt to lift myself off the couch. "The next few days are going to be tough."

He doesn't mention arrangements, but I know what he's talking about. If it really is Jake in that car, I'm going to have to plan his funeral. Just over three years ago, Jake and I planned our wedding, and now I'm left on my own to plan the final big event of his life. We should have been making baby plans.

"I can't fall asleep. I'm afraid that when I wake up, I'll find out he's gone all over again. This time is permanent, isn't it?"

"I'm afraid it looks that way. But you need to take care of yourself and the baby. Jake would have wanted that. You're not alone, you know. Vicky and I are here for you. Whatever you need."

"I know." I avoid his gaze and look instead at our wedding photo. The man I loved more than I've ever loved anyone is gone. He wasn't perfect, but I loved him anyway. *Whatever I need.* Jake is all I've ever needed. I've always known that, but I've never been more sure of it than now. But Craig's right—I need to focus on Jake's baby. He'll know his dad even if he'll never meet him. I'll make sure of that by telling him about him. I'll show him all the happy photos.

Vicky brings in a tray with the teapot, teacups, and a plate of cookies. She pours a cup for me, adding sugar. "Here you go. I'll start supper soon. You need to look after that baby you're carrying." She glances at Craig with an expression I can't read.

She's so kind. On the surface. What is she really thinking?

"I was going to make lasagna. He'll be hungry when he makes it home."

Vicky bites her lower lip, her eyes full of pity, and she speaks softly. "We can still do that, if you'd like. Because it's his favorite."

Craig shifts his legs on the sofa, and I'm sure he wishes he were somewhere else right now. "What do you think, Mallory? We could have Jake's favorite meal in his memory, in honor of Jake."

"No, I couldn't eat." I wipe a tear from my cheek and purse my lips together, trying hard not to break down into a blubbering mess. "But yes, we should do something. For Jake."

"If you give me your recipe, I can do the work. You should get some sleep," Vicky says.

There's no point in arguing with both of them. "It's in my recipe binder in the drawer beside the dishwasher. I'm going upstairs to lie down."

Our house, our dinner, are in the hands of our best friends. The climb up to our bedroom seems never-ending. Nellie tags along. The sight of the empty bed frightens me, with the sun's rays warming the sheets, reminding me that I will no longer feel the heat of Jake's body wrapped around mine. There's no if or maybe about it this time. I'm a 28-year-old widow. I might not have had the perfect marriage I envisioned for myself, but I love Jake, and I know he loved me. In the end, that's important. We would have worked through our problems if we had been given the chance.

The closet and drawers hold Jake's things. They wait for him even though he's not coming back. I touch his clothes, letting my fingers linger on the fabric that once touched his skin. In the hamper, the pajamas he wore last night are covered in his scent. I take it in, breathing deeply, trying to inhale his essence. With the pajama pants on his pillow, I lie down, my face buried in them. And I dream of what could have been.

Maybe if I hadn't gotten pregnant, this would never have happened. It all started when I told him about the baby. Maybe I should have waited for him to be ready to be a father instead of tricking him. We wouldn't have fought if I had waited. *Oh, Jake, I'm so sorry.* This isn't the way it was supposed to be.

When I wake, the image of Jake holding our newborn son is still with me, the dream intruding on my reality. The room is light, but the sun has lost its brightness. The bedroom door is open, and Jake stands there, watching me. I blink and he's gone.

Craig has taken his place.

"Vicky said to tell you supper's ready." His voice is gentle, his eyes glistening. I can tell he's trying to be strong for my sake. "Are you feeling up to joining us?"

As he helps me down the step, the smell of Jake's favorite meal wafts up the stairs and fills my nostrils. In the kitchen, Vicky has the table set for three, with salad and garlic bread in the center. The lasagna sits on top of the stove. It was supposed to be like this, dinner for three, only it was supposed to be Jake, me, and the baby.

"Try to eat. For the baby." Vicky places a piece of lasagna on my plate. "Jake would want you to take care of yourself. Do it for him."

The first forkful sticks in my throat, and hard as I try to swallow, the lump sits in my chest. I may as well have swallowed a rock. But I think of Jake and our baby.

Jake would have said, *I love your lasagna, Mal.* Jake would have wanted me to be okay, to be strong, to get through this. I force myself to eat the plateful of tasteless food as Craig and Vicky eat in silence next to me.

Craig raises his glass of water. "To Jake. You'll always be with us in spirit. We love you, man." Our glasses clink together.

Craig shares some anecdotes of his friendship with Jake, and Vicky adds some of her memories. Most of their stories are upbeat, because Jake was like that. He was a fun, funny, easy-going kind of guy, always looking on the bright side. It's a mini memorial—the three of us remembering all the good things about Jake. Forgetting the darker side of him. The drinking, gambling, secrecy, lies, his background of family violence, his unresolved anger, his jealousy, his OCD.

After dinner, I pull out our photo albums and share moments of our time together, as short as it was. Jake is always smiling. So am I. Because we were happy. Because we'd found each other. Two damaged, lost souls searching for love.

"This is in Jamaica, on our honeymoon." The photo of us holding hands with the ocean in the background was taken by a friendly stranger. We were beaming, the water sparkling like diamonds in the sun, the promise of a brilliant life ahead of us. When did it start to go wrong?

The 10 o'clock news is about to begin. I grab the remote, but Craig takes it out of my hands. "You don't want to see it. Trust me."

"You should turn in, Mallory," Vicky suggests. "You need your strength for the next few days. Take one of the sleeping aids Dr. Falcon prescribed. I'll make some tea. Why don't you go upstairs and get ready for bed? I'll bring it up to you."

By the time I've washed my face, brushed my teeth and hair, and changed into comfortable PJs, Vicky appears with tea, a couple of cookies, and a pill. "Here you go. Do you want me to stay for a while?"

"No, it's okay. I'm going to listen to my book. It'll help me sleep. Thanks, Vicky. For everything."

I want to add, "I forgive you." But it's best if she doesn't know that *I* know about the auburn hairs and the Ruby Red lipstick stain.

She closes the door halfway as she leaves. My eyes spot the key on the dresser. Jake left it there after we came back from the casino. I recall the words he said the day I discovered what was in our locked safe.

The million dollars would take care of the house, the cars, the credit cards, the funeral... It would also take care of Dom and what Jake owes to Gloria and me. It would take care of the bills.

With one paycheck gone and the expenses still coming in, the farm would have to go.

With me staying home to raise the baby, I'm going to need another source of income.

Key in hand, I tiptoe across the hall to the office and insert it into the safe, punch in our wedding date, and check to make sure I hadn't imagined it all. The folder's there, the insurance policy inside. I open it and read carefully, taking in the details.

I'm one million dollars richer.

Chapter Sixty-Five

I t's dark. My heart pounds, and I'm sweating even though the room is set to 19 degrees Celsius. Something has woken me from my nightmare. Jake was driving, with me in the passenger seat and the baby in the car seat in the back, a transport truck headed directly at us. There was no avoiding the inevitable. We were going to crash.

A sudden explosion rocks the house. The illumination through the window tells me we're in for more severe weather. Pulling the covers over my head, I try to drown out the storm and go back to sleep. I'm tired. So tired of it all. The stress of the last several days has been too much. I close my eyes, and Jake's face appears in front of me.

Crrr...ack! Boom! I flip off the covers and head to the window, swaying as though I'm on a boat on a rocky lake. It isn't raining yet, but when lightning emblazons the sky, the clouds seem menacing through the advancing fog, threatening to unleash their fury. Across the road, mist drifts amongst the trees, its fingers trailing through the branches, shadows playing with my mind.

I know I'm safe here. It's Jake's home. Jake's and mine. Jake's and mine and Baby Jakey's home. Vicky is just down the hall from me. Craig is in the den. No intruders lurk outside. Unless Dom, not knowing Jake is dead, has sent his guys to remind us what we owe. I should double-check the doors and windows. With a firm grip on the banister, I descend one step at a time, making my way to the main level, careful not to slip. The sleeping pill brings on dizziness. I can't risk a fall, not with the baby.

Midway down, lightning flashes through the sidelights, illuminating the front entrance. Something moves across the floor.

Me...ow. Just Nellie roaming the house.

We don't need an alarm system with a watch cat in the house. Jake still speaks to me.

I approach the front door, try the knob, and find it locked. Craig would have made sure everything was secure, especially after what happened the last time he stayed overnight. The dining room and living room bay windows are latched. At the back of the house, the room to the den is closed. I won't disturb Craig. I'm sure all this has taken its toll on him. I check the mudroom door, the laundry room window, and the patio doors off the kitchen. All locked. Another crack of thunder resonates through the house. Lightning flashes through the locked kitchen window, shedding brightness on the room. Nothing seems out of place. Vicky must have cleaned up after I went to bed.

Hot chocolate, that's what I need. It'll soothe me so I can sleep. I flip the light switch above the stove and warm milk in a pot to avoid waking Craig with the microwave. Stirring in some chocolate powder, I carry my mug to the living room and sit in the near dark. The clock on the bookcase illuminates the time: 2:20. Jake has been dead for at least twelve hours. *Oh, Jake. If you can read my mind from wherever you are, I love you. Please give me a sign. Please be there, watching over me and baby Jakey.*

Nellie rubs against my legs, then bolts toward the window. Something has caught her attention, and my heart goes out to whatever poor creature might be wandering outside the house with another storm on the way. Russ on the loose? A stray cat? Raccoon or skunk? Squirrel, maybe a bird? Nick and Adam? The thought sends ice down my spine.

"Nellie, what's wrong, girl?" I whisper. "What's out there?"

Meow, meow, meow. She runs back and forth from the window to the door. *Meow, meow.* Nellie's an indoor cat. She likes to watch birds and squirrels, but if she encountered one face-to-face, she'd probably run in the opposite direction. Whatever she thinks she sees, it's got her riled up. I'm surprised Vicky and Craig don't wake up and ask what's causing the commotion. Nellie scratches at the front door.

"Nellie! What's going on?" Through the curtains, only trees and shadows are visible in the mist, set against a dark sky, fog swirling around the lawn and across the road.

"There's nothing out there." But I suspect cats have a sixth sense. That they know more than we do.

Nellie keeps scratching, meowing louder. I scoop her up and unlock the door, opening it just enough to set one foot out. "See, there's nothing."

Three cars sit in the driveway. The cornfield is to the right. Straight ahead, past the long stretch of lawn, are the woods. As I back into the house, Nellie jumps out of my arms and darts across the grass, toward the road.

"Nellie! Nellie!"

She's taken off on me a couple of times before when I've been stupid enough to stand in the entrance with the door open. She'll explore the yard, trees, flowerbeds, but a can of her favorite food usually brings her back in. But I've never lost her at night, in the fog, in the midst of frightening sights and sounds. The boom of thunder should be enough to send her back inside the house, but she keeps running from me.

I follow, barefoot in my pajamas, halfway across the lawn, when I notice the shadow standing still, watching the house. A flash lights up the woods, illuminating Nellie, her back arched, tail in the air, rubbing against something. Someone. The terror rushing through my body is like an electric shock. I'm having a heart attack.

The shadow ambles toward me, and my scream is loud enough to wake the dead. Hopefully, it will wake Vicky and Craig, maybe even the neighbors, Paul and Linda. I race to the open door, lock it behind me, flip on the light switch, and scramble up the stairs to call 911 from my phone, which I think I've left on the night table. The shuffling stops me before I reach the top. When I turn around, the dark shape at the bottom of the stairs elicits another holler from me before I realize it's Craig.

"Mallory, are you all right?" He stares at me, concern etched in his face. "What's going on?"

I join him in the entryway. "It's Nick. Or Adam. Outside."

Craig turns on the outdoor lights while I peer through the curtains. The illuminated scene spooks me more than imaginary evil creatures in the fireplace. It's not Nick, not Adam. Not my neighbor, Paul. I recognized him the moment I saw him, but refused to believe my eyes.

Engulfed by fog, the ghost on my front lawn, moving ever so slowly toward my door, is identifiable in the brightness of the outdoor lights. It's caked in mud and dirt, with leaves and grass hanging off it.

And it's carrying my baby—Nellie. I scream, but no sound comes from my open mouth. My dead husband has returned from the grave, bringing with him the fresh ground he's dug up. And I haven't even had a chance to bury him properly.

Chapter Sixty-Six

The ghost approaches my front porch, and I slip away, the floor reaching out. Craig catches me in time and leads me to the couch, laying me down gently, calling my name. The sound of his voice is hollow, distant. From my vantage point, the staircase is visible through the living room archway. Vicky stands at the midway point of the stairs, frozen, as a key turns in the lock and the creak of the front door fills the quiet of the night.

Vicky's shriek arouses me to full consciousness, and my eyes focus on the archway. A shape blocks the space between the living room and the staircase. "But…but…you're dead," Vicky gasps. "Oh, my God, Jake."

She rushes to the bottom of the stairs and wraps her arms around my muddy, dead husband.

"Jake?" Craig flicks on the lamp switch. "You're alive? We thought you were dead. Thank God! What happened?"

He joins Vicky, slapping him on the back and giving him a big man hug.

Jake pulls away. "Dead? You wish! For Christ's sake, Craig. I'm not gone for two minutes, and I find you here on the couch with Mallory again. What the hell's going on? What are you doing with my wife?"

"There's nothing going on," Vicky intervenes. "Craig and I are here with Mallory because you're dead. The police thought you were in an accident."

"Jake? Is it really you? You're alive?" Coming out of my stupor, I bolt off the couch and wrestle my husband away from the arms of our best friends. Claiming him for myself, the tears stream down my face as I bury it in his dirt-streaked chest.

"I've had one hell of a week," Jake addresses Craig and Vicky, his arms snug around my waist. "You guys won't believe what happened to me, courtesy of some goons and a carjacker. But I'm pretty damn sure I'm alive and kicking."

Jake kisses me, saying how much he loves me. "Everything's going to be okay. Mallory, please, tell me you love me too."

"I...I do, I...love...you." I can't help it, but I'm crying, sobbing, convulsing. "I thought...I thought...you ...were...gone...for...good." Each word is an effort, stuck deep in my pounding chest.

"I'm here, Mallory. I'm right here." Jake holds me, rubbing my back with his hand. "I'm not going anywhere." He kisses my forehead, my eyes, my nose, my lips.

"I'll call the police," Craig says, heading back to the den. "Tell them you're alive."

"I'll let your mom know," Vicky adds, following him. "Get some rest, you two. We'll talk tomorrow."

Jake and I are left alone in our living room, Nellie purring around Jake's legs. "How could you?" I blubber, pounding his chest. "How could you let me think you were dead?"

"I didn't know I was dead." It's the deadpan way he says it. "Nobody told me. If I had known I was dead, I would have let you know, Mal."

My tears of grief, turned to tears of relief, are now happy tears. My Jake is back. Complete with his dark sense of humor.

"I'm glad you're not dead."

"So am I. I'm sorry you had to go through all this, honey. Is everything okay with the baby?"

I nod, my hand on my stomach. He places his hand on mine. Once we're in the privacy of our ensuite, we undress each other, throwing our clothes onto the bathroom tile. In the large glass enclosure, water and soap purge the dirt, pain, tears, and grief. Jake backs me against the shower wall and runs his hands and mouth over my neck, shoulders, all the way down my body, sending shivers, the good kind, through me. His mouth finds its way back to mine, and our bodies join.

"I love you, Mallory. And our baby," he says as we slide down the wall to the wet tiles. We sit under the shower spray until it runs lukewarm, and Jake spews it all out.

"I've had a really bad streak of luck lately. But all in all, I think it's worked out to be more good than bad." My head rests against Jake's chest, feeling his heartbeat. "When I left this morning, I was heading out to see my dad. To tell him I was willing to make amends. Not just for the money, although that's a big part of it. With the baby coming, I want to be sure we're going to be okay financially. I can get Dom off our backs with that money. Get the nursery set up. Put some away for our future. But I didn't get to Mom's place. I stopped at the stop sign down on the 8th line. Some guy was hitching a ride to the city. I figured I'd help him out, pay it forward, since someone helped me the night I got out of the well. Good Samaritan, that's me. But the son of a bitch pulled me out of the Honda, gave me a few good punches, and threw me down the embankment. Then he fucking stole the car. I must have hit my head on the hard ground and passed out. I woke up at the bottom of a steep ravine, right on the edge of the river. I'm just lucky I didn't roll all the way in and drown. It took me ages to climb up the slippery slope, and by then, it was getting dark. I tried to stop the few vehicles that came down the road, but for some reason, nobody would let me in their car. I don't know when I've walked that far, Mal. My ankle hurts something awful, my feet are blistered, and my legs ache so bad. I didn't think I'd ever get home. But all I could think about was how worried you'd be, especially after all the shit that's happened these last few days. I'm gonna make him pay for what he did. First thing in the morning, I'm calling the cops and giving them a complete description of the piece of shit who stole our car and tried to kill me. Send him to prison for a long time, make sure he doesn't do it to somebody else."

"He's not going to do anything to anybody ever again." I gaze into those crystal eyes, set in his hard head. "The driver of an oil tanker was drunk. Hit him head-on. The car went up in flames. They couldn't identify the body. The police said…they said…they thought it was… you."

Jake sits silently, cupping my face in his strong hands. Before he speaks, he roars with laughter, but I can tell it's not because he finds the situation funny. It's the irony of it.

"Poor Schmuck. I guess I'm one lucky guy." He kisses me, and we make love again, in spite of the fact the water runs cold.

Chapter Sixty-Seven

"Is there anything to eat? I can't remember the last time I had a decent meal. I'm starving," Jake says as we wrap fluffy towels around ourselves.

"There's lasagna. We had a memorial dinner for you. Your favorite meal." The tears start again, and I tremble in his arms. "When we thought you were dead."

Jake strokes my head and kisses my eyes, licking the tears away. "I'm so sorry I put you through this. If I hadn't been such an ass... God, I wish I could take it all back. What you must have gone through—"

"Don't leave again. Please... don't leave me."

"We're going to be okay, Mal. We got through this. We'll get through worse if we have to. But we'll do it together." He pulls on his pajama bottoms and says he's going down to get some leftovers.

"No, you get into bed. You must be exhausted after what you've been through. You're the one who died. I'll make up a plate for you." It's the least I can do after I nearly killed him.

Moments later, as he sits in bed propped against the pillows, eating his memorial meal, Jake comments on how happy he is to be alive. "I feel so lucky. Like I've been given another chance."

"Yes, we're both lucky. Very lucky." I let him know I have the cash ready to pay Dom off completely, and Jake can replace my parents' invested money when his own inheritance comes through. I don't even care about the money anymore, but I know Jake's pride will insist on me being paid back.

"Thanks, Mal. I'll make sure to repay you as soon as I can. Mom, too. I swear. There's a couple of things I need to do tomorrow—one is pay off Dom."

"What's the other?"

"I need to send a thank you note and a gift card to some friends of mine."

"What friends?" Does he mean Vicky and Craig? Has he forgiven Craig for what he thinks he did?

"I don't know them. But I stayed at their place. They were very hospitable." He tells me about the cabin where he found refuge after he climbed out of the well. "I'll pick up a $100 dining card for them, treat them to a nice night out. I got their mailing address off a magazine on their coffee table."

My Jake. So thoughtful.

"And I'll suggest they hide their spare key elsewhere. You never know what riff-raff might wander out of a well into your home. Under the doormat, that's just too easy," he chuckles.

Yes, my Jake is back.

"This is great lasagna, by the way."

"Vicky made it."

"Oh." He stops to think for a minute. "Not as good as yours, of course. But then, I haven't eaten properly for days."

* * *

In the morning, we sip our second cup of coffee in the living room, talking about our future. At least, Jake is talking about our future. I'm listening as he makes plans for us.

"I'm so sorry, Mallory. For everything. The secrecy, the lies, the little fling before we got engaged, accusing *you* of having an affair. No more jealousy. And I'll never raise my hand to you again, I swear. When I saw you come back from the hospital, I thought I had finally snapped and become just like my dad. I won't let that happen, Mal. I'm going to get help with my anger issues. I'll join a club or something to deal with my drinking and gambling. AA or Gamblers Anonymous. Both. I'll attend meetings, get therapy, quit cold turkey, swear on the Bible, whatever it takes to get you to trust me. No more hiding things from you. No more wasting money. From now on, it's you and the baby, Mallory. And we'll have more kids, two or three more. We can finish fixing up the house and add on to make room for the family. Especially now that my gambling debts will be paid and we'll have extra cash from my dad. And with the auto insurance, the car will be paid off. Everything's going to be perfect, Mal."

Maybe he's had one too many head injuries, thinking things could ever be perfect.

I take a good, long look at the love of my life. Jake has admitted to being an abusive husband, even though he's never actually hit me. There are other kinds of abuse; I understand that now. I never in my wildest dreams thought I would ever find myself in the position of victim. That sort of thing happens to weak women who allow themselves to be treated that way, I used to think. Not strong, educated women like me. A woman like me would simply walk away from an unhealthy relationship.

Jake grew up with physical abuse, a drunken father, and a mother who ignored what was happening. He broke the cycle when he stood up to his father and threatened to take action. Now, he's terrified of becoming his father.

Marriage is a two-way street. There's a lot of give and take, and a lot of ups and downs. It takes two to make a marriage and two to break it.

"No, this isn't all on you. I'm to blame as well. For not trusting you and not believing in you. From now on, my parents' money is yours, Jake. We're in this together, you and me. And the kids."

I kiss him and tell him how sorry I am about the frying pan. "It just sort of slipped. I honestly thought you were going to hit me. I don't know what came over me. And I know I should have told the police what really happened, but I just couldn't face it. I thought once you sobered up, you'd find a way to get home, and we'd talk...I never expected you'd stumble into a well. Oh, Jake...I almost lost you."

"It's not your fault, Mal. I drove you to it. But Craig..."

"No, not Craig. He had absolutely nothing to do with what happened to you. He's been here looking out for me, helping to find you, along with

Vicky. It was all me—I hit you with the frying pan, pulled up the car to the front door, and dragged you into the trunk." It sounds crazy when I hear the words come out of my mouth. "I'll start seeing Dr. Falcon regularly. Take my medication as prescribed. Get therapy. I promise. I'm so sorry."

"Shh…it's okay. I know you didn't mean to hurt me." He takes my hands from my face and brings them to his, kissing them. "It was an accident. We don't need to talk about it anymore. Although I still don't know how the hell I ended up in the well. Or what happened to my wallet, phone, and keys. Probably Dom's goons," Jake concludes. "Or maybe I wandered off after you dropped me on the side of the road, got mugged, fell in the well. Just bad luck."

He scratches his head, and I wonder what, exactly, Brad did to my husband, and what he expected the outcome to be.

The sound of laughter breaks our private moment. Vicky and Craig come from the den, through the hall, into the living room. "So, do you want to let us in on what happened yesterday?" Craig asks, carrying coffee for the two of them.

Jake repeats the story of the hitchhiker and the fall down to the river, as they sit across from us, mouths open in awe of Jake's luck.

"So, it was a case of mistaken identity," Vicky muses. "He's the dead guy, not you. Jeez, Jake. You seem to always come out on top." A flicker of jealousy courses through me, but I won't let it rise to the surface. "You have no idea how glad I am to have you back."

She gives him a big hug, leaving Ruby Red lipstick on his collar.

"Ditto," Craig adds, putting his arm around Jake's shoulder. "Glad you beat the odds, buddy. More than once. But don't push it. The third time might not be so lucky."

"I'm not taking any more chances, believe me." Jake casts suspicious eyes on Craig. "Mallory and our family are my priority. I'll be extra careful to keep an eye out for her and to keep myself out of trouble from now on." He smiles and winks at me, like we're sharing a secret of some sort. "I'm a lucky man to have Mallory. And now she's having my baby. Let's all go out and celebrate tonight. Dinner's on me."

"That's awesome! Congratulations! We've got some news to celebrate, too." Vicky feigns ignorance about the baby, grabbing Craig's hand as his eyes avoid mine. "I didn't want to say anything before we were sure where it was headed, but…Craig and I are back together again. We've been seeing each other for the past several months."

"And the last few days, going through all this with you guys, the stress has actually brought us closer together." Craig kisses Vicky. "We had a good, long talk last night. After seeing how the two of you have weathered all this and come out stronger than ever, it got me thinking. Maybe being tied down isn't such a bad thing, after all. And last night…." He holds up Vicky's left hand, cornsilk wrapped around her ring finger.

"We got engaged!" Vicky finishes his sentence. "And we want you to be our maid of honor and best man."

"Wow! That's great!" Jake exclaims. "Our two best friends are getting married—to each other. You guys belong together. Isn't that great, hon?" I see genuine happiness, mixed with… relief? in his blue-green eyes, open windows to his soul.

"Congratulations. That's terrific news," I agree. Vicky isn't still hung up on Jake, after all. I don't know why I didn't see it before, but they're perfect for each other. Craig and Vicky. Just like Jake and me.

"We'll leave you two to have some time on your own," Craig says, "and see you tonight. I'll make reservations for 7 o'clock at Michael's."

"Thank you, both of you, for being there for me. I couldn't have managed without you." I hug one, then the other. "You kept me sane through this ordeal."

"Yeah, thanks, guys. Thanks for looking after Mal. I love you guys." Jake pats Craig's shoulder and air kisses Vicky's cheeks.

After another round of hugs, they're gone. "We have the best friends," Jake beams.

"We do." I drag out the frying pan and bring it to the stove, Jake's eyes on me the whole time. "Cheese omelet?"

"Sure, hon. Sounds good. Can I have some bacon with that?"

"Whatever you like, honey. I'll pop in some frozen waffles, too."

"Let me do that. And I'll make another pot of coffee. Or would you rather have tea? Maybe herbal tea's better for the baby."

"Tea would be nice."

We work together in the kitchen, side by side, and the four of us eat breakfast. Jake and I, the baby growing inside me, and Nellie.

Watching him in the kitchen of our home, his curly locks falling onto his forehead, his turquoise eyes pulling me in, I have a hard time thinking of him as abusive. Maybe a little obsessive. Jealous. Controlling. On the other hand, he thinks everything's a big joke. But he's nothing like his father. No, not abusive. Flawed, damaged, only human. And, me? I get a little anxious sometimes; maybe I overreact now and then. I need to loosen up and take things less seriously. But it's nothing that gets in the way of me living a normal life.

Jake and I love each other. We have a good marriage. We're going to make the best parents. It's just been an extra rough week for both of us. We've both made our share of mistakes. Said and done things we regret. Don't all couples? We're not special. No different than anyone else.

Smacking my husband on the head with a frying pan and nearly killing him has been an eye-opener. I try to make sense of it all.

He wanted to kill my baby. I hit him on the head with a skillet. I didn't want to go to jail. He 'tripped' and fell down a well. These things happen. He hid his gambling money from me. I stole it and buried it in the back yard. He haunted me. I nearly lost my mind.

I was verbally and emotionally abused by the man I trusted. He was hit by an oil tanker. Except he got lucky and got carjacked. I thought I was widowed for the second time. He lay dying in a ditch. I thought I was going to bury my husband. He came back from the dead before I had the chance to put him in the cold ground.

Marriage isn't always easy. I'm not sure which one of us got the better deal in this partnership. But we're in it till death do us part. We're meant for each other. No stupid mistake, no amount of stupid mistakes (and we've both made our share) will keep us apart. Everything's *not* perfect. I see that now. But that's okay. We love each other. We'll work things out, as imperfect as they may be. Everything's perfectly imperfect, and that's perfectly okay.

"Did you enjoy your meal?" I ask Jake, his eyes glued to me.

"Yes, thank you. You're an amazing cook, honey." His gaze follows me as I walk to the stove and lift the skillet. His eyes widen, and he backs away. "Honey, what are you doing with the frying pan?"

"Just putting it in the sink to soak, honey. I know you don't like things messy."

"Let it sit on the stove, Mallory. And leave the dishes on the table for now. A little mess isn't going to hurt anything. I'll take care of it later."

He leaves the kitchen and returns with a red rose. "Watch the thorns, honey. I love you."

"I love you, too." I grasp the perfect blood-red rose with care, mindful of the prickly thorns digging into my fingers, and kiss my husband. "We're going to be okay, aren't we? We're going to work things out."

"You bet we will." His lips skim my forehead, my eyes, my nose, claiming my mouth. He leaves no doubt in my mind.

Life's a gamble. Marriage even more so. There are no easy wins, no perfect games. It's all in the roll of the dice. But you can't win if you don't take a chance. Or a second. Maybe a third. This is our chance. I won't blow it this time. You can bet the farm on that. Cash in your chips, claim your lottery winnings.

And take them to the bank.

Acknowledgements

Thank you to those who have made this book a reality, from its inception through to its refinement and to the final copy. It takes teamwork to turn an idea into a published novel.

The idea started with a simple spark. Thank you to Brian Fear for inspiring the premise behind *Where is My Husband?* as I sat in my car in the parking lot of his workplace one night, waiting to pick him up. What, I wondered, would happen if he didn't come out? As well as being my first reader and providing suggestions for the story, Brian is instrumental in promoting my writing to anyone who will listen. I'd also like to thank him for sharing his last name with me. Being a Fear is an added bonus for a mystery/thriller writer. I've been asked several times if it's a pen name. Nope. I'm an actual honest-to-goodness Fear.

Along with my husband (who, by the way, shares only the good aspects of my main character, Jake, and none of the dark side), I'd like to acknowledge our family for being there for me. Thank you to my son, Bryant, for supporting my writing on a daily basis and assisting with all things technical as well as sharing on social media; to my daughter, Brittany, son-in-law, Eric, and grandson, Rowan, for attending book signings and ensuring my presence at Thrillerfest 2023 in NYC; also to my brother, Joseph, for making Thrillerfest a reality for me as a debut author and his continued interest in my writing. I am grateful, as well, to have my sister-in-law, Audrey, my nephews Evan and Reid, my step-nephew and step-niece, Max and Maia, my in-laws, Kim, Jackie, Craig, and Jody, on my team. And to T.C. and Scruffy, my feline family members, thank you for your company as I write.

Thank you to my friends who have shown an interest in my writing path by buying a book, sharing on social media, asking me about my work, or telling others about it. I appreciate my teacher friends' support of my new career path, and the kind words of neighbors in our small community, as well as the encouragement of my social media author friends.

Thank you to the beta readers who shared their thoughts about *Where is My Husband?* to make it a better story. A special acknowledgement to my fellow authors and critique partner friends, Emily Hann and Norah Blakedon, for their expert advice and assistance with my manuscript.

I wish to acknowledge the International Thriller Writers (ITW) organization for accepting me into their Debut Authors Program and inviting me to the debut author breakfast and book signing at Thrillerfest in NYC. What an amazing community of authors!

To my agent, Cindy Bullard of Birch Literary, I thank you more than words can say for making my publishing dreams come true. Your belief in my writing and your continued hard work on my behalf have made this second mystery series a reality.

And finally, to my editor, Shawn Reilly Simmons, thank you so much for loving my book and for your kind words. From helpful edits to an eye-catching cover design, you've added the perfect finishing touches. Thank you to Verena Rose, Harriette Sackler, and the entire team at Level Best Books for bringing *Where is My Husband?* to readers everywhere,

Readers, I can't thank you enough for choosing to pick up this book. I hope you enjoy it!

About the Author

Ivanka Fear is a Canadian writer, born in Slovenia. She earned her B.A. and B.Ed. in English and French at Western University. Prior to pursuing writing full-time, she enjoyed a long career in education. *Where is My Husband?*, A Jake and Mallory Thriller, is her second book. Ivanka is also the author of *The Dead Lie*, A Blue Water Mystery. She is a member of International Thriller Writers, Crime Writers of Canada, and Sisters in Crime. Ivanka resides in Ontario, Canada, with her family and the stray cats that wandered in. When not reading and writing, she enjoys watching mystery series and romance movies, gardening, going for walks, and watching the waves roll in at the lake.

SOCIAL MEDIA HANDLES:
Facebook: https://www.facebook.com/ivankafearauthor
Instagram: https://www.instagram.com/ivankawrites/
Twitter: https://twitter.com/FearIvanka

AUTHOR WEBSITE:
https://www.ivankafear.com/

Also by Ivanka Fear

The Dead Lie, A Blue Water Mystery

www.ingramcontent.com/pod-product-compliance
Lightning Source LLC
Chambersburg PA
CBHW032002130726
47903CB00012B/539